AR OF THE WIND

V. TORIA WILLIAMSON

Published by Neem Tree Press Limited 2022

Neem Tree Press Limited
95A Ridgmount Gardens, London, WC1E 7AZ
info@neemtreepress.com
www.neemtreepress.com

A catalogue record for this book is available from the British Library

ISBN 978-1-911107-50-7 Paperback
ISBN 978-1-911107-51-4 Ebook

Printed and bound in Great Britain

WAR OF THE WIND

VICTORIA WILLIAMSON

SEVEN SEAS
COLLECTION

NEEM TREE PRESS

For Shona and Carolyn, for your support and encouragement over the last twenty-five years. Here's to the next twenty-five years of friendship!

TABLE OF CONTENTS

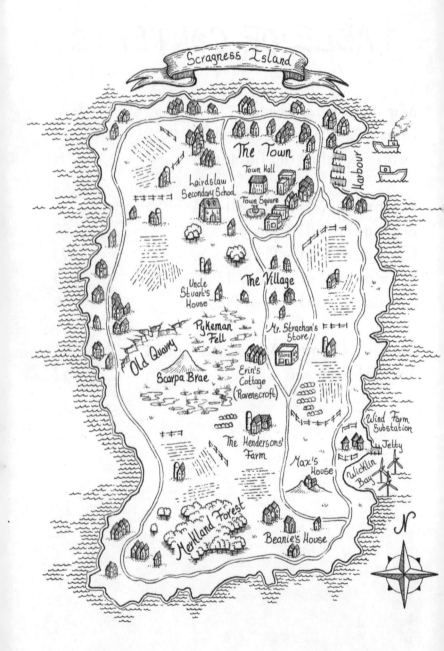

British Sign Language Alphabet

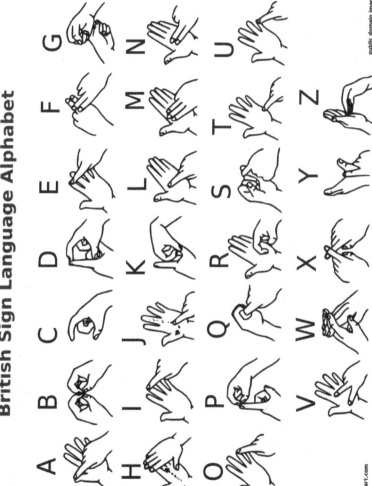

wpllipart.com

public domain images

TWO YEARS BEFORE THE TURBINES

The last sound I ever heard wasn't what I expected.

If I'd been on one of those stupid game shows risking a million pounds on the final question, I'd probably have guessed it would be the cry of gulls.

Those monsters haunted the skies above the island like pale ghosts, swooping down to steal fish from the trawlers coming home to the harbour before the teams could unload. Dive-bombing in unison, they tore at the nets bulging with fresh-caught herring, snatching the silver fish and swallowing them whole as they wheeled back into the sky for the next attack. They kept circling right up until the last crates had been loaded into the packing sheds. Then, once their bellies were full and their wings were straining to stay airborne, that's when they started to laugh.

I could still remember that noise clearly. It was a deep throaty sound that echoed across the scrublands of Pykeman Fell all the way up the slopes of Scarpa Brae. At night I used to hear the gulls circling our clifftop house before turning inland to hunt the burns and rain-swelled backwaters for smaller prey. They were always hungry, always calling out for food with their raw, mocking cry. So, if I'd had to guess the last thing I'd ever hear, the cry of gulls would be the sound I'd have picked to answer the million-pound question.

But I wasn't on a game show when it happened. I was on my dad's fishing boat.

It was just a training run to try out the new deckhand who'd arrived from the Scottish mainland. No way would Dad ever let me out on a real deep-sea trawl till I was old enough to help haul in the net during a storm or steer the boat through a fog whiteout if the sat-nav failed. Too dangerous, he said. The Atlantic waters were too cold and deep, and when sudden squalls rose up, the heavy boat was tossed about like a leaf on a windy day. I was a good head taller than the other boys my age on the island, but still Dad shook his head and said I was too young to be a deckhand. Back then he had hopes of bigger and better things for my future.

That day the Bay was calm, the wind whispering round the masthead like it had a secret to share. Maybe it was trying to warn me what was coming. I wished now I'd listened. The gulls were quiet for once, watching us lazily from the rocks that gaped from the entrance of the Bay like jagged teeth in the mouth of a stone giant. I turned away from the scarred cliffs, shading my eyes against the summer sun and gazing out across the open sea. Dad was leaning over the winch drum, pointing out the controls to the new guy as the trawler net disappeared below the waves.

That was when it happened.

There was a sharp crack, then a harsh whooshing noise, and the winch line suddenly went crazy. One minute it was uncoiling steadily from the drum, the next it was snaking across the deck at a million miles per hour as the heavy net was sent into freefall. Next came the high-pitched shriek of the warning siren, and the rumble of dying machinery as Angus cut the power in the engine room. Uncle Stuart came tearing down from the bridge just in time to see the broken winch cable whip across the deck, snatching at everything in its path and dragging a water pump, a twenty-litre storage barrel, and a spare net over the side with it.

The last thing the cable wrapped itself around before it disappeared below the waves was my leg. And that was when I heard it. It wasn't the gulls or the waves or the trawler's dying engine.

The last sound I ever heard was my dad screaming my name.

EXPERIMENT XO1 – PHASE O

CHAPTER 1

TWO WEEKS BEFORE THE TURBINES

'*MAX!*'

My name was carved deep into the cover of my exercise book like an ugly scar. I took a red pen from my bag and scribbled a bloody outline round the letters, grabbing a bottle of correction fluid and dousing the page in a layer of ghostly paint. I grinned in satisfaction at the mess I'd made.

White noise over a silent scream.

Perfect way to express how I felt about starting another school year. Mr Mason, my school counsellor, was going to have a heart attack.

I tossed the book on the grass beside me to dry and gazed out over Wicklin Bay. The protesters had been cleared off the beach, but if I leaned forward over the edge of the cliff, I could still see them waving their placards behind the sand dunes and kicking at the temporary fencing. I snorted and tossed a rock down, watching it bounce its way onto the sand far below. I didn't get what all the fuss was about. The wind turbines were coming to Scragness Island whether that little band of nutjob protesters liked it or not.

Down at the bottom of the hill, the wind farm substation was almost complete. A group of workers from the mainland crawled like ants across the compound, putting the finishing touches to the row of concrete buildings housing the transformers. Huge steel pylons stood in place behind them, waiting to carry the energy generated by the turbines that would be towed into the Bay in just a couple of weeks.

We weren't just getting any old turbines, though. No communications company would waste their money here. They kept telling us their mobile masts wouldn't get a strong enough signal, and undersea broadband cables would be too expensive to lay from the mainland. After years of campaigning, the government had finally stepped in and offered us the chance to take part in its first combo-tower trials—amazing new experimental turbines with integrated mobile phone masts that would provide next generation coverage for the whole island. Not only were we going to get cheap energy, but we were also going to get free smart phones with the latest X-G technology before it had even been rolled out across the mainland yet.

Who in their right mind would want to protest about that?

"Goodbye stone-age Scragness, welcome to the twenty-first century," I grinned. I couldn't wait to finally get connected to the internet like normal people. It was bad enough we had to make do with landlines instead of mobile phones, but not being on social media like the rest of the world? I was pretty sure that was against my human rights.

Just as I was leaning back on the grass to relax in the sun, a hand brushed my shoulder. I jumped, whirling round in fright.

"What?" I snapped.

"School," my mum said. "You're going to be late this morning."

Actually, that wasn't what she said. There'd be no point in her talking, since I couldn't hear anymore. What she did was wave her hands at me in jerky signs that were meant to mean, "*TODAY SCHOOL YOU LATE.*"

3

Mum wasn't much good at sign language yet, and it didn't help that she had one hand wrapped round my baby sister, Sally, while she tried to talk to me. But it wasn't hard to guess what the concerned look on her face meant this time.

I stood up and stuffed my exercise book into my bag before she could see it. Mum already had lots of little worry lines snaking across her forehead like hairline cracks in a window ready to shatter. One more, and her whole face would collapse.

"OK, OK, I'm going," I grumbled, ruffling Sally's hair on the way past and feeling a cold flash of satisfaction as her tiny face screwed up in a wordless shriek. I wasn't a fan of babies, and all my wee sister had done since she was born six months ago was eat and poop and cry.

"Max!"

Mum mouthed the word this time, pointing to my ear. I nodded, pulling the wire of my hearing aid out of my pocket and waving it at her, pretending to put it in my ear. When she'd gone back inside the house and I was halfway down the road, I shoved it in my bag. No way was I walking to school looking like a space cadet.

I skirted the edge of the Hendersons' farm, resisting the urge to cut across the fields and chase the fat sheep into a mindless frenzy. I was late already, and I still had to stop off for munchies if I didn't want to be stuck with Mum's soggy excuse for sandwiches for lunch.

I jumped over the low wall outside the local grocery store and skidded to a stop.

Oh...crap.

I'd tried to leave so late that all the local kids would already be at school. Looks like I'd miscalculated.

There was a big group of them, all about fourteen like me, standing in a tight circle round a smaller kid who was clutching the woolly hat on her head with one hand and flapping at the kids with the other. I knew who the kids were—I'd been in their class all the way through primary school. I was meant to be in their secondary school class too, until the accident put paid to that. Instead, I'd got stuck in the 'special' class along with every zoomer who couldn't spell his own name or eat her lunch without dribbling it down her chin. That was two years ago, and I was still so mad about it I could scream.

I stood very still, watching to see what would happen.

"Nice hat, Beanie. Can I see it?" Ryan flicked the smaller kid's hand away and grabbed the hat from her head.

I didn't hear him say it, of course, and his back was to me so I couldn't even see him grinning. But Ryan was one of the boys I used to hang around with in primary school, so I knew exactly how much he enjoyed tormenting anyone a bit different, and what he'd be saying to her right now.

"Give. It. Back."

Beanie Lewis pronounced each word so slowly and clearly it was almost like watching a film at half speed with ten-foot subtitles. She was the only person on the island I could lip read, and the last person on the planet I wanted to hold a conversation with.

I could see the other kids laughing as Ryan held the tatty hat up and inspected it. I could guess what he was saying. Even though my ruined eardrums couldn't carry the sound anymore, a voice in my head added the made-up soundtrack for me as I watched.

"God, it's manky, you wee clatbag. Don't you ever wash?"

Some of the other boys grinned as Beanie clutched for her hat, but a couple of them looked uncomfortable when Ryan held it out of reach. That was Ryan's problem—he never knew when to quit.

"Knock it off, Ryan."

A taller boy came out of the shop and snatched the hat off Ryan, handing it back to Beanie. Calum always knew when things had gone too far. That was why he was the leader of the gang I used to hang out with. That's why he used to be my best friend. But that was before the accident.

Beanie made a grab for the hat Calum held out to her, but it slipped from her grasp and dropped into a puddle. My imagination filled in the splash it made when it landed, and then the louder one when Beanie plonked herself down on her knees to rescue it. Calum was about to help her, but then he caught sight of me watching him round the corner of the shop. There was an awkward pause, both of us freezing while we tried to work out whether to say 'hi' or just pretend we hadn't seen each other. Calum glanced down at Beanie in the puddle, then back at me, concern flashing across his face for a split second.

I'd got pretty good at reading people's expressions in the last two years, and I heard Calum's silent message loud and clear. "*I didn't mean to drop it,*" he was saying. "*It was an accident.*"

Calum might be willing to leave the zoomers alone now that I was one of them, but Ryan hadn't finished yet. While Beanie was pulling her hat out of the puddle, he grabbed the packet of crisps sticking out of her schoolbag, bursting it open and sending a hail of flakes across the road. "Hey look, it's raining crisps!" he laughed. I was pretty sure it was something stupid like that he said anyway.

That was when Beanie started to cry.

Some kids looked cute when they cried. Not Beanie. Her face turned bright red, her trusting brown eyes all screwed up, gushing tears. She gulped so hard she looked like she was drowning. Some of the boys in my old gang started sniggering again and nudging each other.

I stared at the ground. Two years ago I might've been laughing along with them. I might've even started it, winding Beanie up to see if I could get a funny reaction. But now? Now I pressed back against the wall as far as I could go and hoped my old gang would move on before the rest of them spotted me.

Calum shoved Ryan away from Beanie, muttering something I couldn't guess at. Whatever it was, it wasn't a compliment. Ryan's grin hardened into a scowl, and when he shook Calum's hand off his arm and turned away, his eyes caught mine and locked on. My guts twisted with dread. I used to be leader of the pack along with Calum. Now I was a zoomer like Beanie, and fair game for Ryan's sick jokes.

Before he could close in on his new target, the shop door opened and an old woman with mad white hair and a nose as sharp as a gull's beak came wheezing out.

"Get away from my Bethany, you evil wee brats! I'll have the police onto you!"

That's pretty much what I thought she said, even though from where I stood trying to read her wrinkled lips it looked like, "Gevaweeyeefhniveets, ahveepeeyieeedwoo."

I used to think that deaf people could just watch someone's mouth as they talked and it was as good as hearing what they said. Now I knew that was just stupid. Even Erin Brody could only lip read about one word out of five, and she'd been deaf since she was born.

As soon as I thought of Erin my stomach knotted again, this time with guilt. She wouldn't have just stood there watching Beanie get pushed around, she would've marched straight up to Ryan Kirkwood and slapped the smile right off his face. But then she'd been picked on her whole life for being different. I was still trying to get used to it.

By the time Granny Lewis had finished waving her walking stick around and helped Beanie up, the kids had run off laughing across the fields. I edged over to the shop, trying to avoid Beanie's sad eyes that followed me accusingly. When the door closed behind me, I sighed with relief. I didn't know why that kid thought I was going to stand up for her just because I'd been stuck in her zoomer class.

I grabbed a packet of crisps and a can of coke from the fridge as fast as I could, trying not to look at the clock above the magazine rack. I knew I was really late now, I didn't need to be reminded. As I put my things down on the counter, I nearly tripped over a pile of placards cluttering up the aisle.

"Protests," Mr Strachan mouthed at me from behind the till. "Wind Turbines. Wicklin Bay."

The grocery shop owner was one of the few people who actually tried to communicate with me. Most people either looked away, embarrassed, or ignored me completely when they worked out that I couldn't hear them.

Mr Strachan held up a sign and pointed to it as I fished in my pocket for a couple of pound coins. '*Keep Wicklin Bay Turbine Free*', it read.

Yeah, really imaginative, well done.

I drummed my fingers impatiently on the counter as Mr Strachan hunted around in the till for change, shaking his head and mouthing, "Disaster," at me like the world was ending.

My parents weren't keen on the wind turbine scheme either, what with the Bay being right next to our house and everything, but what was the big deal? It was just three big towers after all. Nearly everyone on the island was desperate to get on the internet, and with free WiFi for a year and a smart phone each thrown in to sweeten the deal, it was no wonder the vote had come out at ninety-five percent for the government's plan and only five percent against. The turbines would be towed into the Bay in a few weeks no matter how many placards Mr Strachan and his group of angry pensioners waved.

I pocketed my change and sprinted to school. The rain was just starting as I made my way to the wheelchair-accessible unit beside the main building where my enhanced provision class would be halfway through their happy-clappy 'what we did in the holidays' session by now. At least I wouldn't have to sit facing Beanie and her big accusing eyes for long before break. I stopped at the door and gazed back at the main building, feeling the familiar surge of anger at the accident that had dumped me out here with all the 'specials' instead of with my friends from my old life.

This was my life now. This was my new normal, and I thought it would be forever. Two years ago, I'd thought the worst thing that could ever happen to me was losing my hearing. Turns out I was wrong, but I didn't know it until the wind turbines came to Wicklin Bay.

CHAPTER 2

The water closed over my head, shutting out the awful sound of my name being screamed. It was as though my ears had been wrapped in cotton wool. I didn't panic, not right then. I'd been skinny-dipping in the Bay since I was four years old, and I was a strong swimmer. All I had to do was reach the surface where I knew Dad's hands would be waiting to haul me out.

The water surged around me as I fought the pull of the waves, bubbles exploding from my lungs as I collided with the boat's steel hull. I could feel the heat of the engines through the thick plates, the throb of moving parts in the boat's belly dying slowly. Angus had shut the main motor down as soon as the siren had gone off, but it took a minute for the pistons to stop and for the propellers to slow their path through the waves. I could feel the vibration of the great blades cutting their way towards me as I clawed my way to the surface.

That was when I panicked.

I knew right there and then I wouldn't reach the surface in time. My lungs were burning, my heart pounding so hard it felt like it was going to burst. My hands tore at the water above me, my head almost making it above the white spray. But then the winch line tightened round my leg, the waves dragging me back into the boat's slipstream, right into the path of those propellers.

There was a blur of steel—spinning, churning—before my eyes. Then a bomb went off in my head, my skull fracturing on impact. The world spun upside down as the blades flung me against the hull of the ship. More bombs went off on the other side of my head, my eardrums shattering. Everything went strangely still after that. The light on the surface of the water receded, darkness closing in. I drifted down to the depths slowly, the pain and fear ebbing away like surf at low tide, leaving only the memory of a name echoing round my head in a silent scream.

*

"MAX!"

The silent word was mouthed so close to my face I could feel Erin's hot breath on my cheek. I jerked back to reality, flinching from the sea-green eyes that reminded me of the waves sweeping the Bay. Erin Brody wrinkled her freckled nose at me, fixing me with her steady stare.

"YOUR TURN," she signed. Her hands moved so fast the sign was barely more than a blur.

I blinked, the bad memories so fresh, it took me a moment to reboot. Erin folded her arms, leaning back in her chair to watch me, still as a statue. It always unnerved me how fast she could go from restless to calm. She was like the ocean itself, one minute battered by storms, the next all sunlight and tranquility. Her eyes were the colour of deep water, and one was half hidden behind strands of hanging hair dyed bright red and black. She'd done it as a bet for a Halloween party in first year and liked it so much she'd kept it. She thought it made her look edgy, but it reminded me of the 'keep your distance' stripes on one of those poisonous frogs from the Amazon. The rest of her strawberry blonde hair was wound up in a plait at the back of her head like a scorpion's tail ready to uncoil. I sat up warily, taking in the rest of the table at a glance.

Now I remembered where I was: Zoomer Studies 101.

Beanie gave me an encouraging smile, pointing out my place on the board game and handing me the dice. When I didn't take it straight away, she helped me out by rolling it for me and moving my piece like this wasn't the billionth time we'd had to play 'shopping' and I needed help figuring out the rules. God, she loved this game even more than she loved cheese and onion crisps. Her woolly hat was still drying on the radiator, and without it her head had shrunk to half its usual size. Her granny's home haircuts made her look like a baby hedgehog, and Beanie always wore her hat over her ears to stop the mainstream kids from laughing at her.

Yeah, like that worked.

Now her spikey tufts of hair were exposed like an accusation. I should've stood up for her today and not let Ryan pick on her like that. Laughing behind her back was one thing, but pulling her hat off? That was just mean. Ryan needed his backside kicked if he thought hassling a kid because she had Down's Syndrome and looked a bit different was OK.

I ran my hands through my own dark hair, refusing to feel guilty. It had grown again after all the surgery to put my skull back together, but I could still feel the scars where the boat's propellers had struck. My own shaved head had earned me more than enough sideways looks and half-covered sniggers in the school corridors, I wasn't going to put myself in the line of fire again for Beanie's sake now it had grown back. It was bad enough being turned into one of the 'specials' after the accident, I wasn't about to make friends with them.

But it could've been a whole lot worse, I thought.

I glanced over at the fourth member of our group, feeling awkward when his eyes met mine and he grinned back. David was rocking in his wheelchair, drooling down his chin onto a bib that was already half-soaked. There was a light on behind his eyes, but I hadn't been able to work out yet just how many brain cells were home. I wasn't about to try either. Just looking at him made me think of the accident again. If the propellers had got one inch closer to my brain or my fractured skull had splintered badly instead of breaking clean, it could easily be me rocking in that chair.

The hand laid on my shoulder snapped my attention back to class.

"*PROBLEM?*" Mrs Brody signed in front of my face. I looked up to see the question mark being added by my teacher's raised eyebrow. Erin's mother could hear just fine, but she'd learned to sign when her daughter was born deaf. And she wasn't put in charge of us 'specials' because she was slow herself—she was the best teacher in the school. I was lucky to have a teacher who could sign, and Mrs Brody had the patience of a saint with me and my moods, but right now I was too wound up with frustration to feel grateful.

"Yeah, there's a problem," I growled, angry that I couldn't even hear my own voice inside my head. I could only gauge my volume by how much air I used, and right now my words were flying out with the force of machine-gun bullets.

"This game is stupid. I'm just deaf, not a total retard. Why am I playing some pointless kids' shopping game instead of doing calculus and algebra?" I knew fine well the mainstream kids hadn't started that stuff themselves yet, but it made me sound like I had a genuine complaint instead of just whining.

All the zoomers in the class looked up, hearing the sharp edge in my voice. Erin was the only other deaf kid, but she could read

13

the tension in my face like I had a whole novel written across my forehead. Mrs Brody stiffened as soon as I said the word 'retard'. We'd had conversations about that. She'd written whole screeds about the importance of 'inclusive language' and signed at me for hours about respecting others. Whatever. As far as I was concerned you might as well call people what they are. 'Special' was just another way of saying 'freak'.

"THAT WORD OUR CLASS DON'T USE." Mrs Brody's signs were clipped, efficient, annoyed. She hated the labels stuck on the kids in her class even more than the zoomers themselves did. "THIS GAME PRACTISE COMMUNICATION," she frowned. "THIS YEAR OTHER MATHS CLASS. DON'T WORRY, YOU DON'T FALL BEHIND."

I snorted like she'd said something funny. She just didn't get it. I wouldn't care if I was the slowest kid in the mainstream class if I could just be normal again like the rest of the kids. I didn't want to be the special guest stuck at the back of the room with his own personal interpreter.

"HARD, I KNOW," Mrs Brody went on. "YOU SIGN BETTER NOW. NEED MORE PRACTISE, YOU LATER LEARN NEW..." Her hands danced on and on, making shapes that always seemed to be in the wrong order to make any sense. God, I was so sick of sign language. Sometimes I felt like I was getting the hang of it, but not today. Today I just wanted the endless silent flapping in front of my face to stop.

I gave up trying to follow her meaning and stared at Mrs Brody resentfully. The pressure was starting to build behind my eyes. This was not one of my good days, my 'coping days' as my mum called them. Today I felt like I was going to explode with all the anger fizzing round my head.

"*YOU LISTEN?*" Mrs Brody's hands slowed down to make sure I caught her meaning.

"How can I listen when I can't bloody well HEAR?!" I yelled. The fuse of anger fizzled down my arms, my rage exploding when the spark reached my fingers. I knocked the board game off the table with one grand swipe, watching in satisfaction as all the stupid plastic coins and grocery pictures went tumbling across the floor.

Beanie started to cry. She'd been winning.

Mrs Brody didn't react. She just crouched down beside me and held my hand. Erin grabbed my other one, giving it a sympathetic squeeze and nodding like she knew what I was going through. But how could she? She'd been deaf since she was born, she didn't have a clue how it felt to suddenly lose every sound in the whole world. How could she know what it was like to delete an entire digital music collection because looking at the names of the favourite bands I couldn't listen to anymore sent me into a tailspin of grief? To sit across the dinner table from parents who couldn't communicate properly with me, the awkward silences stretching on to infinity? To lose all my friends, the boys I'd once played football with every day, now hanging back when they saw me, whispering behind their hands in voices I'd never hear again?

She had no idea. Nobody did. I was all alone on my desert island of misery with no hope of a rescue ship.

My face felt red hot, my throat burning with the effort not to cry. I snatched my hands back, wishing Mrs Brody would stop being so damn nice when I blew up. A ticking-off I could deal with. Sympathy, not so much.

The bell saved me from making an even bigger fool out of myself in front of the watching zoomers. I didn't hear it, of course, but the bustle of activity as kids searched for jackets and snacks distracted them from me and my drama. Erin helped me pick up the scattered bits of the board game, moving slowly and surely across the floor like an anchored boat in a seething ocean of kids. She always seemed to reflect the opposite of what I was feeling—if I was calm, she was restless, if I was raging, she was still and peaceful. I could not for the life of me figure her out.

When the two classroom assistants pushed the kids in wheelchairs outside, I saw Mrs Brody reach into her desk and pull out a pink form. My heart sank, and I hurried over. "I don't need that," I said quickly as she filled in the boxes. "I'm fine. Really."

Mrs Brody nodded, but I knew I wasn't convincing anyone, least of all her. She popped the form into an envelope and handed it to me.

"*SEE M.R. M.A.S.O.N.*" she signed, spelling out the school counsellor's name with the fingers of her right hand forming the letters against her left. I'd seen his name spelled out for me so many times now I didn't even have to work it out letter by letter. "*MAYBE HELP.*"

"It won't," I scowled back. But I'd just booked myself a one-way ticket to see the school counsellor whether I liked it or not. I rolled my eyes and stuffed the envelope into my pocket, hoping if I wrinkled it badly enough Mr Mason wouldn't be able to read the referral damning me and my temper to counselling sessions with him for all eternity.

The third-year kids were all out in the school yard as I stomped down the wheelchair ramp. The break area backed onto our classrooms, so there was nowhere to go to escape the side-eyes and laughter of the mainstream kids every time the bell rang. Lairdslaw High's head teacher had this dumb idea that the zoomers and the mainstreamers would all sit round a campfire with rainbow-strap guitars at break singing 'Kumbaya' and passing love letters. But that wasn't how it worked out. Of course not. The mainstreamers hung out on one side of the football field, the zoomers on the other, and God help any special kid who was daft enough to wander across the imaginary divide.

It wasn't that the mainstreamers were mean, not exactly. But kids like Beanie with her silly hat and slow speech, and David with his wheelchair and dribbling just made them uncomfortable. Kids who were different, who didn't fit in, made them nervous.

Kids like me.

I stopped at the bottom of the ramp, watching the football game and waiting for my chance to run to the main building when the mainstream kids were looking the other way. Over near the door Calum was hanging out with Ryan and the rest of the gang, drinking coke and glaring at the fourth years who were hogging the football field. At the picnic table nearby, Erin was sitting with a couple of mainstream girls, laughing along with them as they cackled over a fashion magazine. She was the only zoomer who'd managed to cross over and make friends on the other side of the line. Sometimes I wondered if those two mainstream girls were just pretending to be her friends because they felt sorry for her, or because her mother was a teacher.

Erin leaned over the magazine and scribbled something in the corner, and the two other girls bent double, laughing hysterically. They didn't look like they were pretending.

When the kids playing football converged on the goal at the far end of the field, I made my move, keeping my head down as I edged my way round the fence. I was so focused on making it to the double doors without attracting attention, I almost tripped over Beanie. She was sitting slumped on a tree stump, tears sliding down her cheeks like her whole world was ending. A group of girls were walking away, nudging each other and smirking back at her. I was pretty sure they'd been calling her a skelly-eyed scaldhead again.

That poor kid was having a worse first day of term than I was. Without stopping I pulled my packet of crisps out of my pocket and dropped them in her lap. I wasn't sure whether I meant it as some kind of apology, or whether I still felt guilty about looking the other way when she was being pushed around, but whatever, I'd done it before I was even sure why.

She looked up at me like I'd just handed her a winning lottery ticket, her wobbly lip turning into a big smile of gratitude. God, it was worse than her being mad at me. I scowled at her and walked away fast. I didn't want her getting the wrong idea. I'd lost all my friends and I wasn't about to adopt a family of dribbling zoomers to replace them. Not like my parents had replaced their broken son with a brand new, fully functional baby.

But that was a whole other story.

CHAPTER 3

"*So, Max, how are you feeling today?*"

The question was carefully written out at the top of the A4 pad in tiny letters that were almost impossible to read. Mr Mason leaned across the desk and stared at me expectantly. I looked up, seeing my own brown eyes reflected back at me in his oversize spectacles. My gaze was guarded, shut down tighter than a high security jail. "Fine," I muttered, then went back to picking off the wad of chewing gum stuck to the bottom of my shoe.

Mr Mason waited for a bit, hoping for more, then picked up his pen and began scribbling away again. I heaved a huge sigh of boredom and looked out of the window, watching the grey clouds gather in the distance over Scarpa Brae. The weather was doing a pretty good job of summing up how I felt about my first day back at school.

Mr Mason carefully dotted all the 'i's on his literary masterpiece before pushing the pad across the desk once more.

"*Mrs Brody informs me you had some problems in class today controlling your temper. Are you feeling frustrated, Max? Is there anything you'd like to talk to me about?*"

"Nope." I shook my head.

There was a long pause. Mr Mason ran his hand over the hair slicked down with too much gel across his bald patch, then reluctantly took the pad back again. I could tell he was humming nervously as he wrote—his adam's apple was bobbing up and down like a harbour buoy on a windy day. It was funny how uncomfortable folk got when they had to make an effort to communicate instead of just saying the first stupid thing that came into their head. I almost felt sorry for him. He wasn't a real counsellor, just a second-rate R.E. teacher with a couple of free periods a week he had to fill up. It wasn't like he knew how to fix me. No one did. I'd been back and forth to his office for a year and a half now, and he still hadn't managed to get more than a few grunted words out of me. He still hadn't twigged that I kept this game up for as long as possible each session to avoid going back to my class full of zoomers.

I twisted uncomfortably in my seat and looked out of the window again while I waited. The end-of-break bell must've gone off, as groups of fifth-year kids were hurrying back from the bike sheds, stubbing out sneaky cigarettes and chucking the butts in the ornamental plant pots. A sharp stab of envy cut me right to the quick. All the other kids got to do normal things at break like hang out and talk about football and TV, while here I was stuck in a pokey wee office playing the one-word answer game with some total wazzer who smelled of stale coffee and ineffective breath mints. It was so unfair it made me want to hit something as hard as I could and scream at the top of my lungs.

Mr Mason tapped my hand to get my attention, pointing at his notepad again. I drew my fingers back quickly, fighting the urge to slap him right across his baldy head to get rid of all my frustration. I read his stupid note instead. Then I blinked, reading it again.

It wasn't what I was expecting. Our school counsellor had totally excelled himself at randomness this time.

"*Are you worried about the wind turbines coming to the Bay?*" Mr Mason had written. "*Is that what's troubling you?*"

Here I was sitting deaf as a doorknob with my eardrums panned in, and he was guessing I was bothered by a couple of whirly things being built in the Bay across from my house? In the name of…

"What?" I said flatly, not even trying to keep the contempt from my voice.

"I mean, it's…" Mr Mason started saying the words, before remembering the notepad. He scribbled quickly this time, his handwriting looping twice its normal size. "*Are you worried that the wind turbines will affect your family life? Your home? That they'll spoil the Bay?*"

"No, Mr Mason," I sighed, giving him my most sarcastic side-eye. "I'm not worried about the wind turbines any more than I'm worried about being kidnapped by aliens."

Mr Mason was on the wind farm protest committee, and with two weeks to go he was still fishing for a last-minute lifeline to save the island from a sea of evil turbines. A disabled kid who was having anxiety attacks over them being built in front of his house would be the perfect poster boy for their campaign.

"Are we done?" I pushed the pad away and stood up abruptly. Playing 'let's talk about shopping' with Beanie and David was dull, but anything was better than getting tangled up in a turbine discussion with Mr Mason. It was my house that was sitting on the Bay, and I couldn't care less what they built there as long as I got internet access out of the deal.

"Yes, Max," Mr Mason mouthed with an exaggerated nod. He tried to smile at me, but I could tell he was disappointed. I'd been getting that look a lot since the accident, especially from my parents. I stuffed that thought into the strongbox in my head along with all the other baggage from that awful day in the Bay and locked it tight. Closing the door behind me with a silent bang that shook the hinges, I crossed the corridor and hurried out into the rain.

*

It was still raining by the time I stomped up the back steps of my house late that afternoon, scraping the mud off my shoes on the soggy mat before stepping into the kitchen. As usual, the place was a mess. Dirty dishes were piled by the sink, ready to tumble onto the floor where traces of baby food were stuck in the cracks between the tiles. A mountain of clothes overflowed from the laundry basket, the washing machine door hanging open and damp towels spilling into the baby bath.

I thought longingly of Erin Brody's neat cottage sitting snugly on the other side of Pykeman Fell. Mum and I had visited twice a week for six months after the accident, learning sign language and eating Mrs Brody's home-baked scones. Their kitchen was spotless, with gleaming surfaces, a crisp white cloth over the breakfast table and freshly picked flowers on the windowsill. But then the Brodys didn't have a six-month-old baby crying and pooping and ruining everything. They just had Erin, their perfect daughter who got As in school and had mainstream friends and did all her chores without having to be asked twice.

Not like me.

I dumped my bag on the cluttered counter and opened the fridge, drinking straight from the milk carton before Mum could catch me.

She came shuffling down the stairs in her slippers as I rummaged around in the cupboard looking for chocolate biscuits. There weren't any, as usual. Mum gave me a sleepy hug and signed, "*HELLO. YOU GO SHOP BUY PASTA?*"

Oh...the pasta. My heart sank. I'd been too busy trying to keep off Calum's radar at the store this morning to remember. "Sorry, Mum, I forgot. Can we just have something else tonight?"

Mum's face fell. And there it was again. That look of disappointment that followed me around like a bad smell I couldn't scrub off no matter what I did.

"Oh, *Max*!" Mum mouthed silently. "*TONIGHT YOU FATHER HOME, ME COOK. CHIPS BEANS NO GOOD,*" she signed awkwardly. "*HOUSE MESS NO TIME SHOP BUY FOOD FEED BABY COOK...*"

She was tired. Her signs were all mixed up, and I had to guess what she was talking about. It wasn't hard. Dad spent a week at a time at sea, coming home to pack the fish and rest for a few days in between trawling runs. Our family seemed to go off-kilter when he was gone, like a rudderless boat that spun in ever tightening circles as it slowly sank. I knew Dad thought I should help around the house more. Not that he told me that himself, of course, it would be *way* too much to expect him to bother actually trying to communicate with me these days. But Mum kept hinting at it every time the dishes piled up or the laundry basket overflowed. I wished she'd just ask me straight out to do stuff. I was so sick of folk tap-dancing round me like I was made of glass.

Then again, it wasn't like I was eager to do chores even when I was asked outright. I wasn't a skivvy. I was fourteen years old, and I had better things to do with my time than change manky nappies and hoover dried baby barf off the carpet. If Mum couldn't cope then she shouldn't have bloody well gone and had another baby at her age, should she?

"What do you need me to do?" I sighed. There was so much clutter piled up round the kitchen it was hard to know where to start.

Mum pointed to the dishes in the sink with a pleading little smile, and I dragged myself over, making sure I rattled and banged the plates together as much as possible so she'd know I wasn't exactly thrilled about it. Things never used to be like this. Before the baby came and ruined everything, Mum worked down at the post office five days a week. She didn't start till ten, and we'd take our time over breakfast, eating boiled eggs with hot buttered toast and reading the paper together. She'd make my packed lunch while I was putting on my uniform, making sure my sandwiches were cut just the way I liked them. She'd be home by the time school finished too, making dinner long before I needed to raid the biscuit tin to keep my stomach from grumbling. Back then the fridge was always full, the laundry basket never overflowed, and the dishes seemed to magically disappear like a band of kelpies came up from the Bay each night and spirited them away.

Not like now.

I'd gone and got myself broken beyond repair in the accident, and so my parents went and had another baby to replace me. Now my little sister Sally was the centre of my parents' attention, and I'd been pushed to the sidelines, hovering on the edges of our family life like some unwanted ghost of a son they'd once had. Just one more downer to add to the endless list of things that monumentally sucked about my life. I banged a cup against the tap so hard in frustration it shattered in a hundred pieces.

"*CAREFUL!*" Mum signed at me, a pained expression on her face. "*BABY WAKE UP.*"

Everything was always about the baby. I was so sick of that wee troll. "Do you want me to do these dishes or not?" I snapped.

"*HANG CLOTHES PLEASE.*"

"Make up your mind."

Mum looked defeated as she took over the wet sponge, her face crumbling like her chin was going to drop off her head and go sliding down the sink.

I felt like crap.

I emptied the washing machine and heaved the damp clothes into the front yard before I could wimp out and give Mum a hug. I wanted to tell her I was sorry. I was so, so sorry I'd gone and broken my head and now I couldn't hear her describing her dreams over breakfast, or listen to Dad telling funny stories about his fishing trips. I couldn't be the son they wanted. Not anymore. Now I couldn't even wash a few stupid dishes without kicking a temper tantrum.

My chest was aching the way it always did when I tried to force down tears of resentment. I took a deep breath, the smell of wet grass and sea salt soothing away the lump in my throat. The rain had stopped and a crack appeared in the clouds, a long shaft of sun lighting up the Bay. It was so beautiful, that view across the cliffs and out over the wide water, that I felt a sudden shiver of foreboding run up my spine. What if Mr Strachan and his group of protestors were right? What if the wind turbines did shatter the peace of the Bay, ruining the view and killing the wildlife that lived round the headland?

I shook the feeling off and hurried to peg the last of the clothes on the line. It was too late to worry about the turbines coming now. Besides, I had way bigger concerns to keep me awake at night.

The evening wind was rising, rippling up the hill and ruffling the feathers of the seagulls perched on the wall round our front yard. They weren't as big as the monsters that hovered round the fishing boats in the harbour, but they were greedy wee gannets that would take your finger off if you gave them half a sniff of a pickled onion crisp. I grabbed a handful of clothes pegs and chucked them at the gulls one by one, watching in satisfaction as they took off with silent shrieks of outrage. I wasn't trying to hit them, not really. I was just blowing off nervous steam. My dad would be home in a couple of hours, and then I'd only have three short days to try to get him to acknowledge my existence before he disappeared on his boat again.

It wasn't long enough. It never was.

Chapter 4

The darkness gradually gave way to sickly light that ebbed and flowed like waves on the edges of my vision. Each time I surfaced the light grew stronger, searing my eyes as I struggled back to consciousness. My body was numb, my limbs lying weak and useless under the hospital blankets. My head felt like every star in the universe was squashed inside my skull, simultaneously going supernova whenever I tried to open my eyes.

The faces of my parents and doctors swam before me, rippling and blurring together as though I was still trapped beneath the surging waters of the Bay. As I emerged from the sea of unconsciousness they smiled down at me, lips moving soundlessly in words of silent comfort. At first I was too far gone to realise something was wrong. But when the drugs began to wear off, a creeping dread began to claw its way up my spine.

I pushed the fear away, telling myself that my throbbing head was drowning out the sounds of the world around me. I clung to the hope that my parents' smiles were strained by sleepless nights and not the knowledge of something more awful to come. I was desperate to believe that one day soon the doctors would make it all better, they were just waiting till I was stronger so they could operate again.

They were waiting for me to get better alright, but not so they could fix me. They wanted me to be fully conscious when they gave me the news.

I couldn't hear.

And I was never going to hear again.

I couldn't remember how long I cried. I remembered howling soundlessly, banging my fists against the bedframe and knocking over drip stands in a last-ditch attempt to make a noise loud enough to wake the dead air. I remembered Mum holding me when the last of my strength was gone and my fury fizzled out in a whimper of exhausted tears. And over Mum's shoulder I remembered seeing Dad screw his face up, fighting to keep himself together as he whispered my name over and over again into the yawning chasm of silence.

*

"Max?"

Dad tapped my hand to get my attention. I got a fright, snatching it back so fast I knocked the water jug over. It spilled all over the table, drowning the trifle Mum had managed to cobble together at the last minute in between feeding the baby and cleaning our shambles of a living room. She jumped up, fussing over the soggy remains while I moved the ice cream out of harm's way and dabbed at the small lake with a paper napkin. Dad just sat there frowning at me and shaking his head, disappointment etched deep into his face.

Damn. Dad had been home for less than an hour and I'd gone and blown it already.

I could tell from the way he was muttering under his breath and fiddling with his wine glass that he thought so too. Here he was, making such a big effort to bond with his disabled son, and the daft wee zoomer couldn't even get through a family meal without cacking up the whole table. I swallowed down the last of my coke, the sugar tasting bitter on my tongue.

"*YOU OK?*" Mum signed, glancing between me and Dad in concern.

No, I'm not OK, I wanted to yell. *And I'm sick of being asked that stupid question!*

Instead, I rolled my eyes at her and nodded. "Just clumsy." I grinned a big fake smile as I spooned gobs of mint chocolate chip over the remains of her trifle. Mum's face relaxed, and soon Dad's did too. Then we sat in silence, eating the pudding that tasted as thin and watered down as our family life had become since the accident.

It wasn't my fault, I told myself, forcing the ice cream down past the lump in my throat. *I was trying my best.* And I really had been. I'd welcomed Dad home with a hug, chattering away as we set the table together, telling him all about the nest of baby gulls I'd found under the ledge of the cliff a few days back. It was late in the year for hatchlings and I hoped they'd manage to take to their wings before the fierce autumn winds came sweeping up the Bay. Dad had smiled and nodded in all the right places, and for a little while it almost seemed like things were normal again.

But by the time Mum got Sally changed and rescued the over-cooked oven chips, I'd run out of things to say. I couldn't tell Dad what I'd been up to with my friends over the last week, as I didn't have any friends left. I couldn't tell him what I'd been doing at school, as any mention of my zoomer class was a painful reminder for both of us that I'd been kicked out of the mainstream and dumped in the vegetable patch. There was only one safe subject left, one that made Dad's eyes light up with happiness, and that was Sally. And I'd jump off the cliff headfirst before taking an interest in that greedy wee milk vampire.

So, once I'd gone through all my rehearsed lines and run out of new things to say, the smiles and nods from Dad slowly faded into an awkward silence. Mum tried to help out with sign language, but Sally needed to be fed and she ate up Mum's whole attention. Dad and me were left to it, and even though we were sitting right across the table, we might as well have been a million miles apart.

I'd asked Dad questions about his fishing trip, and he'd tried to answer, speaking slowly and clearly like I was foreign instead of deaf, but I couldn't really work out what he was saying. My mind had started to wander, going back again and again to that day in the Bay, picking at the memory like it was a scab over a wound I couldn't heal. And then I'd zoned out, going full on zoomer and wrecking the pudding.

Now the mess was cleared up and our dinner was nearly over, and I only had a short time left before Dad's first night back came to an end. I knew what would happen if I didn't find some way to connect. Mum would fuss over Sally until she finally got her to sleep, and then go to bed herself, exhausted as usual. Dad would veg out in front of the TV with the rest of the wine bottle, and I'd sit in the other chair watching silently with him. He'd get uncomfortable, switching on the subtitles if they were available, and then I'd have to pretend I was reading them and enjoying the programme too instead of wishing for the millionth time we had our old life back, the one without deafness and Sally and this awful loneliness even when we were all in the same room together. I'd have to move fast if I didn't want tonight to end the same way every other night ended.

"Sorry, Dad," I said, hoping my voice didn't come out too loud in the silence, "I didn't catch what you said about your fishing trip. How many mackerel do you think you got this time?"

Dad looked up and started to answer, but then he stopped and pointed to my ear. My heart sank. I knew what he wanted.

I pulled my hearing aid from my pocket reluctantly and put the bud in my left ear, switching it on. At once the silence was shattered by a low buzzing hum that sounded like static between radio stations.

The tension in Dad's face drained away and his shoulders relaxed. He started talking naturally now, his lips moving at their usual speed. As far as he was concerned the problem was fixed and we could all just pretend that day in the Bay never happened.

But I wasn't fixed. The doctors had given me a hearing aid for the left side, telling me the bones weren't so badly damaged there and with practice I might be able to get some use out of it. The ugly piece of plastic that looked like a blob of wax stuck on top of my ear didn't help. All it did was make weird whooshing sounds when people talked. And worse, it made everyone think I didn't have a problem anymore, and they could just go on as normal without making any extra effort for me.

Don't get me wrong, the hearing aid wasn't completely useless. I could hear a soft hissing sound that I guessed was the electric kettle boiling on the counter right behind my head. I could hear a low hum from the CD player Mum had put on to soothe Sally while she was feeding. And I could hear a strange sort of bubbling sound coming out of Dad's mouth. The only thing I couldn't hear was a single word Dad was saying to me.

"Sorry, what?" I interrupted him, wincing at the sudden hissing my own voice made inside my head. "How many kilos of fish did you say you got this trip?" It was just a guess to make it look like I'd actually followed what he was saying.

Dad made his disappointed face again, and I knew straight away that's not what he'd been talking about at all. Before he could go all quiet and retreat back into his wine bottle, I pulled opened the sideboard drawer and snatched up a notepad.

"Write it down, Dad," I said, pushing the paper across the table and hoping I didn't sound like I was begging. "It's much easier if I can just read it."

The disappointed look on Dad's face changed to something else. I couldn't figure that expression out, but he made it every time I asked him to write something down for me. And he never did, not even once.

"Please, Dad?" I gave up all hope of not looking desperate and just begged.

The weird expression on Dad's face got even more fixed and he fiddled with the pen, glancing over at Mum. My heart skipped a beat—maybe this time, *finally*, Dad would stop pretending he could just talk to me like he used to and admit I had a problem. But suddenly there was a weird hissing in my head and I clawed at my hearing aid, pulling the bud out to escape from the burst of white noise. I wasn't scared, though. I knew exactly where that awful din was coming from.

I glared over at Sally, whose face was screwed up in a wordless shriek of fury. Mum had put her down in her chair and leaned over to encourage Dad to write something for me, and that wee brat just couldn't stand losing the attention for a fraction of a second. She screamed and wailed, kicking her feet and banging her fists so we'd all have to stop what we were doing and rush to soothe her.

It worked like a charm. Dad dropped the pen and picked her up, rocking her in his arms and calling her 'my wee princess' over and over. I got up and started scraping the plates into the bin to hide the tears of jealous rage stinging my eyes. Sally couldn't let me have one minute with Dad, not one brief moment to connect and try to repair some of the damage that day in the Bay had done. I hated that wee monster almost as much as I hated my deafness.

Dad slung Sally's changing bag over his shoulder and her upstairs for a bath, escaping the awkwardness of the k I watched them go with a silent scowl. She was his wee prin alright. Her blond hair and blue eyes matched his own so perfectly it was like he was carrying a doll version of himself up to bed. Maybe if I looked like him too, instead of having dark hair and eyes like Mum, he'd find it easier to talk to me. Maybe if I just tried harder, maybe if I...

I dumped the plates in the sink, taking the dishcloth off Mum before she could start on them. "I'll do the washing up, you go and get some sleep."

Mum gave me a grateful hug. "YOU GOOD BOY," she signed sleepily, following Dad upstairs.

But I wasn't good, I knew that for sure. I'd just offered to do the dishes to get the kitchen to myself. I didn't want an audience for the angry tears that were sliding down into the sink. There was no way anyone with this much rage bubbling inside their head could be good. I just hoped I could keep the lid on it for long enough to fix things, or else my anger would come spewing out like lava from a volcano, burning anyone it touched.

But in the end, it wasn't my rage that threatened to tear my family apart.

The winds of change were coming, and maybe that night, two weeks before the turbines, I could sense the warning signals. Soon they would come creeping through the night, whispering poison into the ears of the islanders. Maybe if I'd known that night what was coming, I wouldn't have minded so much that I was deaf.

"Give. Me. The. Green. Pen."

"Mr Mason said we're supposed to colour the Buddhist pictures red. It's the Christian stuff that's meant to be green." I scowled across the table at Beanie, and she scowled right back.

"*GREEN PEN GIVE ME.*" She signed it this time to make sure I got the message, holding her hand out for emphasis.

"Fine, make it whatever bloody colour you want, but keep it down, will you? We're getting stared at." I glanced at the other tables where the mainstream kids were leaning over their own worksheets. Some of them were looking over at us and sniggering. It was my first class with the mainstreamers since the new term started, and already I wanted to slide under the table and die a quiet death. Instead, I snatched up a red pen and took my fury out on the pointless worksheet Mr Mason had inflicted on his Religious Studies class.

Erin grabbed my hand before I could rip a hole right through the table with my angry scribbling. "*B.E.A.N.I.E. RIGHT,*" she signed. "*M.R. M.A.S.O.N. SAY BUDDHIST OBJECT GREEN.*"

I took one look at Beanie's 'I told you so' face and flung the pen down. I didn't know what annoyed me more—Beanie making me

34

look stupid by getting something right, Beanie being even better than me at sign language, or Beanie just sharing the same planet as me, never mind my Religious Studies class.

"DEEP BREATH," Erin warned. "YOU FEEL BETTER." She went on calmly colouring the pictures like it didn't bother her that the three of us were stuck on our own wee zoomer island surrounded by a sea of mainstream sharks. Mrs Brody had sat with us for the first half of the lesson, translating everything Mr Mason said for me and Erin and making sure Beanie didn't eat the felt-tip pens. But then she'd had to go back to teach the rest of the zoomers over in our unit, and we'd been left to fend for ourselves till the bell rang.

"Tastes. Like. Cab-bage."

Beanie tossed the green pen back across to me, lidless and covered in drool. She was grinning at me, a big smear of green pen on her bottom lip. She was joking around now, trying to get me to smile back. It was her way of easing the tension when I got grumpy and the other kids got mean. No way was I in the mood for playing the 'let's see if we can make Max smile' game right now, though. I looked up at the clock. Ten more minutes of this hell to survive before home time. I didn't think I was going to make it.

A wad of scrunched-up paper hit me on the side of the head and I flinched, grabbing it before it disappeared under the desk. I smoothed it out, my heart sinking right down to the bottom of my shoes when I saw the familiar handwriting scrawled across it.

'Space Cadet Party' it read, with two badly drawn stick figures that were meant to be Erin and Beanie getting up to something you only see on dodgy late-night TV.

I glanced across at Calum. He was leaning back in his chair and grinning at me like he'd just cracked the joke of the century. I raised my middle finger till he stopped smirking, then I balled the paper up and threw it back as hard as I could. The paper missed by a mile, hitting Ryan on the chest instead. It was only when Calum tried to snatch it back before Ryan read it that I realised, too late, that he hadn't been trying to insult me. He'd been trying to make me laugh like he used to. Ryan grinned like an idiot when he saw the picture, passing it to the rest of the gang then throwing it to a group of girls at another table. They sniggered, ripping paper out of their notebooks and drawing their own pictures which I was pretty sure included me this time.

Calum threw me a frustrated look and went back to doodling slogans on his schoolbag with a permanent marker.

I grabbed another pen and scribbled furiously on my worksheet again so no one could see my hand was shaking. I wasn't scared of being physically pushed around by the other kids. Even in primary school I'd been the tallest in Calum's gang, with shoulders broad enough to shove my way past the older boys in the lunch queue. It was the laughter I couldn't take. The silent, smirking laughter that had followed me around ever since I came back from the hospital on the mainland.

It hadn't started right away. Calum, Ryan and the other boys in the gang had made an effort at first, calling round at my house like they used to and bringing a football to kick about in the fields. But it had just been too weird for them, the way I couldn't hear a word they said, the way I needed everything written down. It was football that had made us friends and then held the gang together through the first few years of high school. They couldn't exactly write essays to me during a match, could they?

I didn't know what got to me more: being frozen out of the group and treated the same as the other zoomers, or knowing that if I was still in Calum's gang then I'd be sitting there making fun of Erin and Beanie myself.

At least I'd make a better attempt at dirty stickman jokes, I thought angrily as Calum's drawing was thrown back to our desk by the giggling girls at the corner table. I tried to prise the paper out of Beanie's hand before it could upset her, but it was too late. Beanie's smile faded when she saw what was drawn there, and her felt-tip-covered bottom lip began to quiver. She always cried when she didn't understand something. That brought Mr Mason hurrying over, his A4 pad at the ready. "*Is anything wrong?*" he scribbled for me, looking concerned.

It always annoyed me the way he ignored Beanie like he thought she wasn't bright enough to be able to answer for herself. I bet she was the only one in the whole class who'd managed to fill in his stupid worksheet properly.

"Yeah, Beanie thinks your felt-tip pens taste bogging," I muttered, scrunching the paper up and stuffing it in my school bag out of sight. I knew it was pathetic, but I still felt enough loyalty to Calum to keep him from getting detention on my account.

Mr Mason adjusted his spectacles, peering at me closely like I was a puzzle he just couldn't figure out. I wasn't about to make it easy for him. "You do know these things are toxic, Mr Mason, don't you?" I held up the drool-coated green pen.

Mr Mason made his startled rabbit face and ran to rescue the half-chewed pack of pens from Beanie's lunchbox. She wasn't about to give up her new favourite munchies without a fight, and pretty soon the whole class was staring at our table, watching Mr Mason trying to reason with a zoomer high on felt-tip pen fumes.

The jeering eyes felt like they were boring a hole in my skull, the silent sniggering echoing in my head even though I couldn't hear a sound. I gritted my teeth, my hands curling into fists on the tabletop. I wasn't going to just sit there and take it. Just because I was deaf didn't give them the right to laugh at me behind my back.

I knew Beanie felt every bit as bad about being picked on as I did, and any minute now she was going to notice the sniggers being aimed at us. My legs tensed, ready to launch me out of my chair so I could smack the smiles right off those sneering face.

Two soft taps on my hand stopped me before I could do anything stupid. Erin shot me one of her warning looks and shook her head. It always bugged me how she knew what I was going to do before I did it, especially if it was something I hadn't thought through clearly. She'd seen Calum's picture, and she knew that every kid in the class was staring at us and sniggering behind their hands. But instead of looking upset, Erin just sat there calmly folding her pointless worksheet into a tiny origami person. That was her thing—origami. It drove me mental the way she could just filter out the jeering, folding away at her wee sculptures when the world got ugly like she couldn't care less. I wanted her to get mad like I did when the other kids picked on us, but instead all she did was make piles of paper dolls.

Just before she stuffed the figure in her pocket, I caught a glimpse of it. It kind of looked like Calum, except the eyes had been coloured in with red felt tip so it looked like there was blood dripping down his face. Huh. Weird. But I wasn't going to stick around to admire her artwork when the bell finally put an end to my misery.

As soon as the flurry of activity in the class told me it was home time, I didn't hang about. Before Beanie could protest, I swept all her glittery stationary into her bag, grabbed her arm and pulled her to the door. I took the stairs two at a time before ditching her by the drinks machine, rushing for freedom without bothering to say goodbye.

A sea of kids came flooding down the corridor, and the top of Beanie's hat disappeared from view, swallowed up in the mainstream tide. I hoped she'd find her way out before anyone else wound her up so hard she ended up spinning in circles. But I'd already done my good deed by getting her away from the sniggering kids in the R.E. class—no way was I acting as her bodyguard all the way home. I just couldn't face another second of being laughed at.

Granny Lewis will meet her at the gate, so she won't have that far to go on her own, I told myself as I raced into the yard. *Anyway, it's not my problem.*

I already had one annoying wee sister who hadn't learned not to pee herself yet, I didn't need to go adopting another.

CHAPTER 6

By the time I got back home, the crowds were already gathering on the clifftop down the hill from our house. I dumped my schoolbag by the pile of plastic bricks cluttering up the living room floor and peered out of the front window. It looked like everyone on the island had turned up to see the turbines being fixed in place in the Bay.

Seriously people, what's the big deal? I wondered, watching the old folk shake their heads at each other and the kids take pictures like Disneyland had just opened a new park on Scragness. Mr Strachan's protest group was out in full force, waving their placards and no doubt chanting their stupid slogans at top volume. That was one thing I was glad I couldn't hear.

I had to admit I was curious though, and when I saw Mum weaving her way through the crowds with Sally, I made up my mind to go and see what all the fuss was about.

Mum'll translate if anyone talks to me, I told myself as I closed the front door. *It won't be that bad.* It made me kind of nervous though, plunging into that sea of people who were all talking at once without making a sound. It was like that game where you watched a film with the volume turned down and you had to guess what the plot was about from the actors' expressions. Only not as much fun.

"*HI,*" Mum signed awkwardly with her hands full of gurning baby. "*THERE OUR NEW TURBINE,*" she pointed out across the Bay.

"Don't call them that, they're not *ours*," I frowned. If we started calling them 'ours' just because they were opposite our house, the angry protestors might start blaming us for them instead of the other ninety-five percent of the islanders who voted for them.

"Shift yourselves, coming through," I ordered. I pushed a couple of smaller kids aside and got my first clear view out across Wicklin Bay. I got a bit of a shock at what I saw there.

The turbines were huge. Three great masts with vicious-looking blades stood at the mouth of the Bay, guarding the ocean passage like escape was now forbidden. Chalk white against the blue sky and deep-green sea, their central hubs were clusters of strange, knobbly drums and dishes that would soon be transmitting the mobile phone signal across the island from their giant antennae. The high-tech combo-turbines were bigger and meaner than I'd ever imagined, and they were closer to shore than the energy company said they'd be.

No wonder the protestors were so unhappy.

"We'll get used to them soon though, won't we, Mum?" I asked, looking for reassurance. "Mum?"

I turned round, but Mum was busy fussing over Sally who was screaming again as usual, so she couldn't free her hands to answer me. I felt a familiar surge of anger as I looked at that wee face all screwed up with non-stop hunger and neediness. With Mum and Dad, she was all blonde curls and big blue eyes, but whenever I asked for a split-second's attention from them, it was shrieks and tantrums.

41

Things would be so much better without her around, I thought moodily. *I just wish—*

I never got to finish that wish. A tupperware box full of wonky rice krispy cakes was thrust under my nose, and Beanie's woolly hat blocked my view of the turbines in the Bay.

"Chock-lit," she grinned. "Chock-o-lit."

It was more an order to try her baking than an invitation. I guess that was her way of saying thanks for the crisps the other day. I picked one that didn't look like the cherry on top had been licked to death and nodded half-heartedly at Beanie, hoping that would be enough to get rid of her. It wasn't. Granny Lewis joined the tupperware party, handing out thick slabs of shortbread to anyone unfortunate enough to cross her path. Her beady eyes fixed on me and my heart sank as she made a beeline through the crowds.

Another tub of burnt biscuits was held out, and Granny Lewis peered down her sharp beak at me, daring me to say no. I wasn't brave enough to refuse her outright, so I held up my krispy cake to show I was already sorted for munchies.

"But. It's. Short. Bread." Beanie looked at me like I was mad. "Sug-ar. On. Top. Mmm."

"Yeah, thanks Beanie, I'm deaf, not blind," I muttered. Granny Lewis was just as famous as Mrs Brody for her baking, but not in a good way. By the looks of it, Beanie had already licked all the sugar off the carbonised shortbread anyway. I glanced around, hoping I'd not been spotted at the zoomer picnic by the other kids, but as usual I was out of luck.

Calum and his gang were standing a short way off taking pictures of the turbines with their cameras. When Calum saw me with Beanie's cake, he made a face and mimed sticking his fingers in his mouth and barfing. The other boys joined in, and soon there was a whole row of kids along the clifftop all pretending to throw up into the Bay.

Granny Lewis knew they were there, but she ignored them, smiling at me instead, her face all lined and wrinkly like a scrunched-up paper bag. She said something I couldn't guess at, and Beanie set down her tub and signed for her, "YOU GOOD BOY. ME SCHOOL LOOK AFTER THANK YOU."

It was funny the way Beanie made me read her lips when she talked to me, but translated what anyone else said to me into sign language like a pro.

Granny Lewis was wrong, though. I wasn't a good boy; I didn't look out for Beanie in school or anywhere else. And right now, I was wishing she'd drop dead and take Beanie with her to the afterlife so she'd stop embarrassing me. If she knew what I was thinking, I was pretty sure she wouldn't be smiling at me like that.

I walked away fast, hoping if I put some distance between us then people wouldn't think Beanie and me were friends. Calum was still watching me, so I took a deep breath and went right up to the gang. "God, this thing's giving me the boak. Tastes like a dried turd." I chucked Beanie's krispy cake over the edge of the cliff, hoping that would be enough to win me just one second of approval.

It was. On the way down the krispy cake hit a seagull mid-flight, sending it screeching off in another direction. The boys cheered, and even though I couldn't hear the sound, it made me feel like I belonged again for a brief moment. Calum grinned and punched me on the arm. "Nice one," he mouthed. Then he held up his football and asked, "You playing?"

I hesitated, looking at the rest of the gang to see what their reaction would be. A couple of the boys exchanged glances. Ryan rolled his eyes and muttered something under his breath. That was enough to put me off.

"Nah, not today," I shrugged. "Got a ton of homework to do."

"OK. See you." Calum turned away quickly. I could see he was disappointed. I was disappointed too. Didn't he know by now how hard it was for me to act normal when they were all looking at me like I was a freak?

As I watched them head back up the hill, I caught sight of Beanie's face. She was staring at me all sad and hurt, her bottom lip quivering. Guess I should've made sure she was looking the other way before I chucked her stupid krispy cake off the cliff. I rummaged around in my pockets to see if I had any chewing gum left to bribe her with to stop her crying and showing everyone how mean I could be. I hated the way she always made me feel responsible whenever she got hurt. It wasn't my fault she was a zoomer and didn't have any friends.

"ME HAVE CAKE? THEY LOOK GREAT!" Erin came sailing up like a rescue ship, putting her arm round Beanie's shoulder and taking some of the rice krispy cakes from her tub. Beanie beamed when Erin took a big enthusiastic bite, tugging her granny's sleeve to make sure Erin didn't miss out on the burnt shortbread either.

"Thanks. Mrs. Lew-is. These. Are. Love-lee," Beanie translated, though how she worked out what Erin was signing when her hands were full of krispy cake and biscuits I don't know. I do know that the look of reproach Erin shot me as she walked back to her friends hurt like a slap in the face. The two mainstream girls didn't look too happy at the munchies Erin handed them, but with Beanie watching they were too polite to turn their noses up. Not like me.

They regretted it a minute later though, when Calum and his gang walked past and started doing their mimed puking routine. The girls went bright red and put the krispy cakes down like they were diseased or something. Erin went right on eating hers, ignoring the laughing boys like they didn't even exist. Then when she'd finished, she pulled a notebook out of her backpack, tearing out a piece of paper and folding it crease after crease into another wee origami person.

I had no idea how she kept her cool like that. Just watching her zen-like calm made me restless—I wanted to shake her, to make her lose her temper and prove it wasn't just me who felt bad when the mainstream kids picked on the zoomers. But she didn't ever show it hurt. She just went on making her stupid paper dolls and pretending nothing could touch her. It drove me nuts.

A hand tapped my arm, and I looked round to see Mr Mason handing me a note.

"*The group's going down to the substation to protest,*" he'd written. "*Would you and your mother like to join us?*"

I rolled my eyes at him and shook my head. I knew he was just trying to get me to 'join in' and feel 'part of the community', but his clumsy attempts to get me to socialize weren't exactly working in school, so what made him think a fourteen year old would want to hang out with a bunch of pensioners after the bell went? I missed my old friends, but I wasn't *that* desperate to make new ones.

Mr Mason gave up on me and went to join the group heading down the hill to the substation. Mr Strachan looked like he'd brought half the contents of his store to keep them going, so I had a feeling their protest was going to be a long one.

What's the point? I muttered to myself, gazing out at the turbines cutting slow, jagged circles in the restless air. The sun was dipping lower, the gathered people shivering as they took their last look at the metal giants before turning for home. *The turbines are here to stay, it's too late to protest.*

I stood there on the clifftop staring at the turbines long after the crowds had gone, long after Calum and my former gang had left me for their football game, long after Mum had carried Sally home to tell her a story and put her to bed the way she used to do with me.

It was too late now for a lot of things.

CHAPTER 7

It was a bad night.

The wind was restless, rushing up the cliffs and whipping the tree branches in our front yard. I couldn't hear the twigs tapping against my bedroom window, but I could see their shadows dancing across the walls as I tossed and turned in the dark. Sally had been restless too, whingeing all evening and demanding every second of my parents' time. 'Teething', Mum said, like that wee brat needed an excuse for her rotten behaviour.

Worst of all, Dad was restless. He always got like that the night before he sailed. All evening he paced from room to room, making half-hearted attempts to put Sally's baby clutter back in some kind of order. It was like he'd weighed anchor and left us all behind already. Mum was better at dealing with his moods than I was. She pottered around with him, finding wee jobs to keep him busy, like sorting the rubbish bin for recycling and folding the ironing into neat piles. Me? I spent the evening at the kitchen table pretending to do my homework, all the while watching Dad drift further and further away.

I kicked my quilt off and rolled over in bed to check the time. Twelve forty-three. Urgh, if I didn't get to sleep soon then I'd be a zombie in school tomorrow. Huh, fit right in with the rest of the zoomers then, wouldn't I?

I climbed down from my cabin bed, trying not to trip over the schoolbag and piles of books I'd tossed on the carpet. Opening the door softly, I tiptoed down the hall to the bathroom to splash water on my face and hunt in the medicine cabinet for aspirin to soothe the headache building behind my eyes. I popped a couple of pills and turned the light off, trying to remember where the loose floorboards were that creaked as loud as gunfire. I didn't want to disturb anyone. Our resident baby goblin woke my parents up so many times in the night they sleep-walked through their mornings as it was. I suppose I should be grateful I couldn't hear her shrieking her head off, but somehow I didn't feel like getting down on my knees and giving thanks for that one.

I'd got halfway back to my own room when something made me stop dead, the hairs on the back of my neck prickling. I wasn't one to get spooked easily, but right at that moment I had a weird feeling that I wasn't alone. I turned slowly, looking back up the hall.

I was right. I was being watched.

In the moonlit nursery, two huge eyes were gazing at me above a mouth wide open in a silent wail. Sally was sitting up in her cot, ready to wake the whole house. I hesitated for a long moment. Babysitting definitely wasn't my thing, and Sally didn't exactly gurgle with joy when I came anywhere near her. But Dad was heading out on a trawling run early in the morning, and Mum was knackered from running after her day and night, so right now I was the only one awake enough for nappy-changing duty.

"What's up, you wee monster? Got yourself covered in poop again?" I muttered as I tiptoed over to her cot. Sally looked up at me suspiciously, her tiny brow knitting like she couldn't work out if me being there improved the situation or not.

"Let's have a look." I undid the snap fasteners of her night suit and checked her nappy, probably not as gently as she was used to as she started whimpering again and clenching her fists. Yup, a great big number two sat there waiting to be cleaned. Brilliant.

"God, you're a manky wee beastie, aren't you?" I grumbled, dumping her down on the changing mat and hoping I could get her cleaned up before her gurning changed to full scale shrieking. "Come here, and if you pee on me while I'm fixing you then you're going head-first into the rubbish bin."

Sally didn't appreciate speed over gentleness and started thrashing about, spreading poo all over the mat. I tried to clean it off with wet wipes, but she kept wriggling round like I was trying to murder her, getting her legs and my hands covered in big brown streaks.

That was when I snapped.

"What's the matter with you, you wee brat, huh?" I demanded. "You've got Mum and Dad twisted so far round your finger they're ready to break, and here I am trying to sort you out in the middle of the night and you're not even grateful! What more do you want?"

I picked Sally up so her face was right in front of mine. That had shut her up alright, and her eyes were bug-wide in the moonlight. "You know something?" I told her, "you're the worst thing that ever happened to my family. Everything was great till you came along and ruined it. If it was up to me, I'd take you out to the Bay right now and let you sink to the bottom of the ocean. Bye-bye. No more selfish baby Sally. Good riddance."

I didn't mean it. As soon as the words were out I regretted them. Sally's bottom lip was quivering just like Beanie's did when I was mean to her, and it made my heart hurt just as much. I was about to give her a hug despite her manky bum and tell her I was sorry, when I saw a shadow looming on the wall. Dad was standing in the doorway, staring down at me with a face like thunder on a wet day.

In two strides he'd crossed the room and snatched Sally off me like I couldn't be trusted not to fling her straight out the window. Sally liked that rough treatment even less than my attempts at nappy changing, and she started howling for real, letting Dad know just how mean I was to her behind his back.

"There, there, Princess. Daddy's got you."

I knew that's what Dad was saying to her—he said the same thing every time she started crying. I stood there trembling, feeling sick at being discovered. *OK, Dad,* I thought, *you got me. You found out I hate the wee sister you inflicted on me without my consent. Now what are you going to do about it?*

As the long seconds passed and Dad just gazed at Sally, rocking her in his arms like I didn't exist, I almost hoped he would get mad and yell at me. Then, as the silence dragged on, I started to wish he'd take off his belt and beat me the way he said Grandad did to him when he was a boy. It was crazy, but anger, pain, *anything* would be better than being ignored like this.

"Dad?" I was pretty sure my voice was quavering like it did when I was four or five and I'd hurt myself.

No response. Dad just went right on rocking his wee princess.

"Dad?" I tried again. "Aren't you going to say something?"

Dad finally looked up at me, the disappointment written so clearly on his face it was like he'd taken a marker pen to his forehead. "Bed, Max. Now!" he mouthed, and that was all. Not anger, not punishment, not even the slightest interest. Just three words and I was dismissed as if I didn't even matter.

I stomped down the hall, not caring how much noise I made anymore. It didn't matter now that precious wee Sally was awake and bawling the house down. I slammed my bedroom door and threw my clothes and shoes on over my pyjamas. There was no way I would get to sleep now, and I wasn't wasting the rest of the night crying into my pillow. The only thing that was going to soothe my aching head was a midnight walk. Ever since I was little I'd been sneaking out at night to go and sit on the cliffs, watching the stars and listening to the waves crash against the rocks. I couldn't hear the roar of the tide anymore, but the clifftop was still my sanctuary where I could cast my angry thoughts to the wind and let the ocean carry them away.

I clambered out of my bedroom window carefully, gazing down the hill at the new turbines outlined against the dark sky. From here they looked like giant skeletons with three outstretched hands, ready to come striding up the beach towards me. I shuddered, dropping from the sill and sliding down onto the porch roof.

And that was when I saw it. There was a light on in the Bay. A ghostly white flash bobbed up and down once, twice, then winked out.

I froze, peering at the spot where the strange light had disappeared. The Bay was dark once more, only the pale shimmer of moonlight rippling across the water when the clouds parted. But it wasn't the moon's reflection I'd seen. Someone was down there in a boat, floating in the Bay beside the brand-new turbines. I wasn't sure if it was just a fishing boat, or some sleepless islanders having a late-night sail, but after seeing how angry the protesters were today, I had a funny feeling it might be something more.

I almost hoped it was—a mystery to solve was just what I needed to stop my mind chewing itself to pieces over my run-in with Dad.

With a final backwards glance to make sure he hadn't come to check on me, I climbed down onto the front yard wall and stepped into the night.

CHAPTER 8

As I made my way down the hill the night wind picked up, rippling through the grass and sending clouds racing across the face of the moon. My heart was beating just as fast as I reached the overhang where the cliffs fell away to the beach far below. I peered out over Wicklin Bay, watching the huge turbine blades turning slowly against the black sky. For a long moment, nothing else stirred.

And then the light flashed again, brighter this time.

It was coming from a boat, I was sure of it now. Before the light blinked off, I could just make out the faint outline of a cabin and decking before it was swallowed up by the dark. I wasn't sure why, but the sight of that boat sent a shiver down my spine.

What's so weird about a boat in the Bay? I asked myself, trying to ignore the knot of unease forming in my guts. *It's just someone out on a late-night sailing trip, or maybe the energy company sent a patrol boat to make sure the turbines were safe from protestors.*

But I knew none of that was likely. No one was daft enough to go pleasure cruising round the Bay at night. After sundown, the wind swelled and currents swept across the Atlantic, sending rip tides thundering up the beach to crash against the cliff face. And boats didn't just get lost these days. Not with sat-nav and all the fancy gear even the basic rigs were equipped with. So that just left the energy company, but why on earth would they be out there checking the turbines in the dead of night? Mr Strachan's protest group had homemade placards and piles of leaflets, not gun boats and plastic explosives. It wasn't like they could do any real harm to the turbines.

The bright light flashed again, sweeping the Bay from behind the towering masts. It was drifting further round the headland now, nearing the base of the hill where the substation had been built. I watched the beacon approach the makeshift jetty, lighting up the steel pylons and transformer sheds before cutting out again just as suddenly, throwing the whole base into darkness once more. I waited, peering down the hill, straining my eyes in the gloom to catch a glimpse of movement.

There. Down by the substation. Something was coming.

Another light—a smaller, dimmer one—was bobbing round the substation perimeter fence. It paused once, the weak light reflecting off the chain links, before climbing swiftly up the hill to the clifftop. It was heading straight for me.

I shuffled back in the grass, my heart pounding as I watched the light approaching.

What have I got to be scared of? I told myself, trying to shake the growing dread that I had witnessed something that wasn't supposed to be observed. *I live here. I've got every right to be sitting on the clifftop. Stop being such a wimp.* If someone was coming my way and wanted to question me, then I was going to meet them face to face. I took a deep breath and got to my feet. That was when a huge shape leapt out of the dark and slammed into me so hard it knocked me flat on my back.

"What the hell..?" I yelled, fighting off the mound of wet fur and teeth pinning me to the ground. If I hadn't been so spooked by the lights I'd seen, I would've known right away there was something familiar about the smell of the monster attacking me, but it took me a minute of struggling to realise the creature was licking my face instead of eating it.

"Twister?"

Oh, for God's sake, I'd nearly peed myself over a cuddlefest with my uncle's dog.

A moment later two strong arms pulled me upright and brushed me down, and in the flashlight's steady glow I saw my Uncle Stuart grinning back at me.

"Hi, Max," he mouthed.

Uncle Stuart sat down in the grass beside me and pulled a small notepad and pen from his coat pocket. Positioning his torch on the grass between us so I could read his messages, he started scribbling away before I even had time to say hello back.

"*What you doing out here so late? Sally keeping you up?*"

"Nah, went and got myself baby-proofed a couple of years back, remember?" I laughed, pointing at my ears. Uncle Stuart was the only one I could joke with about the accident, even though he'd been there and seen the whole thing. Instead of looking serious like Dad did on the rare occasions it was mentioned, Uncle Stuart just smiled back and started writing again.

"*What do you think of your new view? Bit ugly if you ask me, and Twister's not keen.*" He patted the overexcited dog that was still trying to lick a hole in my face as I read the notepad.

"It's not the best, but if it means I can get on the internet like the energy company promised then they can build as many as they like," I shrugged. "I'm pretty sick of stone-age Scragness, and it's not like there's much else to do around here."

I didn't need to say any more. Uncle Stuart knew all about my problems with Calum and the gang, and how much I hated my zoomer class in school. I could tell Uncle Stuart anything. He didn't try to fix me like I was some broken thing that needed put back together before he could feel comfortable around me. He just listened. Not like Dad.

Maybe it was the difference in age that made it easier. Uncle Stuart was much younger than Dad, and sometimes when he was messing about with the barbeque in the back yard or playing football with some of the local guys, you'd think he was still a teenager himself. And the best thing about Uncle Stuart was that he was always ready to talk to me. He even carried that wee notepad around with him everywhere he went on the island, just in case he bumped into me.

We patted Twister for a bit until the daft German shepherd calmed down, then we sat in silence, watching the turbine arms turning slowly in the dark. But it wasn't like the silences I had with Dad when we both squirmed uncomfortably, searching for something to say. This was friendly, easy. If Dad made even a fraction of the effort Uncle Stuart did to talk with me, we wouldn't be having problems. We wouldn't have had that showdown in the nursery tonight, and Dad wouldn't be lying in bed right now thinking his son was a monster who'd painted a target on his baby sister's head.

Before I could swallow the lump forming in my throat, Uncle Stuart picked up the pen and started writing again. It was like he could read my mind.

"How's your dad doing? Things any better?"

I knew exactly what he was asking. Uncle Stuart worked on Dad's boat with him, so he wasn't asking about fishing, or Dad's health, or anything pointless like that. I rubbed Twister's ears, trying to decide if I should just come clean and tell him about tonight's nursery drama. It wouldn't exactly make me look like the good guy, but I was pretty sure Uncle Stuart would understand.

"It's getting worse," I admitted. "Dad just won't make any effort to talk, you know? He hasn't bothered learning any sign language, and he refuses to write anything down for me. I just don't get why he doesn't even try—it's like he's blaming me for being deaf or something, like the accident was my fault."

Uncle Stuart fiddled with the pen, gazing off into the Bay for a bit before writing again. "*He doesn't blame you, Max, he blames himself. He feels guilty about what happened, and how everything got spoiled for you. He can't forgive himself for bringing you out on the boat that day.*"

"So you keep telling me," I muttered. "But it's not like I hadn't been on the trawler before, and there was no way anyone could've known the winch line was going to snap. It was just a stupid accident. Anyway, if Dad does feel guilty, he's got no right taking it out on me. You should see the way he looks at me any time my special needs class is mentioned—it's like he wants the ground to open up and swallow him so he doesn't have to admit to the world his boy's disabled."

I hated the 'd' word almost as much as Mrs Brody hated the 'r' word, but right now it was the only one that seemed to fit.

"*He isn't embarrassed by you, Max! No way, don't even think that.*" Uncle Stuart's handwriting got all scrawly the way Mr Mason's did when he was trying to get his point across quickly. "*He just...*" Uncle Stuart paused, chewing the end of the pen. "*It's complicated. When he was at school...*" He stopped again, the last word trailing off into a doodle while he tried to think of a way to end the sentence.

"When he was at school…what?" I prompted. There was something hiding just below those words, some secret I was close to uncovering. Mum grew up on Scragness, and she talked about what she and her school friends got up to all the time. But Dad was from Aberdeen, and I'd never heard him mention his time at school even once. If I could just find out what secrets Dad was keeping, then maybe I'd have the key to unlocking him and getting him to open up to me again. I missed him so much it was driving me crazy.

But Uncle Stuart was his brother's keeper alright. "*Sorry, Big Mac,*" he wrote, "*but you need to talk to your dad about it. I know it's tough right now, but things will get better, I promise. I'll have a word with him myself and see if I can get him to stop being so stubborn, but in the meantime, keep at it. I know it's not easy, what with Sally and everything.*"

I nodded and looked away, disappointed. I wasn't going to be solving the puzzle that was my dad tonight after all. Uncle Stuart sensed the shift in my mood, and stood up, putting Twister back on the lead again. "*Daft mutt's had his walk, better go get some sleep,*" he wrote on his notepad. "*Got fish to catch at first light. Best get yourself back to bed too—you don't want to give the other space cadets in school a head start tomorrow, do you?*"

I couldn't help laughing at that.

"*See you later, Big Mac.*"

Big Mac. Huh. I liked how he still used my old nickname from before the accident, even though Ryan had changed it last year to 'Mad Max'.

Uncle Stuart let me read the last line he'd scribbled on the notepad by torchlight before closing it and putting it back in his pocket ready for next time. He was onto about his twenty-third pad by now, and I knew he kept them all too, the way some people store their old cinema tickets or birthday cards. I watched him disappear with Twister down the other side of the hill, the torchlight fading into the night.

It was only when Uncle Stuart had gone I realised I'd forgotten to ask him about the strange lights I'd seen out in the Bay.

EXPERIMENT XO1 – PHASE 1

CHAPTER 9

ONE MONTH AFTER THE TURBINES

"Urgh, what is that even supposed to *mean*?" I grumbled.

I hit pause on the laptop video and slumped in my seat, admitting defeat. When I looked back up, Erin was grinning at me. *So* not helpful.

"YOU OK," I complained, forming the words clumsily with my hands. "YOU UNDERSTAND EVERYTHING. ME THINK SHE TRY FLY LIKE BIRD." I flapped my arms around for emphasis. Erin's grin widened. "HOW ME LEARN CHEMISTRY WITH BIRD WOMAN?"

I'm pretty sure that's not really what I said. I was getting better at reading sign language, but my own signing was still all over the place. Erin seemed to get the message, though.

"NEED MORE PRACTISE," she encouraged. "DON'T READ EVERY WORD, READ TOTAL MEANING."

I nodded at the woman on the frozen screen and scribbled on the back of my chemistry notebook, "*As far as I can see she means 'Clear the runway, get ready for takeoff'*."

Erin laughed and chucked her exercise book at me. I caught it and scribbled a rude word in the margin of her science report before she could snatch it back. So much for us working on our communication skills.

This term Erin and me were spending a lot more time in the mainstream classes so we'd be ready for our exams in two years. Only problem was, Mrs Brody couldn't come with us to translate as she had to teach her own class, so she'd got hold of all these educational videos that explained our coursework in sign language to make sure we'd keep up. Huh, so Erin could keep up, more like. As far as I was concerned, our science subjects were hard enough without me having to learn them in a foreign language.

"SHE SAY THAT," Erin signed, pointing out a passage in the chemistry textbook.

"'In a solution, the dissolving substance is called the solute'," I read aloud, before signing, "NO WAY. SHE PRETEND SHE BIRD WOMAN."

Erin rolled her eyes and went back to scribbling answers on her worksheet. I shut up and started on my own work, leaning over her shoulder and copying her when I got to the bit I'd missed. By now I could read Erin's silent warnings pretty clearly. There was only so much joking about sign language she would take before she suddenly snapped and got defensive. And I had pushed her right up to the line today.

"YOU OK?" Mrs Brody signed, stopping at our desk on her way round each group.

"Yes, Mrs Brody," I said at the same time as Erin signed it. I wasn't sure whether she was asking about our chemistry work or whether we were getting on OK with each other, but right now I was happy to lie about both. Mrs Brody shot us a questioning look, then moved off to help David and Beanie with their own maths work. I was glad she wasn't going to push her whole 'you two need to work together more' agenda today.

It wasn't that I didn't like Erin. She was super smart, with a wicked sense of humour and a smile that could knock you sideways. The problem was the whole communication thing. Being deaf, she hadn't learned to talk like ordinary folk—her speech was all slurred and mumbled like she was talking through a mouthful of toffee, and her constantly moving hands and exaggerated expressions had made her the butt of our gang's jokes in primary school. Some of the mainstream kids made an effort to understand her, but others just laughed at her. That didn't stop her. She just went right on talking, making her point whether folk had the decency to listen or not.

I guess that was what made me uncomfortable around her. She wasn't embarrassed by her disability the way I was. When kids laughed at her, mimicking her voice or pretending to sign rude words, she just looked at them like they were slime on the sole of her shoe. Me, I wanted to hide under the nearest rock when they started their 'let's all pick on the space cadets' routine. I just wished she would quit using that mouth-full-of-sticky-toffee voice of hers all the time when she could write things down for people instead. I hated the way it made her sound less smart than she really was. I hated the way it drew attention to her.

And to me by association.

Before I could finish my mental list of 'things that bug me about Erin', she leaned over and started correcting the spelling on my worksheet, putting in all the extra letters where I'd spelt 'dissolve' and 'assorted' with only one 's'. I grabbed her sheet, turning all the 'o's in her words into stick figures, and before we knew it, we were having a pen fight to see who could get more ink on the other's hands. Mrs Brody looked up from her maths group and shook her head once. That was all it took. We settled back down and finished off our own worksheets quietly.

"*Hey,*" I nudged Erin when I was done and scribbled in my chemistry notebook so Mrs Brody wouldn't see. "*What's up with Beanie today? She's been all grumpy. She didn't even celebrate winning that board game this morning. Is she sick or something?*"

I didn't like seeing Beanie so sad. Usually she did my head in being so upbeat, trying to make me laugh when I was grumpy and getting way too excited over stupid things like board games and new glitter stickers. But not today.

Erin glanced over. Beanie was sitting all scrunched up and defensive in her chair like a hedgehog, fiddling with the corner of her worksheet over and over until it ripped. Then she started crying. Not noisily, like she usually did when she got upset or overexcited, all huffing and puffing for breath. This time it looked like she was trying not to draw attention to herself. It worked too, as Mrs Brody didn't look up from the group she was talking to. David leaned forward in his wheelchair, his hand wobbling as it reached out to pat hers awkwardly.

God, things must be bad if even David managed to take five minutes off dribbling down his uniform to comfort her.

"*It's Calum's fault,*" Erin scribbled on my notebook. She looked annoyed. I instantly tensed. We were going to have a falling out over this, I could read the warning signs a mile off. "*Him and his minions were winding her up this morning, saying mean things to her.*"

"*What was he saying?*" I wrote back carefully, trying not to look like I was gearing up for a fight.

Erin's pen raced across my notebook like a speedboat, leaving angry words floating in its wake. "*He told Beanie that her granny was old, and when she died social services would come from the mainland to put Beanie in a children's home.*"

"What?" I gasped, trying to work out if I'd read Erin's scribbled words right. I grabbed my pen again and wrote, "*No way would Calum say anything that mean. The gang goes too far sometimes, especially Ryan, but not Calum. He'd never say that. God, that's just—*"

"*Evil?*" Erin underlined the word three times and shot me a look. "*Yeah, that pretty much sums up those… TOSSERS.*" She threw down her pen and signed the last word for emphasis. I knew it, as she'd taught it to me just last week.

My hands were curling into defensive fists, and I had to loosen them before I could write back. "*Calum and the guys are alright,*" I insisted. "*They gave you a hard time in primary school, but they were just wee kids then, they didn't mean—*"

"*Stop making excuses for them!*" Erin interrupted, her sea-green eyes blazing as she scribbled furiously. "*You were just as bad in primary school, always laughing at me and Beanie behind our backs and making stupid jokes. You'd still be hanging around with them now saying nasty things about us if they hadn't dumped you for being deaf.*" Her pen was zooming across the page, and it took me a minute to read what she'd just written.

"*They didn't dump me! I just…moved on,*" I wrote, my own pen slowing to a lame stop. It was a lie and we both knew it. But I had to keep telling myself that if I could fix my friendship with Calum and the boys, there'd be hope for me and Dad. "*Anyway, how do you know what he said to Beanie when you couldn't hear it?*" I went on the attack now that I'd been argued into a corner. "*For all you know he told her a joke and she didn't get it, so she started crying as usual. She probably made that story up to get sympathy, and*

64

you fell for it." I was clutching at straws to defend Calum, and it was getting more obvious by the minute.

"*BEANIE TELL ME,*" Erin signed so slowly there was no way I could miss her meaning. "*SHE NEVER TELL LIE. NOT LIKE YOU.*"

Before I could sign a reply, Erin put her worksheet down on her mother's desk with a silent thump, sitting down at Beanie's table to help with the group's maths work. Just like that, she was calm again, looking all mild-mannered and chilled-out. But I could see the tension in her shoulders when she leaned over to help David grip his pen, and the hard set of her jaw when she straightened Beanie's squint hat. It wasn't just her sign language I was getting better at reading.

The lunchtime bell rang before I'd worked out how to fix the mess I'd made. At least I'd get an hour to myself to cool down. I used to go home for lunch before Sally was born. Back then Mum would make me scrambled eggs or hotdogs and we'd watch TV together. But not now. Now I came back to dirty dishes and a list of chores a mile long that needed done before I could even rummage up a basic lunch of instant noodles.

What with Sally needing an endless supply of nappies and baby gear, money was too tight for school dinners every day, so now it was mostly soggy sandwiches thrown together with whatever could be found in the cupboard. I hated sitting at the zoomer table in the lunch hall surrounded by sniggering mainstreamers, so I ate my sandwiches up on the rocks near the harbour, watching the boats come in and the anglers cast out at high tide. It wasn't much fun spending all that time on my own every day, but it wasn't as lonely as being at home with Mum and the baby, or sitting by myself in the lunch hall.

If we just had the smart phones and internet access we were promised I'd have plenty to keep me entertained at lunchtime, I thought resentfully. Everyone on the island was hacked off about the delay. We thought we'd be connected as soon as the turbines came, but the energy company had packed up and left the day after everything was in place. They said the project would be overseen by a group of government specialists who'd be coming to distribute the phones soon, but what exactly did 'soon' mean? Tomorrow? Next week? Next year? At this rate I was going to be ninety before I got connected to the rest of the world. And if the government group wasn't here yet, how come I kept seeing lights out in the Bay at night, and how come that boat kept docking at the substation jetty? Who'd been coming and going under cover of darkness these last few weeks?

I could always take a look during the day, I told myself for about the millionth time. It wasn't like walking around outside the fence was illegal. I could go there now and eat my lunch right outside the padlocked gate if I wanted to. But there was something weird about that place. Maybe it was the silent humming of the generators I could feel but not hear that set my teeth on edge. Maybe it was all the creepy high-voltage machinery that stood in rows like something out of a sci-fi horror film that unnerved me, or the way the station always looked so strangely empty.

Maybe though, it was the turbines themselves that made me nervous.

Think I'll just stick to the harbour, I decided. *I can't be bothered walking all the way back from the Bay.* It was a lame excuse, but better than admitting to myself that the turbines with their skeletal blades and ghost-town substation totally creeped me out.

I was just putting my pencil case back in my schoolbag, when Mrs Brody waved to summon me and Erin to her table. "YOU GO HOME WITH HER ," she told us, pointing to Beanie. "HER BOX CARRY SCHOOL."

I groaned inwardly as I read the signs. The school was holding a fundraising bring-and-buy sale at the end of next month, and it was a fair bet that Granny Lewis had half the planet's second-hand junk hoarded in her house waiting to be donated.

"YOU [SOMETHING] HELP HER CARRY."

"What does that word mean?" I asked, copying the unfamiliar sign Mrs Brody had used. She smiled and wrote 'volunteer' on the pad on her desk. I opened my mouth to protest, then closed it again just as quick. Mrs Brody used 'volunteer' the way other folk used 'ordered at gunpoint'.

"NOW? AFTER SCHOOL FINISH WE CARRY BOX?" Erin surprised me by not immediately doing what she was told. Despite being Beanie's best friend, she clearly didn't fancy the idea of being force-fed burnt toast and twenty-year-old jam in Granny Lewis's pokey wee kitchen any more than I did.

Mrs Brody signed something to Erin really quickly, her hands moving too fast for me to catch the whole meaning. It was something to do with 'not being well', and 'keeping an eye on', so I guessed Granny Lewis wasn't feeling up to walking Beanie back and forth to school today, and was worried that she'd get picked on without a bodyguard. That was probably what happened this morning with Calum and the boys, and Mrs Brody didn't want it happening twice in the same day.

Erin nodded at her mother and went to help Beanie put her worksheets away. It wasn't like Beanie couldn't do things for herself, but Erin was always acting like her big sister, helping her with her schoolwork and making sure she kept track of all the half-chewed stationary in her pencil case. I had a sneaky feeling sometimes Erin just did it to make me look bad by comparison. Whatever, I wasn't about to add 'personal slave' to my list of babysitting and box-carrying chores.

I waited by the door, hanging back when Erin and Beanie came out so it didn't look like we were leaving together. I wasn't the only one avoiding them, though. Just as we passed through the main gate I saw Erin's two mainstream friends ducking behind the bike shed so she wouldn't see them. Maybe they'd finally realised hanging out with a zoomer, even one as smart as Erin, wasn't going to do much for their popularity.

Or maybe it was something else.

The atmosphere in the school yard had changed over the last couple of weeks, the temperature dropping to permanently frosty, and not just because autumn had arrived. It was like the divide between the mainstream kids and the zoomers had grown to the size of a black hole. Now everywhere I looked, I saw hostile faces staring back at me, waiting for an excuse to attack.

Nah, I was being paranoid.

But still, as Erin and Beanie crossed the road into the town square, I hurried to catch up with them. Beanie wasn't the only one who felt like she had a target painted on her forehead because she was a zoomer. For now, there was safety in numbers.

CHAPTER 10

All the way through the village and past the Hendersons' farm, what Calum had said to Beanie bugged me. Ryan and the other boys had wound her up plenty of times before, sometimes even taking her crisps or juice off her when Calum wasn't looking. But Calum never did anything mean to the zoomers, not since I became one myself, and he always stepped in before the gang's messing about went too far. I just couldn't believe he would say something so sick to Beanie. It wasn't like him at all.

"Beanie, are you sure about what Calum said to you this morning?" I asked, grabbing her arm so suddenly she nearly tripped. "Did he definitely say that stuff about your granny dying and the children's home and…"

I trailed off, seeing Beanie's eyes go bug-wide. Oops, I probably should have led up to that subject a bit more gently instead of stomping straight in with my size nine shoes.

"That's. What. He. Said," Beanie nodded, her chin wobbling dangerously close to a full-scale meltdown. "He. Said… He. Said…"

"OK, OK, I was just checking."

"YOU ASK THAT AGAIN WHY?" Erin signed angrily, guessing from Beanie's expression what I'd asked her. "C.A.L.U.M. WRONG," she said, finger spelling his name. "DROP IT."

"ME KNOW," I signed back quickly. "BUT C.A.L.U.M. NOT NORMAL. ME WORRIED. NOW EVERYONE NOT NORMAL. LAST WEEK J.O.A.N.N.E..." I stumbled over the fingerspelling and went on, "HISTORY SHE PULL HARD GIRL HAIR. WHY? NO REASON. YESTERDAY LUNCH J.O.H.N.N.Y. KICK SMALL BOY. STRANGE! BEFORE HE ALWAYS QUIET, HE LIKE..."

I couldn't remember the sign for Buddha from the R.E. class, and my signing was getting more and more tangled, so I just waited to see if Erin understood what I was trying to say. She worked it out pretty quick, and after screwing up her forehead for a bit, Beanie got what I'd said too.

"Every-one's. Mean." She nodded. "Mean. Mean. Mean."

But Erin didn't look convinced. "KIDS ALWAYS MEAN. BEFORE YOU DIDN'T SEE. BEFORE YOU MEAN TOO," she signed to me. "NOW YOU SEE KIDS MEAN NO FUN, HUH?" She raised an eyebrow.

I quit right there and then. Erin had put up the Great Wall of Past Resentment between us again, and no amount of me talking sense was going to bring it down this side of home time. Pushing all thoughts of the other kids' weird behaviour to the back of my head, I followed Beanie and Erin down the road, psyching myself up to face whatever mush Granny Lewis was going to serve up for lunch. If the worst came to the worst, I always had Mum's soggy tuna rolls in my bag as backup.

Beanie's house was at the far end of the fields, about a mile inland from mine. Sitting at the base of the hills, it caught the run-off whenever there was a heavy storm, and the front garden was submerged under a foot of water. I jumped over the puddles to the front door with Erin, but Beanie just squished through the miniature lake flooding the yard like she didn't even see it anymore. She made sure we wiped our feet carefully on the mat before we stepped inside, even though she was the one with a layer of mud stuck to the bottom of her shoes.

The house was small and cramped, with yellowing wallpaper and a faded carpet that looked a hundred years old. The smell of overcooked spaghetti hoops and burnt toast wafted down the narrow hall, summoning us to the kitchen whether we were hungry or not. Granny Lewis was bent over the cooker, trying to stir the pot and butter the toast simultaneously with her arthritic hands, and making a hash of both. She looked paler than usual, but seeing as she was about two hundred and eighty-three, she was halfway to decomposing anyway.

Beanie ran to give her a big hug, and I couldn't help wondering as I watched Granny Lewis wince in pain just how long the old woman had left. Calum's words this morning may have been cruel, but that didn't mean he was wrong. Beanie didn't have any other family, and when Granny Lewis passed on it was pretty certain she'd get taken into care on the mainland. I bet that thought kept them both awake at night.

Before I could get my sandwiches out of my bag, I'd been hustled to a seat at the kitchen table and served a big plate of carbonized toast and mushy pasta hoops.

"Thanks, Mrs Lewis, this is great," Erin said slowly, her mouth forming the words clumsily out loud so I could read her lips. She took a big bite of toast and a spoonful of spaghetti hoops and tried not to make it look like she was eating cardboard and worms covered in tomato sauce.

Oh, you great big fibber, I thought smugly. *And after you being so high and mighty earlier about me not always telling the truth.*

Beanie chatted away as we ate, telling Granny Lewis all about the board game she'd won that morning and the stall she'd been put in charge of for the bring-and-buy sale. She signed as she went along so Erin and me could keep up too, even though we could read her lips. It bugged me that she'd picked up sign language almost effortlessly from hanging around with Erin in primary school when I was only just getting the hang of it now after so much practice.

"You finished, pet?" Granny Lewis patted my hand and pointed at my plate, mouthing the words carefully. I nodded, feeling guilty at passing back the lunch I'd barely touched, but I was more annoyed by the fact she managed to communicate with me without making it into a huge effort like my dad. Granny Lewis had never been bothered by Erin and me being deaf, and Beanie was so good at reading sign language she might get a job as an interpreter one day if she could only speed up her own speech to more than three words a minute.

"Wash. Dish-es," Beanie ordered. "Then. Back. To. School." She wiped her hands on the clump of kitchen roll her granny handed her, but seemed totally oblivious to the tomato sauce moustache she was wearing. Everybody thought Beanie got her nickname from the hats she wore, but I was pretty sure it was because she never ate things like baked beans without getting half of them stuck to her face.

Erin cleaned the plates at the sink while I did my best to dry them with a damp tea towel and Beanie directed me to their proper places in the cluttered cupboards. God, Granny Lewis had enough cups and dish-cloth mountains to open three thousand charity shops. She tried to help clean up by scraping the plates

72

into the bin, but she was tired and struggled to lift them. When we were done and she was handing out chocolate fingers from her biscuit tin, I could see her hands shaking. Things were not looking good for Beanie and her chances of staying on the island past Christmas. I wasn't Beanie's biggest fan—she attracted the mainstream kid's laughter like bees to a picnic and she took her board games way more seriously than a gambling addict—but still...I didn't like to think of her crying herself to sleep in a mainland children's home, with her face all screwed up like Sally's when I was mean to her.

"YOU READY?" Erin tapped me on the forehead to wake me up from my daydream, and pointed to the boxes sitting in the hall. "YOU CARRY HEAVY BOX," she signed, nudging it towards me. "YOU ARM LONG LIKE MONKEY."

Huh, I wasn't *that* tall. But I took the biggest box without complaining, relieved to find it wasn't nearly as heavy as Erin thought. It looked like Granny Lewis wouldn't be parting with her entire crockery collection for charity any time soon.

We trudged back up the lane with our boxes and bags, hoping it was going to stay dry till we got back to school. When we reached the main road, I looked round to see Beanie stomping determinedly off up the hill, swinging her carrier bag full of mangy stuffed toys for the sale.

"Hey, Beanie, where you going?" I called. She yelled something back silently from way off in the distance, but I couldn't see what it was. I exchanged glances with Erin, but with our hands full of cardboard boxes we couldn't sign anything, so we turned back and followed Beanie up the hill to the clifftop. Mrs Brody may have told Erin to keep an eye on Beanie, but I was pretty sure there was some law that said I should get paid at least minimum wage for being her minion for the day.

"Beanie, wait up!" I grumbled. "What are you going this way for? It's much longer."

"Want. To. See. The. Tur-bines," she said, turning towards me so I could read her lips.

"You can see them every bloody day," I complained, "they're not going anywhere. We're going to be late for school."

"Want. To. See. Them."

Urgh. I'd learned from my time in the zoomer class that when Beanie got something into her head, it was best to go along with it.

We walked along the clifftop, gazing down at the huge masts with their long blades slowly spinning in the wind. They didn't look so spooky in the daytime, but even in the pale autumn sunshine they made me uneasy. Further up the hill I could see my house where my mum was busy hanging out the washing in the yard. I set my box on a rock for a moment to wave as we passed, feeling bad that I was helping Granny Lewis out but couldn't be bothered going home at lunchtimes to help my own mother with the chores. If heaven existed, then I was definitely not going there.

When we got to the end of the cliff walk where the hill sloped down to the wind farm substation, Erin stopped suddenly, putting her box down. I put mine down again too and signed, "*TOO HEAVY? ME CARRY?*"

"*NO...*" Erin shook her head, staring down at the cove where the headland met the Bay. "*LOOK THERE. YOU SEE? YOU THINK THAT WHAT? SEAWEED?*"

I peered down at the tangled mass of black objects covering the rocks like a thick blanket of tar. "*NOT SEAWEED. TOO DARK. LOOK LIKE...*" From up here I couldn't quite figure out what it was. It hadn't been there yesterday when I'd taken Twister out for a walk while Uncle Stuart helped Dad put up a new fence

74

round the back garden. Whatever it was, it had arrived last night. And that couldn't be good.

"LET'S GO. AFTER SCHOOL COME BACK. WE LATE." I didn't really care about missing class. But if we didn't turn up on time, Mrs Brody would keep us back after the home-time bell, and then there'd be much more chance of me bumping into my old gang. With the other kids behaving weirdly, I wasn't sure if I was ready to test my faith that Calum hadn't started picking on the zoomers himself.

"Don't. Like. It." Beanie turned and ran down the hill so fast I thought she was going to trip and go rolling headfirst into the substation fence. I was just about to pick up my box to go chasing after her, when Erin grabbed my hand.

"LOOK." She held up something black she'd found lying at the edge of the cliff. It was a dead bat, its body shrivelled and deflated between its outstretched wings. It looked like it had exploded, as though all of the air had rushed out of its lungs at once killing it stone dead mid-flight. I looked back down into the cove, my stomach knotting as I realised what it was that lay spread out on the rocks.

"Bats!" I said out loud, forgetting for a minute to sign. "God, there's so many of them! What the hell happened?"

Erin didn't need me to sign to know what I was thinking. "DON'T LET HER SEE," she signed quickly, pointing at Beanie and dropping the dead bat over the edge of the cliff. "SHE UPSET."

Beanie wasn't the only one. We grabbed our boxes and ran after her, catching up at the bottom of the hill. Beanie was pressed up against the substation fence, staring in fascination at the generators and power lines that I knew were humming ominously even though I couldn't hear them.

"Beanie, come away from there," I said more sharply than I meant to. "You'll get in trouble if you hang around here." It was a weird thing to say, I mean, there weren't any laws saying we couldn't look at the substation from this side of the fence, were there? But somehow I felt instinctively that there was something bad about this place, and we should stay well clear of it.

"There's. Men. In. There."

"I don't see any. Maybe the power company's sent folk back to do some maintenance work. Come on."

But Beanie hung on to the fence, pointing through the wire netting. "No. There's. Ar-my. Men."

"HERE NO SOLDIER, NOT [SOMETHING]." Erin signed.

"NOT WHAT?" I asked.

"Military base." Erin mouthed several times till I guessed the meaning of the sign. "THIS WIND FARM POWER STATION, REMEMBER?" she told Beanie, using the signs I'd learned from her in the weeks since the turbines were towed into the Bay.

Beanie shook her head stubbornly. "I. Saw. Sol-diers. There."

And she was right. A soldier in camouflage gear came striding out of one of the huts, a gun slung over his shoulder. He didn't look happy, not one bit. Another soldier appeared, then another. They were yelling something that I was pretty sure was 'clear off', but I wasn't sticking around to ask why. I snatched up both boxes, Erin grabbed Beanie by the hand, and we legged it as fast as we could over the scrubland. We didn't stop till we were halfway across town, red faced and panting with our chests on fire.

I didn't know why we were so scared. We hadn't been doing anything wrong, but something about that substation had been so weird it set our hearts racing with fear. The turbines had come and now there was a whole beach strewn with dead bats, and a platoon of soldiers with guns occupying the power station without anyone's permission.

Bad things were happening on Scragness that had never happened before, and I had a terrible feeling they were about to get a whole lot worse.

CHAPTER 11

I ran all the way back home when the bell rang.

I wasn't being chased by mainstream kids, or by soldiers, or anything conjured out of my overactive imagination. I just wanted to find out what had happened to all of those bats. I could've asked Mrs Brody about it, or better yet, Miss Morrison our biology teacher. But something made me bite my tongue every time I felt the urge to put my hand up and tell my teachers what I saw. Maybe I was scared of getting into trouble for going near the substation, or of being accused of making things up. Or maybe I was more afraid they would take me seriously, send people to investigate, and find out the problem was real.

I only slowed down when I reached the clifftop, my heart beating faster as I leaned over the edge and looked down into the Bay.

"What the..?"

The colony of dead bats carpeting the rocks had gone. I stood there for a long time, blinking in confusion. *I didn't imagine it, did I? I mean, Erin was there, she saw it too. There were hundreds of them!*

But the beach was empty, the low tide exposing a strip of sand leading up to the small jetty. The only things covering the rocks around the cove were seaweed and the white spatterings left by the gulls.

No, I was wrong. The beach wasn't empty. Two soldiers dressed in camouflage gear came out from behind the rocks, carrying a big crate full of something black between them. They carried it up the jetty to a small boat moored in the deeper water, lifting it carefully inside. Then they turned, looking back down the beach. I followed their gaze.

A man was kneeling on the shingle, his white hair a sharp contrast to the black ankle-length coat that he wore. He didn't look like a soldier, and there was something about the way he was examining one of the bats, turning it over and over in his hands, that made me think he must be a scientist. He stood up, scribbled some notes on the clipboard he carried, then took a last look around the deserted cove. I jumped back when his eyes swept the cliff, hoping I hadn't been seen. I didn't know why those men made me feel like I was doing something wrong by watching them, but something strange was happening down in the Bay, and I didn't want any part of it.

I stayed crouched in the grass until all three men got back in the boat and it had motored halfway round the headland. Then I walked slowly up the hill, chewing my lip all the way home. *Maybe Uncle Stuart knows what's going on,* I thought, seeing his dusty blue pickup parked in the back yard. *He walks Twister out by the cliff every day, he must've seen something.*

But when I opened the back door, I knew straight away that no one was going to pay any attention to my story. Uncle Stuart, Mum and Dad were all standing round the kitchen table, their arms folded and their faces grim.

They were arguing. Fiercely.

I stood in the doorway for a long moment, wondering what the hell was going on. Dad *never* argued with Uncle Stuart, he was the most easy-going guy on the planet. Mum treated him like her little brother, fussing over him and force-feeding him chocolate biscuits whenever he dropped by. But not today. Today everything was all wrong.

"What's going on?" I demanded. "What's everyone yelling about? Has something happened?"

They stopped shouting and turned to stare at me like I'd just walked into a posh dinner party stark naked.

"*NOT NOW*," Mum signed. "*GO UPSTAIRS DO HOMEWORK. WE TALK.*"

"You're not talking, you're fighting!" I insisted. "What's going on?"

Uncle Stuart fumbled in his pocket for his notepad, but he still had Twister on the lead, and the daft dog was hiding under the kitchen table to escape from the noise. By the time he'd managed to untangle the lead and retrieve his notepad, Mum had started quarrelling again, wagging a finger in his face, and Dad was scowling so hard I thought his whole forehead was going to cave in.

Sally was squirming in her high chair, yelling her head off and trying to wriggle onto the floor. I wasn't sure whether Twister was trying to hide from the angry voices or from Sally screaming. I couldn't coax him out, so I did the next best thing and got rid of the noise right above his head. I bundled Sally up, carrying her outside to the bench by the back gate and rocking her in my arms until she stopped crying and just lay there all huffy and confused.

"Get used to it, munchkin," I muttered. "This is the way things are going to be now you've come along and screwed everything up."

But that wasn't fair. Mum and Dad didn't start arguing after Sally was born. They only started arguing a month ago, after the turbines came. It had begun with daft wee things I barely noticed, like a sharp glance over dinner or a disagreement over whose turn it was to put

Sally to bed. Next time Dad came home from sea it was bigger things, like Dad blowing his top when he couldn't find his toolkit amid the kitchen clutter, and Mum bursting into tears and yelling right back at him. Mum wouldn't tell me what the arguments were about afterwards, she'd just shrug and say everything was fine. There was no point trying to get anything out of Dad. It drove me mad that I couldn't hear what they were saying to each other. I mean, how was I supposed to help fix things when I had no idea what was going on?

I just hoped it was because they were both tired, what with Sally keeping them up at night and Dad being away so much. I had to keep reminding myself that a new baby was tough for my parents, because I had this awful suspicion that it was somehow all my fault. I was the one who'd gone and messed things up for my family by getting my ears broken. I was the one who made conversations awkward and embarrassed them by being a 'special needs' kid. Maybe now that Sally was here to take my place, they'd decided I was more trouble than I was worth and that's what they were arguing about.

Uncle Stuart came out of the back door pulling Twister by the lead and looking totally hacked off.

"So what was all that about?" I demanded, trying to keep my voice down now that Sally had gone to sleep in my arms. "What were you and Mum and Dad yelling about?"

Uncle Stuart tied Twister's lead to the back fence and sat down beside me, pulling his notebook out and scribbling for a bit while I waited impatiently. Finally, he handed it over to me.

"*I need you and your mum to look after Twister for me this week while we're away at sea since my usual dog-sitter's going on holiday,*" Uncle Stuart had written. "*But your mum's not happy about it, she thinks Twister's a danger to the baby.*"

"Oh, right," I said when I'd finished reading. It didn't seem like such a big deal to me. Not something that needed all that yelling and finger pointing anyway. "Twister's a big softy, he'd never hurt Sally. And Mum always said if you needed us to look after Twister anytime it wouldn't be a problem."

"*That's what I thought,*" Uncle Stuart wrote back, "*but your mum's changed her mind. I can't take him with me though, and I can't leave him with the Hendersons as the farm dogs bully him.*"

I snorted at that. Twister was a big teddy bear alright. As tall as a baby elephant and nearly as fat, Twister cacked himself whenever he crossed paths with the two tiny Jack Russells at the Hendersons' farm. What a wimp. The thought of him doing anything worse to Sally than licking her to death when Mum wasn't looking was ridiculous.

"She said it was alright, though?" I asked. "Us taking Twister while you're away, I mean?"

"*Yeah, but your mum and dad aren't keen. They want him kept outside in the back yard, so I just hope the weather's good. Twister doesn't like getting wet.*" Uncle Stuart rubbed his eyes when he'd finished writing, leaning over to pat the dog curled up at his feet chewing his shoelaces. Everyone was looking tired these days, like they'd forgotten what sleep was for or something.

"Don't worry, Uncle Stuart, if it rains I'll make sure Twister sleeps in the shed. I'll look after him."

"*I know you will,*" Uncle Stuart smiled as he wrote. "*Thanks, Big Mac, you're a good kid.*"

There it was again. Someone calling me good when we all knew it wasn't true. If I was such a good guy then how come my parents looked at me all the time like I was a disappointment? If I was good then how come I made Beanie cry so often? And if I was good, then how come I was a liar like Erin said?

"Uncle Stuart!" I remembered, just as he was getting up to go. "You haven't seen anything weird down by the Bay these last couple of days, have you?"

"*Weird how?*"

"Like, dead bats weird. Nothing like that?"

"*No. I was down on the beach with Twister yesterday and didn't see anything unusual. Why, what have you seen down there?*" Uncle Stuart tapped his pen impatiently on the notebook while I read, clearly ready to put it away and head home.

"Nothing," I shrugged. "Some guys at school said there were some dead bats on the rocks this morning, that's all. I wondered if anyone else had seen them." Uncle Stuart was tired and distracted. Now didn't seem like the right time to go launching into a story about soldiers with guns and that weird scientist guy I'd seen down on the beach.

"*Probably just kids making things up, else the protest group would be straight over here with their placards and leaflets, wouldn't they? Listen, I've got to go and prep the boat for tomorrow morning. See you next week, OK?*"

Uncle Stuart gave Twister one last pat before he got back in the pickup and drove off, leaving me sitting on the bench with a dog licking my ankles and a baby drooling down my neck.

CHAPTER 12

I was still sitting on the bench daydreaming an hour later when Dad came out to check where Sally had got to. He looked a bit surprised to see me holding her while she slept, but at least he didn't rush to take her off me like I was some kind of baby-eating monster. He just smiled awkwardly and hovered by the bench, patting Twister and fiddling with the lead to make sure it was knotted tightly to the fence. I waited to see if he would say anything, but although he glanced at me a couple of times like he was about to speak, he looked away again when I met his gaze. It was infuriating.

"So how come you and Mum don't want us looking after Twister?" I asked to break the ice. "You know he'd never hurt anyone, he's too soft."

Dad just shrugged and nodded at Sally. "Not safe," was what I think he mouthed.

"But it's not like we're going to starve him then plop Sally down in his feeding bowl," I grumbled. "I don't see why he can't just stay in the house."

Dad mouthed something else that I didn't catch, then when he saw me frowning he pointed at my left ear.

"Dad," I sighed, "I've told you a million times the hearing aid doesn't work, it just makes funny noises that don't mean anything." I pulled my hearing aid from my pocket and plugged it in anyway. Anything to keep Dad happy. I hadn't worn it in weeks, and as soon as I switched it on, I could tell that something was different.

At first I thought the strange low humming coming from the ocean was the sound of waves breaking on the rocks. But my hearing aid wasn't strong enough to pick up subtle sounds like the rushing tide or the crash of surf. Listening to the sharp hiss of Sally crying was pretty much all this ugly blob of plastic was good for. Luckily right now she was still asleep, giving me a dead arm and soaking my school shirt with drool. Totally adorable, right? Huh.

Anyway, the sound wasn't so much loud as persistent, humming away inside my head so low it was like a wasp had crawled into my ear and was building a nest at the back of my skull.

Maybe it's the gulls? I thought, searching the tree branches where they normally perched. Today they were nowhere to be seen, and the yard seemed strangely empty without the great white seabirds staring down at us. It was weird—those greedy beasts were always hanging round our house looking for scraps under the barbeque or rummaging in the bins. Come to think of it, I hadn't seen the gulls circling the headland in weeks.

Ever since the turbines came to the Bay, I realised.

"Max?" Dad tapped my knee and said something, but all I heard in my ear was a faint burst of static.

"Sorry, what?"

Dad pointed to Sally, back at the house, then awkwardly mimed eating. He looked really embarrassed about it, like a wee boy who'd been forced to dress up as a shepherd for a school nativity play. He hated play acting. It was always Mum who read the stories when I was small, putting on funny voices and doing sound effects. Dad was a TV man, not a book fan.

I handed Sally over carefully so I wouldn't wake her, then grabbed the notepad that still sat on the bench. Uncle Stuart had forgotten it in his rush to get away from the argument.

"Dad, have you seen any dead bats down at the Bay?" I asked. "I saw a whole heap of them at lunchtime today, but they're all gone now." I held up the notepad for his answer, but he just shook his head. I wasn't sure whether he meant he hadn't seen the bats or he didn't want to write anything down.

"But don't you think it's weird that the birds have gone?" I pointed to our roof. "I've hardly seen a single one since the wind farm came. You think the turbines have scared them off?" I waved the notepad again hopefully.

Dad held Sally between us like a shield, smiling apologetically like it was physically impossible to pay attention to both of us at the same time. That really made me mad.

"Why won't you just *talk* to me?" I demanded, shoving the notepad into his hand. "It would make everything easy if you'd just write things down."

Dad looked hurt, like I'd accused him of being a crap father or something. But he just stood there staring at the notepad dumbly like he wasn't sure what he was meant to do with it. Mum came to the door with Sally's bottle and rescued him before I could start a major row over it. If Dad had escaped from me any faster his shoes would've left skid marks on the grass.

"DINNER HALF AN HOUR," Mum signed. "YOU SET TABLE PLEASE?"

"In a minute, I'm taking Twister for a quick walk," I called back, untying his lead from the fence. "I won't be long." I needed to get away from my parents and Sally to loosen the angry lump

86

forming in my throat. I hurried off before Mum could ask me if I was alright.

Twister went daft with excitement when he realised I was taking him out, but his enthusiasm quickly dried up as I headed down the hill to the clifftop. He hung back as I leaned over the edge and studied the beach, checking to make sure there were no more armed soldiers or mad scientists there. It was all clear. Now I could go down and take a closer look. If no one else was going to pay any attention to the dead bats and vanishing birds, then I'd have to do my own investigating.

Twister dug his heels into the grass when I started down the winding cliff path to the beach.

"Stop being such a wuss, it's not that steep," I told him, pulling on the lead till he followed me reluctantly. I didn't know what his problem was, he'd been this way a million times before. Uncle Stuart usually had to keep him on the lead to stop him running down and diving headfirst into the sea. Maybe the weird sound was getting to him too. It was stronger out here on the exposed cliff path, the low humming pulsing back and forth between both sides of my head like the tide rushing in and out. It didn't dawn on me what the sound was until I'd picked my way carefully down the path and stepped onto the beach.

Then I looked up, and the sight hit me all at once. The three great masts towered over us, their long arms spinning slowly with each gust of ocean wind. As I stared up at the metal giants, the pulsing in my ear seemed to get louder, filling my head until it was hard to think straight. It was clear now where the strange noise was coming from.

It was the turbines that were making the sound.

A strange sensation shivered its way down my spine, like the sick feeling I got when I stood too close to the cliff edge and imagined myself falling headfirst down to the beach far below. Twister was trembling, pawing at his muzzle and butting his head against my legs in fear. There was something very wrong with the sound the turbines were making, but it was too low and faint for me to make out what it was. When my stomach started clenching with anxiety, I decided I'd heard enough noise for one day. I yanked my hearing aid out and stuffed it back in my pocket

"Come on, boy, we'll have a quick look round then go back for dinner, OK?" I gave Twister an encouraging pat and led him across the rocks, peering in the cracks to see if I could spot anything the soldiers might have missed earlier. I wanted something real to take home to show my parents. I needed proof there was something bad going on down here before anyone would believe me.

It was Twister who found something, only it wasn't what I'd been expecting.

Down in the cove, someone was kneeling by the rocks. Before I could stop him, Twister had pulled the lead from my hands and dashed over.

"Twister, come back!" I yelled, panicking at the thought of a soldier pointing a gun at him. Twister might be soft as a marshmallow, but most people wouldn't know that if they saw a seven-stone German shepherd galloping at them at a hundred miles an hour. The figure leapt up in fright, but a second later she pulled back her hood and I saw a familiar fringe of red and black striped hair falling across sea-green eyes.

"Erin!" I gasped. "YOU HERE WHY?" I signed to her. Most people preferred the coastal walk near the harbour where the path down to the beach was less steep.

"ME INVESITGATE," she signed back before giving Twister a pat.

"DEAD BAT YOU FIND?" I asked.

"NO, STRANGE. DEAD BAT ALL GONE." Erin shook her head.

I grabbed Uncle Stuart's notebook from my pocket and began scribbling in it. "*If you think magically vanishing bats is weird, then just listen to this,*" I wrote. I told her all about the soldiers and scientist on the beach, and how it looked like they'd been piling the bats into crates and packing them onto their boat. By the time I'd finished, Erin's eyes were wide.

"TAKE AWAY BAT TELL PEOPLE NOTHING WHY?" she wondered.

"*To get rid of the evidence, obviously,*" I wrote.

"EVIDENCE?" Erin pointed to the word in the notebook then signed it with a frown to show she was asking a question.

"*That the experimental turbines are killing the local wildlife,*" I wrote. "*The protest group would be all over a story like that in a heartbeat. And it's not just the bats, it's the birds as well. I haven't seen a single seagull round my house in ages. And then there's the weird sound I heard when I put my hearing aid in.*"

"WHAT SOUND?" Erin asked. "HEARING AID HELP YOU HEAR?"

"*No, not much. But there's a strange kind of humming coming from the turbines that makes me all shivery and nervous. You haven't heard anything?*"

Erin gave me a dead stare that screamed, 'WELL, DUH!'

"*I don't mean heard, more like...felt?*" I wrote slowly, trying to work out how to make the question clearer. "*It's sort of like that feeling you get when you're in a nightmare, you know? When everything starts to get scary and...*"

It wasn't the withering 'You're totally mental' look Erin was giving me that made me stop. I finally noticed what she'd been

89

doing when Twister dashed up, and it was almost as weird as those soldiers hoovering up the carpet of bats. Snaking across the rocks all around us was a line of mini origami figures all held in place by pebbles pinning their feet down. There must've been hundreds of them standing back-to-back like domino pieces ready for an epic knock down.

"*OK, so this is totally normal,*" I wrote, giving Erin my best side-eye. "*You going to tell me what it's for before I call the men in white coats to take you away?*"

Erin signed something I didn't understand, then took the notebook from me and wrote, "*Call it my therapy.*"

"YOU MAKE PAPER PEOPLE TAKE THEM BEACH HOLIDAY, YOU THINK THAT THERAPY?" I used the new sign I'd just learned and raised an eyebrow at her.

"THAT NOT THERAPY. THIS THERAPY." She took a cigarette lighter from her pocket and grinned at me wickedly.

"SERIOUSLY?"

"SERIOUSLY. WATCH THIS."

Erin knelt down and clicked the lighter, setting the first origami figure alight. A moment later the mini person behind caught fire, then the one behind that, and pretty soon the flame was spreading down the line like dragon's breath, gobbling up the origami people one by one. I had to admit it was pretty cool. If this was Erin's way of blowing off steam every time she got hassle from the mainstream kids for being deaf, then I was totally up for joining her therapy sessions.

I was grinning along with her until I took a closer look and realised who the people were meant to be. Erin was really good at art, and she'd coloured each of the figures so it was clear what they were wearing. One was Calum, dressed in the red tracksuit he got for his last birthday, followed by his gang and the two mainstream girls she used to hang around with before they started ignoring her. Every few rows another tall figure stood out clearly. It was lots of versions of me in my blue school jacket.

I stepped back so Erin could see my hands. "*YOU WANT SAY SOMETHING TO ME?*" I signed angrily.

"*NO.*" Erin smiled back, a bit too smugly. "*YOU DON'T WANT HEAR.*"

"*THAT MEAN WHAT?*" I demanded. "*ME THINK YOU ME FRIEND.*"

"*FRIEND?*" Erin's smile finally vanished. "*YOU THINK ME YOU FRIEND? PRIMARY SCHOOL YOU C.A.L.U.M. LAUGH, CALL ME B.E.A.N.I.E. D.A.V.I.D. ZOOMER,*" she scowled, using the sign for 'astronaut' to mean 'zoomer'. I guess it was as close to 'space cadet' as sign language could to get.

"*PRIMARY SCHOOL YOU MEAN, NOW YOU DEAF SOMETIMES STILL MEAN. IN CLASS ME HELP YOU, AFTER SCHOOL YOU IGNORE ME B.E.A.N.I.E. YOU THINK US [SOMETHING]?*"

At first I thought she'd signed 'sick', then I realised she meant 'diseased'.

"*FRIEND SHOULDN'T DO THAT,*" she finished at the speed of light. "*WE NOT FRIEND.*"

Erin's signing was so fast it took me a minute to work out her meaning, but when I did I finally realised why every other figure she was burning was a miniature version of me. If I'd stopped to think about it for even half a second, I might've worked out that I probably deserved it. But instead I just let the familiar anger flood my veins, turning my brain into a big mushy soup of resentment.

"God, you can be such a cow, Erin," I snapped out loud. "No wonder your stupid mainstream friends dumped you."

I didn't expect she'd be able to lip-read any of that, but she must've got the gist of it, as her face turned white and her eyes went glassy like she was fighting back tears. Great, I'd gone and done it again. Hurt someone without even trying. As superpowers went, mine totally sucked.

Before I could get all soppy and apologise, I grabbed Twister's lead and marched back up the cliff path. I was tired of feeling responsible for everyone else's problems. Right now I had more than enough of my own to worry about.

EXPERIMENT X01 – PHASE 2

CHAPTER 13

SIX WEEKS AFTER THE TURBINES

The next time Uncle Stuart dropped Twister off at our house for Mum and me to look after, the row was even bigger.

I didn't know what the big fuss was about, Twister was no hassle last time he spent the week at ours. I should probably say 'last time he spent the week tied to our back fence', as Mum wouldn't let him near the house while I was at school, and I couldn't even talk her into letting him sleep in the kitchen at night. He got a bit grumpy and growled at me sometimes when I came out to feed him, but I probably would've been in a bad mood too if I'd been tied up in the yard all week.

I didn't tell Mum and Dad about the time I couldn't get him back on the lead after a walk and he went chasing the Hendersons' sheep round the field, or the time he raced up to a woman pushing a pram and snapped at the wheels. He was just letting off steam, and I was pretty sure he wasn't really trying to hurt anyone. All the same, I kept my mouth shut.

It wasn't like I had anyone to talk to anyway. Dad was out at sea most of the time, and when he was home, he was restless and fidgety like he just wanted to get away again. Mum was the opposite. She was so close to falling asleep on her feet she could barely stand upright. It was weird, I mean, I knew looking after a baby was tough and everything, but after seeing Mum and Dad and Uncle Stuart rowing like that, I'd done my best to pitch in at home and smooth things over. I'd washed dishes like a skivvy, done the laundry after school and even got up in the night to change Sally to give Mum a break. But nothing I did seemed to make any difference. Dad was still irritable, Mum was still really tired, and I was still miserable.

I couldn't even escape at school—that was even worse. All of our teachers were grumpy and half asleep, and the kids growled at each other in the corridors like dogs in an alley. It was totally bizarre. There were actual fights in the school yard, and it had got so tense in the mainstream classes I was starting to feel like I was on the wrong side of some kind of war. It wouldn't have been so bad if Erin was still talking to me, but the only things she'd signed to me since I saw her on the beach were rude words when her mother wasn't looking, and a few brief chemistry explanations to help me with my classwork when she was.

Those weird noises I heard from the turbines must be keeping everyone awake, I thought as I sat on my bed in the dark, staring out into the Bay. *If they could just get a good night's sleep, they wouldn't be so bad tempered all the time.*

I couldn't hear the noise the turbines were making, but I was wide awake all the same. I wasn't sure whether it was my parents being so tired and grumpy that was worrying me, or whether it was their row with Uncle Stuart that was keeping me from sleeping, but I'd given up tossing and turning by midnight and spent the next half hour looking out of the window.

I wouldn't be so bored if I could just get on the internet and watch videos, I grumbled to myself, swiping my new phone on and checking for the hundredth time if we had any signal yet. The phones had arrived in the post last week. Everyone had been sent one, and I was so excited when I ripped open the box, I nearly dropped our family's phones on the kitchen floor. Mum was a lot more careful, though—she actually read the letter that came with them. When she showed me what the government group overseeing the project had written, I almost died of disappointment. They'd discovered problems with the signal from the integrated combo masts—some technical crap about the spinning rotors causing scattering patterns that weakened the transmission, but they said they were working on it and we'd have full X-G coverage on the island in a few weeks. In the meantime, even though we couldn't make calls, send texts or go online, the phones all came preloaded with apps that worked despite the signal problems.

I was the only one who wasn't impressed by that. The combo masts' signal was clearly strong enough to update the news app the old folk loved, and the guys working on the boats down at the harbour were already addicted to the constantly updated weather app. Mum found a cute little nursery rhyme app on hers that sang baby songs to lull Sally to sleep, and I'd even caught Mr Strachan playing some juiced-up version of Soduku under the counter at his store the other day. The kids at school were hooked on the games app that had everything from *Angry Ducks* to *Sugar Crush*, and every time I met Uncle Stuart walking Twister round the cliffs now, he had his earbuds in and was listening to the radio app. Those stupid apps were so popular everyone on the island was carrying their phones wherever they went, despite not being able use them for anything else yet.

Everyone except me.

I wasn't into the games. They just made me think of all the times I used to spend at Calum's house playing *Night Raid 4* on his G-Box with the gang. I didn't need any more reminders of everything I'd lost in the accident. The whole point of getting a phone was to hook me back up to the outside world so I wouldn't feel so lonely all the time. If I could just text Calum and the guys and share photos and dumb jokes with them online, maybe I'd have a way of getting back into the gang.

If that government group could just get their stupid X-G problems fixed and get me on the internet, there was one app I could download that would change my life. Mrs Brody showed me a magazine article last week about a text app for deaf people, where folk could talk into their phone and it would come out as text. How awesome would that be? No more awkward silences with Calum and the gang. No more sitting on my own in the mainstream classes feeling totally out of things. And no more wasted evenings struggling to communicate with Dad over the dinner table when he was home.

That app could fix everything, but it wasn't included on my smart phone. I'd have to sit in my lonely wee bubble watching life pass me by for another few weeks while the rest of the island held their app party without me. I chucked my useless phone back on my bed in disgust and went back to gazing moodily out at the night.

I used to love the view from my bedroom window. On winter nights when it was too cold to go out walking, I'd spend hours after dark looking up at the stars or watching the moonlight shimmering on the water. It used to be peaceful, calming. But now it was different. Now there were ghostly white masts and huge revolving blades staring menacingly back at me from the mouth of the Bay.

Tonight, it wasn't just the turbines that ruined my view of the sea. Three figures were standing on the clifftop, still as statues as they gazed out across the sea.

"What the..?"

I opened the window and leaned out, trying to get a better look at the trio at the edge of the cliff. They were too far away for me to make out more than their dim outlines in the darkness.

It's probably the soldiers again, checking up on their turbines.

But I couldn't see guns slung over their shoulders, and one of the shapes was smaller, half-sized in the moonlight. It was clearly a kid standing between two adults. It looked as if they were all holding something small and rectangular in their hands, but from here I couldn't see what. If it hadn't been so late, and if they hadn't been standing so strangely still, the sight wouldn't have sent shivers down my spine the way it did.

Something's not right, I muttered, pulling on my shoes and coat and sliding down onto the porch to get a closer look. Every nerve in my body was telling me to go straight back up to bed and close the curtains, but there was no way I'd get to sleep now. I took a deep breath and jumped onto the wall, hurrying across the front yard and ducking behind the gate.

When I raised my head to look, the figures were gone.

One minute I'd seen them clearly, the next they'd melted back into the night. Now all I saw as I gazed out across the Bay was the turbines turning slowly and steadily in the breeze. The clifftop walk was deserted. I drew my coat tighter round me and headed back up to the house, my neck prickling creepily the whole way.

I didn't climb back up to my room straight away, instead I skirted round the fence to the back yard to give Twister a quick pat. He was lying with his head on his front paws, his collar attached to the fence by a long leather lead. But he wasn't asleep. He was wide awake, watching me in the moonlight as I approached.

"Hey, Twister," I whispered. "You lonely out here all by yourself?"

I couldn't be sure, but it seemed like Twister started growling as I got closer. The hair was standing up on his neck like he'd just got an electric shock, and his eyes were narrowed to slits above his trembling muzzle.

"What's up, boy, you see a ghost?" I reached over to give him a reassuring pat.

That was when he lashed out, his teeth snapping for my hand.

"Hey!" I yelled, leaping back as he lunged at me. His teeth grazed my knuckles, scraping the back of my hand and drawing blood. Twister was on his feet now, straining on his lead to get at me, drool dripping from his jaws. He looked totally manic. I stood there in shock, clutching my throbbing hand and wondering how the hell this big teddy bear could've turned into the snarling beast that was two inches of leather away from eating me alive.

Maybe Mum and Dad were right about Twister being a danger to Sally after all. Maybe they knew something I didn't.

CHAPTER 14

Next morning, Twister was back to being a total softie again. I kept my distance when I brought his breakfast out though, watching him just in case. His tail wagged so hard when he saw me, he knocked one of Mum's plant pots over, and when I finally edged forward to pat him, he went daft with joy, butting his head into my chest and licking my neck like a lollipop.

"You didn't like being locked out here by yourself in the dark, did you?" I asked, rubbing his belly when he rolled onto his back. "I bet that's why you were so grumpy yesterday."

But that didn't explain the sudden personality transplant Twister had last night. From now on I'd need to keep a careful eye on him, and not just for Sally's sake.

Mum came to the back door in her slippers and waved to get my attention. "*YOU GO SHOP BUY MILK PLEASE?*" she signed apologetically. "*BREAD TOO. EGG TOO. YOU DON'T MIND? YOU GOOD BOY.*"

I loved how she said it like I had a choice in the matter. It was either go to the shops or eat a bowl of dry cereal for breakfast.

"Let me get my jacket." I headed into the house and rummaged around till I found my green hoodie stuck down the back of the washing machine with a bundle of other clothes I'd forgotten to wash. Looks like I wasn't getting the hang of this whole housework thing as well as I thought. I was just going out again when I noticed something strange about the way Mum was making breakfast for Sally.

"Mum, what are you doing?"

Mum held up a box of baby rusks sleepily and nodded at Sally.

"I mean, what are you putting in it?"

"FRUIT JUICE," Mum signed with a yawn. "MILK FINISHED."

"That's not fruit juice!" I snatched the bowl off her before she could spoon it to Sally. The wee troll took one look at her food disappearing and starting bawling. For once I didn't feel guilty.

"Look what you've put in it!" I yelled, holding up the bottle Mum had poured into the baby bowl. "How could you be so stupid?"

Mum took one look and her face turned white. Dad had left an old juice bottle full of white spirit by the sink, and he must've cleaned his paint brushes in it after covering the fence in wood preserver, as the liquid inside was dark orange. It didn't look that much like fruit juice to me, but then I wasn't massively sleep deprived and walking around like a zombie. Even so, I couldn't believe Mum had done something so careless.

Mum picked Sally up and hugged her, dangerously close to tears. It seemed like everyone was on the verge of a nervous breakdown these days. "It's OK, Mum, no harm done," I tried to reassure her, but my own heart was hammering too fast for me to sound convincing. Sally loved her rusks. You could soak them in sulphuric acid and she'd still gobble the whole lot down. If I'd gone straight to the store instead of into the house for my hoodie first, she would've eaten at least some of the rusks and white spirit Mum gave her.

God. I didn't want to think about that.

"I'll put Dad's bottle in the shed," I said, pouring the mushy rusks and paint stripper down the sink. "I know you're tired, but just be careful next time, Mum, OK?"

Mum nodded, all flustered and upset. Her hands were trembling when she got another bowl out of the cupboard for Sally, being extra careful to make sure the orange juice bottle came from the fridge this time.

"You need anything else or is this everything?" I held up her list.

"**THAT EVERYTHING. YOU BACK SOON PLEASE?**" she signed anxiously. It was pretty obvious it wasn't me she was worried about. Looks like I'd be on babysitting duty the whole weekend while Mum got her head sorted out.

"I'll be quick as I can. I'll take Twister with me, he could do with a walk."

Mum didn't look too happy at that. I had a feeling if it was left up to her, Twister would spend the next five days tied to the fence like a convict while she yawned her way round the house half asleep. I didn't think that would do his temper much good, so I took Mum's shopping list and untied Twister from the fence before she could object.

I was halfway up the road by the Hendersons' farm before I realised Twister wasn't the only one acting weird. There was something wrong with the sheep too. They were huddled together in one corner of the field, shivering like a big blob of white jelly. Twister strained at the lead when he saw them, growling and snapping at the air.

"Twister, stop it!" I ordered, grabbing his collar to pull him back. It was like he didn't even hear me. Froth was foaming round his muzzle, his lips drawn back in a furious snarl. That scared the hell out of me. Twister was the kind of dog who tried to befriend anything that moved and ran from a fight with his tail between his legs. I'd never seen him like this. Any second now he was going to tear his lead out of my grasp and go running off into the field to do…I didn't know what.

And that's why I was scared.

"I said STOP IT!" I snapped, bringing the end of the lead down hard on Twister's nose. I'd never hit him before, but now I didn't have a choice. Twister's muscles went instantly slack and he cowered back, his eyes wide with pain and shock.

"I'm sorry, boy, but you can't act like that around the sheep. Mr Henderson would be out with his shotgun in a heartbeat if he saw you eying up his flock like that."

I was pretty sure Twister was whimpering now instead of growling, and I patted his head cautiously, heaving a sigh of relief when he nuzzled my hand and tried to clamber inside my jacket. "I'm sorry," I said again, feeling like I was some kind of monster. "Just don't scare me like that, OK? Come on."

All the fight had gone out of him, and Twister followed me past the sheep without a struggle. I looked back when we reached the top of the road, feeling the same chill of foreboding that had crept up my spine when I'd seen the beach covered in dead bats.

Something's gone wrong with the animals on the island, I thought darkly. *And I bet it's got something to do with the turbines out in the Bay.* There was nothing I could do about it, though. So far, I had no real proof.

Mr Strachan's store was halfway to the main town, near a row of cottages on the edge of Pykeman Fell. I glanced over at the neat gardens as I tied Twister to the bike rack, wondering if I should call in at Ravenscroft and tell Erin about the weird figures standing on the clifftop last night.

Nah, I decided. *We'll probably just get into an argument about how it's actually all my fault for being such an evil bully back in primary school.*

I snorted at that, but I didn't really feel like laughing. If I talked to Erin about what I'd seen then I'd end up telling her about Twister too, and I didn't want anyone else knowing about his behaviour. If folk started worrying about him acting vicious, well…next thing you know they'd be talking about solutions. The permanent kind the vet provides.

"Don't worry, boy, as long as you keep your temper under control then it's just between you and me, OK?" I whispered, giving him a final pat before taking Mum's shopping list out and heading into the store. With it being Saturday morning, it was busier than usual, and I had to squeeze past a group of old folk clogging up the middle aisle to get to the bread. It was the same bunch of pensioners who stopped by every weekend. They were all part of Mr Strachan's wind farm protest group, and today it looked like they had something particularly serious to argue about.

Mrs Thompson was waving her umbrella in old Aggie Brown's face, and Mr McCormack was going so bright red with rage it looked like his head was going to blast off into outer space. Behind them one of our school dinner ladies was quarrelling with the delivery boy, and Mr Harrison from the bank was pushing and shoving a young couple who were trying to reach the powdered milk. God, it looked like World War Three had just broken out in the bread aisle.

Maybe they've seen the soldiers and the animals that are acting weird? I thought, clutching at the hope that the adults were going to deal with the problem. *Maybe they're trying to decide what to do about it?*

I inched closer to see if I could lip read anything useful, but everyone was arguing at a million miles an hour, and I backed off when I nearly got my eye poked out by Mrs Thompson's umbrella. Glancing round to see if Mr Strachan was going to come and referee the boxing match, I caught sight of a small figure peering out from behind the vegetable rack.

"Beanie!" I grinned. It was the first time I'd ever been glad to see her. I needed a translator right now, and I wasn't fussy about who did the job for me. "What are they arguing about?" I asked. "Is it the turbines?"

"No. Not. The. Tur-bines." Beanie shuffled her feet and played with her fingers the way she always did when she was nervous. I was too busy trying to work out what the fight was about to notice at first that something was up with her.

"So what is it? Something to do with the soldiers on the island?"

"No." Beanie shook her head. "It's. The. Milk."

"The…what?"

"MILK. TODAY NO MILK," she signed.

"Why not?"

"COW SICK."

"What, all of them?" That was hard to believe. There was a small dairy farm on the other side of Scragness that supplied the islanders with fresh milk, but even if that had problems there was always the ferry from the mainland that supplied the shops twice a week. "What about the boat?"

"TODAY BOAT LATE NO MILK."

"And that's what all the arguing's about? God, some people need to get a life."

I was disappointed and a bit disturbed all at the same time. There was no way those old folk should be flipping out over a day's disruption to their milk supply; Scragness was pretty remote, and we had the odd shortage now and then. But this aggression was something new. It was like their fuses had been lit and it wouldn't be long before they all blew up and took the whole island with them.

"So we have to use the powdered stuff today," I shrugged, grabbing a tin from the shelf and sticking it in my basket.

"Don't. Like. Pow-der."

Beanie looked upset. She had a habit of taking anything that messed with her daily routines personally, and she looked close to a full-scale flake-out over not getting her morning bowl of Weetbites. At least, that's what I thought was bugging her. Then she began pulling the coins out of her purse, counting them carefully and muttering something that looked like, 'Too expensive'. I finally realised what was wrong.

"Hey, Beanie, where's your granny? Didn't she come with you today?"

"She's. Fine." Beanie said it just a little too quickly for me to believe her.

"Yeah, I didn't ask how she was, I asked *where* she was."

"Home. She's. Fine." Beanie went back to counting her money like ignoring me would make me magically go away. It wasn't the fact she was here on her own that was odd, I mean, it wasn't like Beanie needed her hand held going to the shops. It was just that her granny was a bit overprotective, and I couldn't remember a time I'd ever seen Beanie go anywhere on her own. And Beanie was definitely looking shifty, like she was hiding some big smelly secret that was going to stink the place up when it came out.

I was just going to offer to walk her home and check if Granny Lewis needed a doctor, when two police officers came marching into the store to break up the fight. Mr Strachan finally appeared from the back rooms where he'd been phoning the local station on the landline, and between them they managed to separate the group of bickering old folk. I thought it was all over until one of the police officers suddenly grabbed my arm.

"Hey! This has nothing to do with me! Let me go."

The officer said something angrily to me, showing me a rip in her jacket then pointing outside. I had no idea what she was on about, and I pulled my arm away and backed off. Even though

I used to hang about with Calum and his gang, we'd never done anything that had got us into real trouble before. The thought of getting mixed up in a police report scared me stupid.

"I'm just here to get some stuff for my mum, leave me alone."

Folk on the mainland thought there were about three people and a couple of sheepdogs living out here on the island, but there were a lot more of us on Scragness than that, and I didn't know half the people here. I certainly didn't know this police officer, and she clearly didn't know I was deaf. I tried telling her and pointing to my ears, but she had that weird look on her face that I'd been seeing a lot of recently, like she was tired and angry and ready to blow a fuse.

Mr Strachan came to my rescue before I publicly humiliated myself by starting to cry. I wasn't a coward, but I'd got so wound up with the crap that was going on at home and in school that I didn't know how else to deal with it. Mr Strachan explained something to the police officer, and she grumbled something back and pointed outside again. Mr Strachan turned to me.

"Your. Dog," he mouthed clearly. "He's. Biting." He held up the arm of the officer's jacket so I could see the teeth marks that had ripped through to the lining.

Oh. Crap.

"Sorry." I couldn't think of anything else to say, so I just began jamming the rest of the things Mum needed into my basket at top speed, hoping I could get out of there before it occurred to the police to get the dangerous animal outside put down. While they were all busy taking statements from the old folk, I quickly counted up the prices and stuffed my groceries into a couple of bags. Mr Strachan just nodded at me when I pointed to the pile of cash I'd left on the counter. At least there was someone on the island who still trusted me.

When I got outside, Twister was straining on his lead, barking at the police car parked in front of the store. He growled at me when I approached, his muzzle twitching.

"Come on, boy, don't do this to me," I pleaded, holding my hand out and praying Twister wasn't going to chew it off. "If you go biting police officers they'll have you put down for sure."

Twister sniffed my hand suspiciously, then his face relaxed, his tail wagging and his tongue lolling out to lick me.

"Good boy." I patted him in relief and untied his lead. In the distance I could see Beanie halfway down the road to the Hendersons' farm, stomping along with a bagful of groceries that I'm not entirely sure she paid for.

I should go with her and check Granny Lewis is OK, I thought. *She wasn't looking too great a few weeks back.* But that road went by the sheep fields, and I couldn't risk Twister flipping out again on the way home. I turned away reluctantly and led Twister up the path to the edge of sea instead. The coastal walk was longer, but there were no sheep out that way and it might burn off some of Twister's nervous energy.

The walk by the coast didn't work out so great either.

Twister whined and strained on his lead the whole way, desperate to run down to the rocks and go paddling in the water. I was too scared to let him off the lead. What if someone else walked past and he went nuts and took a bite out of them? It would be my fault for not keeping him under control. And then it would be my fault if he ended up on the vet's table. I felt sick at the thought.

I'd nearly got him home when it happened.

We were rounding the headland where the wind farm substation sat when Twister yanked so hard on his lead he pulled it clean out of my hands. One minute he was walking beside me, the next he was galloping full speed towards the substation fence, scrabbling at the bottom for a way in.

"Twister!" I yelled, "get back here!" I dropped the shopping and lunged for his lead, but it was too late. He'd found a loose section where the wire netting didn't quite reach the ground, and wriggled his way under it before I could stop him. I could only watch in horror as he bounced across the compound with his tail wagging, sniffing the humming generators and lifting his leg to pee on the base of a pylon.

"Twister!" I groaned, "you're going to get us both in trouble!" The thought of the soldiers with their guns scared me far more than the police at the store. Unless I could get Twister back before we were spotted, this wasn't going to end well. And that meant I was going to have to climb in there and get him myself.

I took a deep breath and gripped the wire netting with both hands, my heart pounding in my chest.

CHAPTER 15

At first I thought the substation was deserted.

Blinds were drawn over the windows of the nearest hut, and its door was sealed tight with a heavy padlock. On top of the second hut was a bank of dishes and aerials that looked like something from one of those NASA spaceship documentaries. Whatever was in that hut must've been important, as the door was solid steel, and metal bars were welded across the window. But when I tiptoed round a row of big grey boxes connected to the pylons with high-voltage cables, I stopped dead. The door of the third hut was standing open. I just caught sight of Twister's wagging tail as he disappeared inside.

Crap to the power of infinity.

"Twister, come back!" I hissed. I'd got used to judging the volume of my voice by little hints like the hum in my throat when I talked, but it was hard keeping my voice to a whisper when I couldn't hear it. "Twister!" I called again, a little louder.

It was no use. If I wanted the stupid dog back, I was going to have to go in there and get him. I could only hope this was the soldiers' day off.

I crept to the door of the hut and peered inside. I thought it would just be a shelter for the generators, or maybe a storage hut for maintenance gear. I didn't expect anyone to actually be *living* in there.

There was a camp bed set up by one wall, and Twister was sniffing the boots by the locker and lapping up cold coffee from the cup on the floor. Filling the rest of the hut was a desk cluttered with computer equipment, document files in enormous folders and a mountain of graph paper. I was pretty sure it all belonged to that weird scientist I'd seen down on the beach. But I wasn't about to stick around to find out.

"Twister, get over here!" I grabbed the end of his lead and managed to drag him out from under the camp bed where he'd been trying to reach the remains of a digestive biscuit. He fought to get back under, pulling on the lead and sending me stumbling back into the desk. I knocked over a whole bundle of folders, and computer printouts spilled to the floor in a waterfall of paper.

"Crap!" I muttered, scooping the folders up with one hand and smacking Twister with the other. "Stop that! Look what you've gone and done!"

Twister's tail went limp and he looked up at me like I was the world's biggest party pooper, but at least he wasn't trying to bite me. As I was stuffing the paper back into the folders as best I could, the words on one file caught my eye. I riffled through it, blinking in surprise as I scanned the reports.

'Wind Turbine Noise Pollution Analysis'
'Wildlife Disturbance Metadata'
'Bat Population Loss Critical Cutoffs'
'Detrimental Health Effects of Low Frequency Exposure'

My hands were shaking by the time I got to the end of the file, but there was something else I had to see before I made my escape. A black briefcase was sitting half open on the edge of the desk, a dark red folder sticking out of it. When I opened the lid fully, I could see the word 'Confidential' stamped across the front. I drew the file out, my heart pounding as I turned the pages. Inside the top sheet read:

'Military Weapons Research Base 12,
Scragness Island, Scotland:
Experiment X01 – Subliminal Population Control by
Infrasound Carrier Wave.'

I didn't know what all of those words meant, but I did know it
was something bad. Mr Strachan's protest group had talked about low
frequency noise pollution, so I already knew the turbine sounds could
make people anxious and mess with their sleep—I'd seen the effect
firsthand on Mum these last few weeks. But this top-secret military
file was about something else entirely, something far, far worse.

I turned the pages slowly, chapter headings jumping out at me
like neon warning signs.

'Phase One –   General Raised Aggression through
                Subliminal Suggestion by Turbine Infrasound
                Carrier Wave.'
'Phase Two –   Sleep Deprivation. Aggression Escalation.
                Initial Trial of Targeted Combo Mast
                Command Response.'
'Phase Three – Main Trial of Targeted Combo Mast
                Command Response: Hypnotic Neo-Cortex
                Control. Automatic Response to Signal.'
'Final Phase – Weapon of War Trial Run. Total Community
                Breakdown. Final On-Site Data Harvest –
                In-Depth Combo Signal Control Study,
                Violence Analysis and Casualty Statistics.'

I clutched the edge of the desk as I read, feeling dizzy. The
soldiers weren't here to guard the turbines from the protest group.
They were here to carry out some sick experiment on the people

of Scragness. That mad scientist down on the beach had turned the experimental combo towers into some kind of mind control weapons test, and we were the guinea pigs.

Before I could flick through the charts to the last few pages marked 'Final Phase', Twister began tugging at the lead again.

"Shh, Twister, sit!" I ordered, patting him to get him to settle. "I need to read this—just another minute and then we're out of here, OK?" But then I realised he wasn't looking up at me for attention, he was looking at the door.

Someone was coming.

I shoved the red folder back into the briefcase, straightening the files on the desk and hoping it didn't look like they'd been messed with. Peering out the door to check the coast was clear, I edged my way round the transformer banks with Twister, praying we'd make it to the loose bit of fence before we were discovered.

We only got halfway there before we were caught.

Just as I rounded the corner of the second hut, I ran straight into three soldiers with their guns pointed right at my head. I froze in panic.

The soldiers waved their guns at me, barking orders I couldn't hear and backing me up against the side of the hut. Over at the makeshift jetty, a boat was moored that hadn't been there when I sneaked in. That must've been what Twister heard. For about the billionth time in two years, I cursed the stupid accident that had silenced my whole world.

"Sorry, I can't hear you," I stammered at the soldiers. "I'm deaf."

I wasn't sure whether it was my words or the instruction from the man behind that stopped them, but suddenly the soldiers lowered their weapons and stepped aside to reveal their leader. The white-haired scientist was standing there with his arms folded across his long black coat, looking me up and down with eyes as pale as the sky in winter. From a distance I'd thought he must be an old man, but up close he looked younger, even though something about the way his papery skin clung to his bones made me think of a skeleton dressed in leather. I backed away with a shudder.

Twister cringed away from him too, trying to squeeze between me and the hut wall. Great—the one time I needed him to do his werewolf impression and he wimped out on me. I gulped and looked back at the scientist, wondering if he'd guess what I'd been doing and what the punishment was for reading top-secret military files.

"*YOU HERE WHY?*" he asked. Only he didn't say it out loud, he signed it.

My mouth dropped open, and for a long moment I just stared at him. Then I noticed the telltale curve of hearing aids over both his ears, almost hidden beneath his chalk-white hair.

He was deaf too.

I moved my hands to sign back, but the soldiers raised their guns again and I put them back down quickly. *Idiot! If he's wearing hearing aids then they probably work, don't they?*

"I'm not trespassing, honestly!" I said out loud instead. "At least, I didn't mean to. My dog got under the fence and I had to come in to fetch him."

The scientist clearly heard what I said, as his eyes narrowed in annoyance. "*SHOW ME,*" he signed. It was definitely an order.

I led the scientist and the soldiers to the fence, pointing out the loose bit at the bottom where Twister had crawled in. They examined it closely, darting glances at me as though trying to work out whether I was telling the truth. My shopping bags were still sitting on the other side of the fence though, and that's what convinced them in the end. They stood muttering together in a group for a bit, then the scientist gave some orders, and one of the soldiers hurried off. A minute later he came back with a set of tools and a coil of wire and started work repairing the loose section of fence.

"*COME HERE,*" the scientist signed. He grabbed me by the arm and led me towards the padlocked gate, the other two soldiers keeping their guns trained on me all the way. The brief spark of relief that I was going to be released without any hassle fizzled out a second later when the scientist started throwing questions at me at the speed of light.

What was my name?

Where did I live?

Who were my parents?

Where did I go to school?

How did I lose my hearing?

Were there any other deaf people on the island?

Where did Erin live?

What had I seen in the compound?

Had I gone into any of the huts?

I struggled to keep up with his signing, answering truthfully until he asked about the substation. There was no way I was telling him what I'd seen in that hut. I stuck to my story: I just came in to get my dog and was heading straight out again.

The scientist didn't look too convinced by my innocent act, and he stared at me like he was trying to bore a hole in my head to see the answers he wanted.

"*HEARING AID WHERE?*" he demanded suddenly, frowning when I told him it didn't work very well. I shrunk back when he reached out and patted my pockets. At first I thought he was checking for my hearing aid, but then he asked, "*YOU PHONE WHERE?*"

"Um, at home," I stammered. "I can't text my friends or surf the net yet."

The scientist's pale eyes narrowed to suspicious slits. "*YOU DON'T PLAY PHONE GAME?*"

I shook my head, too scared to work out why he was asking something so totally random.

For a long moment it seemed like he was trying to decide whether to release me or keep me prisoner, but eventually he nodded at the soldiers and they slung their guns back over their shoulders, opening the padlocked gate.

"DON'T COME HERE AGAIN," the scientist warned me. "THIS PRIVATE. GET OUT."

I was just making my escape when the scientist grabbed my arm again. I turned round with a shudder of dread.

"DON'T TELL OTHER PEOPLE YOU SEE US," he signed slowly and clearly. "YOU TELL, ME GET VET EXAMINE DOG," he pointed to Twister. "VET SEE DOG VIOLENT. VET MAKE DOG SLEEP. UNDERSTAND?"

I gulped and nodded. If it was meant as a threat, then it was a good one. What he added next was just plain weird, though.

"YOU WEAR HEARING AID, CARRY PHONE."

He stared at me intently. It was clearly another direct order.

I grabbed my shopping bags and headed up the hill at a run, not glancing back until I got Twister safely onto the clifftop. When I finally looked over my shoulder, the substation was deserted again, standing as silent and empty as a miniature ghost town. Only the tarpaulin pulled across the boat in the jetty suggested that there might be someone in there, hiding out in those innocent-looking huts and experimenting on the islanders with their soundwave weapons.

I gazed out across the Bay at the three huge turbines turning in the autumn wind, and shuddered.

CHAPTER 16

I didn't hear the ambulance racing down the road past our house.

It was only when Mum dropped a bottle of baby formula into the sink in surprise and rushed to the window that I ran outside and saw the flashing lights disappearing round the bend at the bottom of the hill.

"Oh, crap!" I groaned. "Granny Lewis!"

I'd been meaning to go and see if she was alright for days. Beanie hadn't said much in class for over a week, and she'd been sad and withdrawn during her favourite board game sessions. She didn't even smile when I gave her half my Mars bar at break the other day. That should've been a big red flag, but after what happened at the substation, I'd been so preoccupied I hadn't even noticed it waving right in front of my face.

Erin should've gone to check on her ages ago, I thought as I pulled on my shoes. *Beanie's her friend, not mine.*

But I knew it wasn't Erin's fault. I was Beanie's nearest neighbour, and if my head hadn't been stuck so far up my own backside, I might not have ignored all the signs that she was in trouble.

"*GO SEE,*" Mum signed, still in her dressing gown even though it was half four in the afternoon. "*WE HELP MAYBE?*"

"Yeah, bit late for that," I muttered, grabbing my jacket and heading out the back door.

The sharp sea air nipped at my ears as I ran down the hill. The autumn sun sat low in the sky, casting long shadows of the turbines across the grass. Their blades spun with grim determination, the huge metal towers staring back at me silently from the mouth of the Bay. If I closed my eyes and turned my face to the wind, I could almost hear their menacing laughter.

I stuck my hands in my pockets and jogged down the road by the fields, trying not to look at them. No one would believe me if I told them what I'd seen at the substation. Dad would chew my head off for trespassing before I even got to the bit about the secret files, and Uncle Stuart would laugh and say my imagination was running away with me. Mum might believe me, but she'd wring her hands and die of worry before she ever got round to doing anything about it. That just left my friends. The non-existent friends I didn't have anymore.

Erin would believe me.

The thought popped into my head before I had a chance to smother it.

Erin would know what to do if I told her about the scientist and the experiment with the turbine signals.

"Shut up!" I muttered to myself. It didn't matter if she'd believe me or not. Erin wasn't talking to me anymore, not after I'd called her a cow and made her cry. My chest ached with guilt every time I thought of it, but I was too proud to apologise. I was sick of being sorry. Sorry for myself, sorry for the accident, sorry for Sally coming along and ruining things, and sorry for not caring enough about Beanie to make sure her granny hadn't died in her sleep. More than anything, I was sick of feeling like some kind of selfish monster.

"It's not my fault!" I said to the wind, wishing I could hear my own voice or believe the silent words. "It's not my job to fix things."

By the time I reached Beanie's house, I'd almost convinced myself that helping her wasn't my responsibility. That was until I saw Granny Lewis being loaded into an ambulance on a stretcher. Erin and her mother had their arms around Beanie, who was clutching her favourite stuffed rabbit and bawling her eyes out while Mr Brody talked urgently with the paramedics.

When the doors closed and the ambulance drove away, Erin's father turned and saw me standing awkwardly at the end of the lane, unsure what to do. There was no point in trying to tiptoe away unseen now, so I hurried over and asked, "Is Granny Lewis OK? Will she be...I mean, is she going to...?"

Mr Brody turned to face me so his back was to Beanie and she couldn't see him signing. 'SHE SICK. VERY BAD. WE WAIT HEAR NEWS.'

"Where are they taking her?" I asked, watching the lights of the ambulance fade into the distance. "Are they going to the hospital?" The main medical centre on the island wasn't much bigger than a mini hotel, with a small cluster of rooms for overnight cases and a maternity ward with one midwife. The thought of Granny Lewis lying in that pokey wee clinic didn't exactly fill me with hope for her chances.

"HOSPITAL FIRST," Mr Brody signed slowly so I'd understand. "THEN HELICOPTER MAINLAND."

"But what about Beanie?" I asked. "Is she going too? Or will she stay with you?"

"YOU ASK WHY?" Erin signed at me behind her father's back. "YOU DON'T CARE."

I winced, not sure if I was more annoyed by her managing to lip read what I'd been saying or by her being right. I hadn't cared enough about Beanie to check on Granny Lewis when it mattered. This was all my fault. I lifted my hands slowly, and signed back the one phrase I hated more than any other.

"ME SORRY."

Erin just glared at me, putting her arms round Beanie again and helping her into Mrs Brody's car. Her father's eyes narrowed for a minute, as though he was trying to work something out, then he signed quickly to me, "TONIGHT YOU COME OUR HOUSE EAT DINNER."

"Uh…thanks, Mr Brody, but I don't think that's a good idea…" I trailed off, embarrassed. I was pretty sure Erin had told her parents all about our argument, as Mrs Brody had spent the last couple of weeks trying to get me and Erin to work together in class, without much success. Mr Brody saw his daughter scowling back at me from the car window and gave me an encouraging little smile. I wished my own dad would smile at me like that, just once.

"YOU COME SEE B.E.A.N.I.E. YOU TALK. MAKE EVERYTHING OK."

I couldn't help smiling back. He was giving me a chance to make it up to Beanie and to Erin. I couldn't exactly say no to that, could I?

"OK, Mr Brody, thanks. I have to go home and finish some chores first, though. I'll be round in about an hour, is that OK?"

"GOOD." Mr Brody nodded, patting me on the shoulder then getting into the car. I didn't watch as they drove away. I knew Beanie was still crying and Erin was still scowling, but somehow I felt if I could just keep that little spark of hope alight, then maybe Mr Brody was right and I would be able to make it up to them after all.

I ran all the way up the hill home, panting the news to Mum that Granny Lewis was being taken to the mainland and Beanie was staying with the Brodys. She wasn't over the moon that I was going to Erin's for dinner as it meant she'd be left on her own yet again with Sally, but I promised I'd make it up to her by doing all the laundry tomorrow. I'd been doing so much around the house these last few weeks to try to keep Mum and Dad from arguing that she almost believed me.

I rushed through my maths homework without checking my answers, and then made a half-hearted attempt to sort out the mess in the living room before I left. I wasn't exactly in a hurry to get to Erin's house, but I was worried if I left it too long then I'd chicken out and not go after all. I had to get things sorted with Erin—I wasn't sure I could face another week of being given the cold shoulder in my zoomer class on top of everything else. And I needed to make things right with Beanie or my guilty conscience would never let me sleep tonight.

"I'm off, Mum. Will you be OK with Sally till I get back?"

"*YOU GO.*" Mum nodded absently, feeding Sally with one hand and trying to make herself a sandwich with the other. "*ME FINE.*"

I wasn't entirely convinced that was true, but I left her to it anyway and walked down the road to the Brodys' house before the last of the daylight disappeared. Mr Strachan's store was closed when I passed, the shutters drawn down over the darkened windows. Somehow the sight made me nervous. Mr Strachan usually stayed open till at least half eight on a weekday, and sometimes as late as ten at the weekend. The store closing early was yet another small sign that something was going wrong on the island, and I had no idea what I could do to help fix it.

I skirted the small parking lot at the back of the store and headed up the lane to the row of cottages at the edge of Pykeman Fell. Erin's house was the one at the end, painted custard lemon and surrounded by a hedge of prickly bushes, their purple flowers long since withered in the autumn wind. It was only when I pressed the bell that I realised it was nearly a year since I'd last been here, when Mrs Brody gave Mum and me sign language lessons. I never stopped by to see Erin on my way home from school, or offered to go round at the weekends to work on our joint school projects. I didn't even drop in to say 'hi' when I went to the store. No wonder she was mad at me.

"HELLO," Mr Brody smiled when he opened the door. "COME IN."

The smell of chicken fried rice wafted from the kitchen, making my mouth water. The last time I'd had a meal that didn't come out of the freezer, a can, or a microwave bag was before Sally was born. I hesitated for only a moment on the doorstep, then followed him eagerly down the hall.

Erin was helping her mother spoon rice onto plates at the cooker while Beanie set the table slowly, her eyes red-rimmed from crying. I hovered in the doorway when they all turned to look at me, embarrassed by the sudden attention.

"Hi, I, uh…" I trailed off, wishing now I'd rehearsed an apology on the way over. I mean, how did you say, 'Sorry for calling you a cow, Erin, and ignoring you except when you do my work for me in class?' or, 'Sorry I didn't check to make sure your granny wasn't dead, Beanie, it's just I'm totally embarrassed by you and the other zoomers and don't want to be seen with you outside school?'

I couldn't think of a single thing to say that would make anything I'd done alright. So I just gave Beanie a hug instead. She sniffed and buried her head in my shoulder, and I knew I was forgiven.

One down.

But Beanie was the easy one—she was too kind to hold a grudge or stay mad at anyone for long. That was why she was such an easy target for the school bullies. She just kept giving them chance after chance to hurt her. It was Erin who was going to be hard work. I disentangled myself from Beanie's woolly hat and looked up in time to see Erin turn back to the rice with a grin on her face.

Maybe getting her to forgive me wasn't going to be as hard as I thought.

Maybe all I had to be, was a bit kinder.

CHAPTER 17

It was the strangest dinner I'd had in years. Not because it was weird being there—I'd spent months in the Brodys' kitchen last year learning sign language with Erin and her mother. And not because the food was bad or anything—Mrs Brody could cook like a pro, and I had more second helpings of fried rice and cherry scones than my stomach could comfortably hold. No, it was strange because it was all so…normal. I'd almost forgotten what a normal family dinner was like.

Mr and Mrs Brody were just as happy talking with us in sign language as they were speaking to each other, and sometimes Erin would make a comment out loud too, though she usually had to say it a couple of times before her parents understood. No one looked uncomfortable or embarrassed when something had to be repeated, and no one was disappointed with me if I didn't understand a sign or I needed something written down. For the first time in nearly two years, I didn't feel like a complete freak just because my ears didn't work anymore.

It was a nice feeling, a warm glow in the pit of my stomach that didn't just come from Mrs Brody's baking. I wanted to hold on to it forever, but I knew when I went home it would evaporate. As soon as I sat down to a family meal with my parents, with my dad all embarrassed by my attempts to communicate, my mum tired and distracted, and my baby sister screaming for attention and ruining everything, the happiness would be gone in a flash.

The ringing phone saved me from beating myself up for thinking Erin's family was much better than mine. I knew it was ringing because there was a little red light on the handset that was flashing. Mrs Brody had told Mum and me about a messaging service that deaf people could use over the phone, and Mum had offered to get one for our house, but what was the point? Nobody over the age of ninety used landlines these days. What was I supposed to do with it? Ask Calum and the gang to give up their football games and Friday nights eating chips down by the harbour so they could sit around at home calling me with stone-age technology?

Only that smart phone speech-to-text app would give me the chance to hang out with my old gang like I used to. I was so desperate to get on the internet and download it onto Dad's mobile and so we could have normal family dinners like the Brodys I felt like I was going to burst with impatience.

Mr Brody talked on the phone for what seemed like ages, and Beanie looked like she was going to suffocate from holding her breath for so long. But when he hung up there was a big grin on his face, and Beanie nearly hugged him to death when he told her the news.

"What is it?" I asked Mrs Brody. "What's going on?"

"HOSPITAL SAY GRANNY NOT TOO BAD. JUST VERY TIRED. STAY MAYBE TWO WEEK THEN HOME," Mrs Brody signed to me and Erin.

"GREAT!" Erin signed before joining in the hugfest, and I was left to finish off the last of the scones and jam all on my own. I didn't mind.

It was only when we'd cleared the table and I was helping Erin and Beanie do the washing up that I noticed Mr and Mrs Brody looked really tired too. And I mean *really* tired, like, Mum-trying-to-stay-awake-in-front-of-the-TV-after-being-up-two-nights-straight-with-Sally tired.

"*YOU OK?*" Erin frowned at them.

Huh, if I'd noticed something, then it was a fair bet Erin had already got there first.

"*FINE. JUST TIRED. BED EARLY.*" Her mother smiled back weakly.

"*OK. WE FINISH CLEAN. GOODNIGHT,*" Erin signed, glancing at the clock with a worried look when her parents headed upstairs. It was barely half past seven. And it wasn't as if they had a screaming baby keeping them up all night. Maybe Sally wasn't totally to blame for my parents' tiredness and arguments after all.

"*THAT NORMAL?*" I asked Erin, nodding in the direction of the stairs.

Erin shrugged and fiddled with the dish towel. She may have forgiven me, but it was clear she didn't entirely trust me with her secrets yet. I let her keep them. I had plenty of my own to worry about.

Beanie was bustling about, putting things away in the cupboards and making sure the surfaces were all wiped clean. If her relieved grin got any wider her whole head was going to split in two. It was clear she'd been in Erin's kitchen a million times before, as she knew where everything was kept. Funny, it hadn't occurred to me till now that Beanie's signing was so good because she spent a lot of her time at the Brodys'. Maybe that was why Erin had fallen out with her two mainstream friends—maybe they just didn't want to spend their weekends hanging out with a zoomer who couldn't pass for normal the way Erin could.

Huh, if that's what happened then she's better off without friends like that, I thought, trying not to feel too guilty about hoping the speech-to-text app would get me back my mainstream friends who were *exactly* like that.

Erin and Beanie finished putting the dishes away while I hovered awkwardly, not sure if I'd already outstayed my welcome. I was desperate to tell Erin everything I'd seen at the substation, but I couldn't just blurt it out, not when she was still looking at me so warily.

"More. Scones?" Beanie asked me, holding up the last of Mrs Brody's baking. Just then my overfull stomach gurgled loudly in protest, and Beanie giggled when she heard it. Erin cocked her head to one side and threw Beanie a questioning look, and Beanie quickly signed something that made Erin laugh too.

"THAT MEAN WHAT?" I asked, adding the unfamiliar sign that Beanie had just used. Beanie and Erin exchanged furtive glances, then they both started giggling again. I had a nasty feeling I was the butt of their joke somehow.

"OK NOW ME GO HOME," I signed quickly. "DINNER GOOD THANK YOU." I grabbed my jacket and headed for the hall, a familiar knot of anger fighting for space in my food-filled stomach. The mainstream kids laughing at me behind my back was bad enough. The last thing I needed was the other zoomers doing it to my face.

Erin came after me and grabbed my arm before I made it to the door.

"STAY LONGER?" she said, opening her eyes wide to try to make it look like a question rather than an order. "COME UPSTAIRS YOU HELP HOMEWORK."

I couldn't help raising an eyebrow. Erin could do her homework in her sleep, she didn't need me messing up her physics equations for her. It was a rubbish excuse to get me to stay and we both knew it. She smiled sheepishly, then hurried up the stairs without looking back to see if I was following. Beanie took my hand on the way past and pulled me upstairs with her just in case I hadn't already made up my mind.

Erin's room was every bit as tidy as I expected it to be, with books stacked neatly in alphabetical order on the shelves and not a stray sock to be seen on the freshly hoovered carpet. Not like my room. There was a vase of wild flowers sitting on her nightstand, and a small fold-out sofa bed already made up for Beanie in the corner. The only thing I hadn't been expecting to see was the huge fish tank taking up half the space along one wall.

I did a double take when I saw it, staring in fascination at the colourful clownfish and bright yellow angelfish swimming in and out of the long plant strands. Two black and white eels slid along the stone chips at the base of the tank, while a crab with giant claws eyed me lazily from behind a model shipwreck. It was like watching an underwater ballet in slow motion.

Maybe this is Erin's real secret, I thought to myself. *Maybe this is how she can stay so calm when the mainstream kids are mean to her.* If I had a tank like this to stare at all day, then maybe I'd learn to let go of all my anger and chill out just like Erin.

"YOU LIKE?" Erin nudged me and pointed at the tank. I nodded, trying hard not to add it to my long list of 'reasons why I'm jealous of Erin Brody'. I'd been asking my dad for a tank for years. I'd almost talked him round too, but then Sally came along and everything suddenly became 'too expensive'. I pushed the thought away before it could give me even worse indigestion, and pointed at the triggerfish that was swimming round its own sectioned-off part of the tank.

"HE ALONE WHY?" I asked.

"HE HUNGRY EAT EVERYTHING." Erin mimed chomping the smaller fish with her hand.

"Cool!" I said out loud without meaning too.

"I KNOW, RIGHT?" Erin grinned, and signed something to Beanie. She laughed again, and before I knew it, I felt left out once more, like there was some joke they were sharing at my expense.

"THAT MEAN WHAT?" I asked, making the sign they'd been using when they glanced at me. I didn't recognize it, and I had a nasty feeling it was something insulting.

"THAT YOUR NAME," Erin giggled, "YOU [SOMETHING]." She made the sign again.

"MY NAME M.A.X," I said, fingerspelling my name as fast as I could before my hands could ball into angry fists.

"NO YOU [SOMETHING]." Erin was nearly bent double with laughter by now.

"What does that sign mean?" I demanded, looking at Beanie this time and trying hard not to lose my temper. Beanie grabbed a small chalkboard from a shelf before I could blow up and wrote 'whale' on it, turning it round to show me.

"You think I eat too much?" I snapped, too annoyed to use sign language now. "If you think I'm a greedy git then why did your parents bother inviting me to dinner, huh? Just so you could laugh at me, is that it?"

Erin's smile had faded, and she was shaking her head now and trying to get me to look at her hands while she signed something else. I turned away angrily, about to leave them to it, but Beanie grabbed my arm and stepped up so close I couldn't look anywhere but her face. "You're. Not. Fat. Max," she mouthed slowly and clearly. "You're. Just. Ver-ee. Tall."

"So why are you calling me a whale instead of using my name?"

"Whale. Just. Means. Big," Beanie said. "You're. Big. Max."

"Oh." I looked back at Erin, and she signed quickly, "FINGERSPELL TOO SLOW. WE GIVE EVERYBODY SHORT NAME."

"Oh," I said again, not entirely sure yet I wasn't being made fun of. "YOU NAME WHAT?"

Erin signed something else I didn't understand, and Beanie wrote 'ladybird' on the chalkboard for me. Erin held up her strand of red and black hair so I'd get why. I bit my lip to stop from saying that I thought 'poisonous frog' suited her better.

"YOU GET GOOD NAME," I scowled at her. "ME GET BAD NAME WHY?"

"WHALE SEA KING." Erin looked surprised. "NOT BAD NAME."

That shut me right up. Maybe they hadn't been laughing at me after all. "What's your short name, Beanie?" I asked. "Is it an animal too?" I stopped myself just in time before I asked her if it was 'hedgehog'.

When Beanie shook her head and made the sign for 'hat', I couldn't help smiling. It suited her perfectly. "Have you given everybody in school a name?" I asked Beanie. She signed something quickly to Erin and they both nodded. "So…does everybody know what you call them behind their back?"

Beanie looked at me like I was mad and shook her head hard.

"OK…" I was grinning too now. "What do you call Mr Mason?"

Beanie patted her head, making the sign for 'bald'.

"Ha!" I snorted. "Perfect. What about…Mrs MacPherson?" I mouthed our head teacher's name slowly so Erin could catch it too. She made another sign I didn't know, and Beanie wrote 'dinosaur' on the chalkboard. I chuckled at that one too. Mrs MacPherson was about eighty years old and thought we were all living in nineteen fifty-seven.

"OK, what do you call…" I began again, warming to the new game I'd discovered.

By the time we'd gone through the names of most of our teachers and half the mainstream kids, there were tears of laughter running down my cheeks. I had to hand it to the girls, they knew how to make the most of the secret language they shared. And I loved having a way to get my own back on the bullies without anyone knowing. Erin and Beanie let me help them come up with signs for the mainstream kids they hadn't named yet, and the happy glow in my belly burned even brighter when I felt included for once instead of watching from the sidelines.

When I'd wiped my face and got my breath back, I made up my mind there and then to tell Erin and Beanie everything I knew about the substation and the scientist's experiment. They'd shared their secret names with me, and now it was my turn to share my secrets with them.

"LISTEN," I told them when we'd all stopped laughing and Beanie was rummaging around in her overnight bag for her pyjamas. "NOW ME TELL YOU SERIOUS THINGS."

Erin and Beanie looked at me curiously as I grabbed a pad of paper from the bookshelf. This was too important a story to trust to my messy sign language or Beanie's translation. I needed to tell them everything I knew in my own words.

I took a deep breath, and started writing.

EXPERIMENT XOI – PHASE 3

CHAPTER 18

EIGHT WEEKS AFTER THE TURBINES

The next time I saw the strange white-haired scientist again, it was in the last place on earth I'd been expecting.

It was at school.

If I'd known the bring-and-buy sale was going to be such a disaster, I'd have stayed at home and pretended I didn't know anything about the turbines or the military experiment. After what happened at the bring-and-buy sale, there could be no more pretending.

I talked Mum into coming with me despite her being dog tired. She was going a bit stir-crazy stuck in the house all day with the baby, and after the weird incident with the orange juice, I wasn't keen on leaving her alone with Sally for too long. After spending half an hour trudging round the assembly hall staring at tables full of the most useless tat the islanders could find to donate, I was beginning to regret it, though.

"*YOU THINK WHAT?*" Mum signed, holding up an ugly green vase that had a big chip on one side.

"Mum," I groaned, "that looks like someone's blown their nose onto a pottery wheel. You're not seriously thinking of buying any of this crap, are you? What do you think, Sally? Do you want a big bogey vase on your bedside table instead of your teddy bear?"

Sally wriggled in my arms and blew a dribbly bubble that I was pretty sure was a 'no'.

"TONIGHT MONEY BUY SCHOOL BUS," Mum signed. "ME BUY SOMETHING."

"Yeah, but can you try to find something that isn't manky or five hundred years old?" I grumbled, even though that's what she'd been trying to do for the last half hour without success. Then she caught sight of a table piled with baby clothes, and her tired eyes lit up.

"Sally's got so many dresses and sleepsuits the cupboards are going to explode!" I reminded her.

"NOT SALLY CLOTHES, BUY A.L.S.I.O.N. P.A.K.R.E.R. CLOTHES," Mum said, fingerspelling her best friend Alison Parker's name and getting it hopelessly muddled up.

"Why can't you just use the word for journalist?" I sighed in exasperation, showing her the sign and trying not to drop Sally at the same time. "I'll know who you mean."

I'd been trying to get my mum to use shorthand names the way Erin and Beanie did instead of muddling her way through fingerspelling, but she was so tired and confused these days she kept forgetting everything I told her. Alison Parker was a journalist living in Glasgow who'd grown up on the island and gone to school with Mum. She'd had a baby boy about five months ago. Every morning Mum said she was going to send her a parcel of baby clothes, and every night she forgot all about it.

Mum rolled up her sleeves and went rummaging again, and I jiggled Sally up and down to keep her amused as I studied the people milling about the hall. A lot of parents had turned up to support the school fundraiser, digging around in the piles of tat with fake enthusiasm and making small talk with the teachers while their embarrassed kids hung out by the orange juice stall.

Everything seemed weirdly normal if you weren't looking carefully for the telltale signs that something was up.

I could see them clearly, though.

The parents had smiles pasted onto their tired faces, but they were irritable and snappy with the kids running the stalls. The haggling over prices was getting out of hand at some of the tables, and Mrs MacPherson our head teacher was running round like a demented chicken trying to smooth things over. The rest of the teachers were wandering around like zombies, clutching their coffee cups like caffeine was the only thing standing between them and eternal sleep. They'd been like that for weeks now, turning up to class late and stumbling through their half-prepared lessons. They were so bad tempered I was scared to breathe too loud in case I got into trouble. I mean, Mark McNab got suspended last week when he was five minutes late for assembly, and Jenny Gibson got three days' detention just for sneezing in Biology.

Seriously.

You'd think the kids would've noticed by now that something was badly wrong, but they were in a worse state than the adults. There was something kind of feral about the way they were slouched round the orange juice stall, eyeing up the smaller kids like they were just itching for a fight. Mrs MacPherson had sent more kids home for brawling in the last two weeks than she'd done in the last two years. She was blaming it on the kids spending too much time playing with the addictive games apps at night and not getting enough sleep, but when she'd threatened to ban the new phones from school there was nearly a riot. She'd backed off and said she was just banning them during class, but that didn't stop most of the kids fiddling with them under their desks when their tired teachers weren't paying attention.

Calum and his gang were leaning against the wall by the stage, their hoodies pulled up and their eyes fixed on the smart phones in their hands. The gang loved games, but it had always been social before—playing *Jungle Quest* together as a team, or holding epic *Space Battle* tournaments on a Friday night after chips down at the harbour. Now they barely spoke to each other, and the only time they tore their eyes from their screens was to size up the other kids walking past. I couldn't help thinking they looked like a pack of wolves just waiting for the hunting call.

One small spark, that's all it would take to set this hall alight, I thought with a shudder.

Everyone was on edge, but it seemed like no one wanted to admit that anything was up. Even Mr Strachan's protest group had gone quiet after that pensioners' wrestling match in the store. Mr Mason was still standing by the main doors handing out protest leaflets to parents robotically, but all the fight had gone out of him. I didn't know whether to feel sorry for him or shake him awake so he'd see what was happening.

Maybe I should tell some of the adults about what I saw at the substation? I thought for the hundredth time. *Maybe I should go to the police?*

But I didn't have any real proof that the scientist was up to something bad. I kicked myself for not thinking fast enough to swipe the top-secret red folder when I'd had the chance.

Maybe if I told Mrs Brody about it she could do something?

Erin hadn't been keen to tell her parents about what I'd seen at the substation. Now I knew why. I glanced over to where Erin's mum was helping a couple of zoomer kids count change at their stall. Mrs Brody was so sleepy Beanie had to keep correcting her arithmetic.

God help us.

I was just going to head to the munchies stall for a snack to keep my mind off things, when a hand brushed right past my cheek, making me jump.

"Hey!" I yelled, nearly dropping Sally. "Watch it!"

I turned to see an old lady backing off like I was a rabid dog. She'd just been trying to pet Sally, but I hadn't heard her come up behind me. Mum stepped in quickly to apologise for me, and I fumed silently as the woman's startled look turned to one of pity. I hated it when people assumed I was soft in the head just because I couldn't hear them.

The old lady fussed over Sally, mouthing a bunch of stuff to me I couldn't understand while I did my best to keep my wee sister out of her reach. If I couldn't trust my own mother not to do things to hurt her then I certainly wasn't about to trust any of these strangers with her. God knows what mad ideas that weirdo scientist had put into their heads with his experiments.

"*HEARING AID*," Mum signed, looking embarrassed as I continued to ignore the baby-mad granny. "*MAYBE HELP HEAR.*"

"Mum, you know it doesn't help," I protested.

"*DOCTOR SAY PRACTISE IMPORTANT.*" Mum gave me a pleading smile.

The last person who'd told me to wear my hearing aid was that scary scientist down at the substation. I still wasn't sure why, especially as I'd told him it didn't work well. And why did he care whether I carried my new smart phone around with me either? That was just weird. Without the internet it wasn't much use, but I'd brought it with me tonight anyway to give me something to do while Mum went dumpster diving for the least tatty thing she could find. I'd spent the last half hour playing *Sugar Crush* one-handed while I rocked Sally with the other. I had to admit, it was pretty addictive. Even Sally had her eyes glued to the screen watching the colourful sweets being swapped about, and she hadn't cried once. If I'd know how useful a babysitting tool the phone was going to be, I'd have rescued it from my bedroom drawer ages ago.

Mum pointed to my ear again, and I gave in. I stuffed the earpiece into my left ear and gave the old woman a fake grin for Mum's sake. I knew she was just trying to get me to act more normal around people, but I resented it. I couldn't pretend to have a 'normal' conversation—I was deaf, and no amount of wires in my ear was going to change that. It wasn't like anyone else round here was acting normal these days anyway. The noise of chatter and footsteps in the hall made weird whooshing sounds in my ear as soon as I switched the hearing aid on, and I winced at the weird humming that seemed to be coming from every direction at once.

"Max!"

Another hand grabbed my arm and mouthed my name in my face, but this time it was someone I was really glad to see.

"*NEED TALK NOW*," Erin signed. "*COME HERE.*"

"Er, but…"

"*NOW!*"

I handed Sally over to Mum and followed Erin over to where David sat in his wheelchair at the back of the hall. His parents were over by the zoomer stall talking to Mrs Brody, and they looked a bit more awake than the other adults. Taking a couple of weeks' break from the island must've done them some good.

"Hey, David, so you're back. Good trip to the mainland?"

David had been away for a fortnight, and I felt kind of bad that I hadn't even noticed he'd gone till Beanie pointed it out to me in class this morning.

David nodded enthusiastically. At least, I think it was a nod. I mean, his head wobbled a lot, and he kind of looked like he was grinning most of the time because of the amount he dribbled, but

I think he was glad to see me. It was only when he leaned over the wee desk on the front of his chair that I realised he'd gone and got a shiny new computer when he was on the mainland. As he hit some of the keys on the pad, selecting words from a drop-down menu, a message flashed up on the screen.

"Hi, Max. I got a new computer for talking to people. Cool, huh?"

Oh. Wow. It hadn't even occurred to me this kid could even *think* in complete sentences, never mind communicate by computer.

"Yeah, David, very cool." I blinked, trying to scrape my jaw off the floor. "Er… it must've been really expensive."

David went back to hitting keys, and after a bit a new message appeared.

"Uh-huh, cost like a billion pounds. Had to sell my wee brother to pay for it."

David dribbled some more, and I realised with relief that he was laughing. I grinned back, and Erin shot me one of her 'I told you so' looks. This time I definitely deserved it.

"ME HIM DISCUSS WHY PEOPLE ANIMAL ACT STRANGE," she signed. "ME TELL DAVID YOU GO SUBSTATION SEE WHAT. DAVID THINK MAYBE TURBINE SIGNAL CAUSE STRANGE THING, UNDERSTAND? DAVID HAVE THEORY—"

"Wait, what?" I spluttered out loud. It wasn't the fact that Erin was using the shorthand sign 'wheels' for David, though that was pretty funny. And I wasn't struggling to understand the sign for 'theory' either, as Erin had taught me that one in our Chemistry class weeks ago. It was something else she'd said that make my eyebrows shoot right up into my hair.

"D.A.V.I.D. HAVE TURBINE THEORY?" I asked, fingerspelling his name slowly to make sure I'd got her words right.

I stared at the zoomer who was looking back at me patiently with a line of drool down his chin.

"YES, **D.A.V.I.D.**" Erin signed back with a big exaggerated flourish. "*HE BRILLIANT SCIENTIST. HE NOT STUDY 3RD YEAR PHYSICS, HE STUDY 5TH YEAR. YOU NOT NOTICE. YOU IN CLASS HAVE HEAD UP BUM.*"

I opened my mouth to protest, but then I realised she was right. Not only had I assumed David couldn't even understand the pictures in a science book never mind the words, I'd pretty much thought he had the same IQ level as Sally.

I am totally, without question, the biggest tool on the entire planet.

After all my complaining about other people not making the effort to communicate with me and assuming I was stupid, I'd gone and done exactly the same thing to a kid I saw in school every day. I'd had a hard enough time after I lost my hearing, but it was nothing to what David must have to put up with, even from other zoomers like me.

"LISTEN!" Erin snapped her fingers in front of my face to get me to focus. "*DAVID SAY HE SEE INTERNET SIGNAL ON COMPUTER. SO PHONE WI-FI NOT WORKING BIG LIE. READ THEORY.*" She pointed to David's miniature computer screen and nodded at him, and David clicked on his menu page, selecting a message he'd already shown Erin.

I leaned over and scanned the words scrolling up the screen.

"I've been doing a lot of research on infrasound—that's sounds lower than the human ear can hear. The tips of turbine blades can reach up to a hundred miles an hour, and the difference in wind speed at the top and bottom

of the turn can produce a really low frequency
pulsing sound."

"Uh-uh," I nodded as I read, hoping it was going to get a bit
more useful and less like one of my school science lessons.

"There's lots of documented cases of turbine
infrasound noise pollution making people and
animals anxious. Over time it builds up and causes
sleep deprivation which leads to aggression and
health problems. That's what's happening with
the wildlife."

"OK, I get why the protest group is so worried about the
turbines," I said, "but could the wind farm be causing all the weird
stuff that's being going on? I mean, could the signals actually change
people's behaviour without them knowing it?"

David just pointed to the computer screen again. I kept reading.

"Since the turbine infrasound waves are too
low to hear, they could maybe be used to send
subliminal messages to people without them being
aware of it. Maybe the scientist has some kind
of device in the substation transmitting signals
across the island on the turbine carrier waves?
That would explain what all those aerials and
dishes are doing on one of the huts."

By the time I finished reading I was grinning like a loony.
"That's exactly what's happening!" I said breathlessly. "David, you're
a genius! It must be that scientist who's sending signals out and
making the people and animals act weird. But that report I saw said
worse things were going to happen in the next stage, and something
about 'targeted combo mast command response'. What does that
mean? How can you target a signal that's just being blasted out
across the whole island? And—"

142

Erin tapped me on the shoulder with an annoyed frown, and I remembered she couldn't hear what I was saying to David. I patted my pockets, but couldn't find a pen for the notebook in my jacket, so I signed at the same time as I was talking. I'd already told Erin everything I'd read in the scientist's secret file, but she liked to be included in the conversation, same as I did. I explained to David what I'd read in the documents, trying to find the right signs for Erin to describe what was supposed to happen at each new stage. From what I could remember, it seemed like we'd just finished phase two of the experiment.

I'd just got to the bit about the final phase and how it might all end in violence, when I caught sight of something that made me freeze like a statue, the blood running cold in my veins.

A pair of pale eyes was frowning under a thick crop of white hair. The scientist from the substation was talking with my mum and staring at me like I'd just volunteered to be the main course on his dinner menu.

"Oh, crap!" I gasped.

From where he was standing across the hall, he could see everything that I'd been signing.

CHAPTER 19

The piercing stare seemed to stretch on to infinity.

Then very slowly and deliberately, the scientist drew a mini clipboard from his long black coat, and scribbled some notes. I waited, my heart pounding. Erin was tugging my arm impatiently, trying to get me to answer the questions she was signing, but I couldn't take my eyes off the scientist. He'd just seen me admit I'd read his secret files, and now he was going to make something happen to punish me. Something bad.

Before I could work out what that something might be, another disturbance at one of the stalls got everybody's attention. Beanie was stuck in the middle of a tug of war over a plate with the old lady who'd been cooing over Sally. Mrs Brody was trying to reason with her, but Beanie had gone red in the face and tears were sliding down her cheeks—big warning signs she was only a few moments away from a full-scale meltdown. Erin took one look and legged it across the hall to help. With people gathering round to see what was going on, the white-haired scientist was hidden from view.

"Look, stay here, David, I'll be back in a minute, OK?" I told him, scanning the hall nervously. I wasn't sure if the scientist had put Erin and David on his hit list now that I'd told them his secrets, but I couldn't take any chances. I hurried after Erin, pushing past the spectators crowding round the zoomer stall.

"SHE PAY MONEY," Erin was signing. "YOU GIVE HER PLATE."

"It's. Gran-ee's!" Beanie sobbed, clutching her end of the plate tighter. "These. Are. Her. Things."

"GRANNY GIVE AWAY PLATE, SHE DOESN'T MIND," Erin tried to soothe her. "GRANNY COME HOME SOON."

Beanie whimpered and looked pleadingly at Mrs Brody. She was clearly still upset after seeing her granny rushed away in an ambulance and was clinging desperately to reminders of her. Bringing Beanie to the charity sale to take her mind off things and then asking her to sell off her granny's old crockery probably wasn't the best idea Mrs Brody had ever had. Guess that's what happened when a mad scientist's secret signal interfered with people's higher brain functions.

Some of the parents were muttering and shaking their heads as they watched the fight. The feedback from their voices buzzed loudly in my hearing aid. I couldn't make out exactly what they were saying, but whatever it was must've embarrassed the old lady. She let go of the plate reluctantly, but Beanie wasn't expecting the sudden release and lost her balance, falling down hard on her knees. The plate dropped to the floor and broke into pieces.

Beanie stared at it in shock, her face turning from red to white.

This was not going to be good.

Erin and me both rushed over to pick her up, trying to avert the coming Beanie apocalypse.

"DON'T WORRY," Erin signed, scooping up the bits of plate and showing Beanie they fitted back together like a jigsaw. "GLUE STICK TOGETHER LIKE NEW PLATE."

"Your granny wanted to help raise funds for a school bus," I reminded Beanie, checking to make sure she hadn't skinned her knees in the fall. "What's she going to think when she comes back from the hospital and finds all the stuff she's tried to get rid of piled up on her kitchen table?"

Beanie pouted, fingering the broken pieces of plate and not looking entirely convinced by our reassurances. I guess she still hadn't forgotten Calum's mean words about her granny dying and Beanie being taken into care on the mainland.

But then I saw something else that drove all thoughts of Granny Lewis straight out of my head. The white-haired scientist was standing by the main doors, typing away on some kind of handheld device. Then he clipped a tiny microphone to his hearing aid, and began to talk into it.

And that was when I heard it.

Well, not *heard* exactly—it was more like a low pulsing vibration that whooshed and throbbed in my left ear, sending chills up my spine until I was shaking and breathless. All around me parents and teachers shivered, the younger kids clutching the hands of the adults and looking disoriented.

What the hell is going on? What did that scientist just—

Suddenly I didn't care anymore. It was like the big bubble of rage about the boating accident suddenly burst in my chest, spilling all of that red-hot anger into my bloodstream. I was mad at everything that had happened to me. It was so unfair I'd lost my hearing and my best friend had dumped me from his gang. It drove me crazy that my parents had gone and had another baby to replace me, and I had to watch Dad fuss over her while he acted like a stranger to me. It was torture to have to sit in a class full of zoomers day after day while the mainstream kids made fun of us behind our backs. My life was spiralling out of control, and I wanted to reclaim it.

My hands curled into fists, my breath coming out in shallow gasps. I wanted payback. I wanted to hurt someone, someone smaller and weaker than me who I could pummel with my fists until my rage was spent. My eyes narrowed, scanning the hall for a suitable target. Then I saw him. That drooling, shaking wee freak who wobbled around in his wheelchair all day doing Einstein-level physics. If David wasn't in my class making the rest of us look stupid, I wouldn't have lost all my friends.

I was almost choking with anger, and it was all David's fault.

I needed to get rid of David.

I took a step towards him, and then another. On the other side of the hall, Calum and his gang peeled away from the stage where they'd been hanging out, heading for David with grim faces and clenched fists. I was back in their team, accepted again, and we were all focused on the same goal: sort the problem that was David once and for all.

But before I could take another step, a hand reached up and yanked the hearing aid from my ear. The sound was cut off abruptly, the pulsing in my head vanishing as suddenly as it had begun.

"What..?" I muttered groggily, shaking my head from side to side to try to clear it.

"*YOU DO WHAT?*" Erin was up in my face now, signing like a lunatic. "*EVERYONE SLEEP! EVERYTHING GO CRAZY!*"

I looked around, feeling disorientated and dizzy. Most of the adults and younger kids were standing still, gazing off into space like someone had flipped the 'off' button in their brains. Mum was staring vacantly at a blue snowsuit on the baby clothes stall, jiggling Sally up and down on her arm while my wee sister squirmed and wailed. Mrs Brody was leaning over a tub of cash, counting the same pile of coins over and over again like she kept forgetting what she'd just done. And over in the corner where David sat in his wheelchair, Calum, Ryan and the rest of the gang were closing in.

"Oh, crap!"

I bombed across the hall, but it was too late. By the time I got there, Calum and the boys had overturned David's wheelchair and were swarming in a group, battering their fists into something that lay on the floor.

"Get your hands off him!"

I dragged Calum and Ryan off, shoving the rest of the boys back until I got a clear path though the scrum to the centre. I was almost sick with relief when I realised it wasn't David they'd been pounding into the floor. He was lying a few feet away, staring with wide eyes at the remains of his new computer the boys had turned into a broken pile of casing and smashed chips. Behind us by the door, the white-haired scientist unclipped his microphone, put his handheld device in his pocket, and began taking notes again, watching us all the while.

All around the hall folk came back to life again like nothing had happened. Parents and teachers rushed over, righting David's chair and helping him sit back up. Mrs Brody and his parents fussed over him, checking for bruises while the gang of boys stepped back, distancing themselves from the mess of broken circuits on the floor.

"What happened?" Mrs Brody gasped. She stared at the smashed computer, then up at me like she couldn't make sense of the mess.

"Didn't you see it?" I demanded. "Didn't any of you see it?" I turned to the other parents and teachers, but they shook their heads, bewildered.

"*THIS HAPPEN HOW?*" Mrs Brody asked, signing at the same time to make sure I understood. I opened my mouth to reply, but Calum got there first.

"David fell over," he said, rubbing his hand across his eyes like he was confused. I knew that was what he said as his words were slow, deliberate, as though he wasn't quite sure what was going on himself. "His computer broke."

"That's not true! It was Calum and the other boys who did it! They knocked David over and smashed his computer!"

Calum gaped at me like I'd just punched him in the face. Then he frowned and muttered something that looked like, "Why would you say that?"

"It's true! I saw you do it, you liar!"

Calum backed away from me like I was some kind of lunatic, and I could see some of the adults exchanging glances and shaking their heads. They clearly thought I was making it up as well.

"THIS JUST ACCIDENT," Mrs Brody signed. "BOY KNOCK HIM OVER ACCIDENT. ME STAND THERE," she pointed at the table. "ME DIDN'T SEE FIGHT."

"I'm telling the truth, Mrs Brody," I insisted. "Ask Erin—she saw it too!"

But Erin was still at the zoomer stall trying to calm Beanie down. Beanie had her hands clamped over her ears and was rocking back and forth in distress. Whatever that mad scientist had done, she clearly didn't like it.

The scientist...

I turned to the doors.

The man in the black coat had gone.

"Excuse me, excuse me!" I pushed my way past the parents and teachers and ran into the corridor. Apart from Mr Mason standing by the main entrance with his leaflets, the passage was empty. Hung all along the corridor were posters advertising the upcoming

149

Halloween party in the town hall, the pictures of skeletons and witches staring back at me with dead eyes.

"Mr Mason!" I hurried up to him. "Did you see someone leaving? A man in a long black coat with white hair?"

"Hello, Max," Mr Mason smiled at me, the bags under his eyes bulging behind his spectacles. He took a pen from his shirt pocket, hesitated between a pile of leaflets for the protest group and the other pile advertising the Halloween party, then decided the party leaflets made better scrap paper and started scribbling on the back. I hopped from foot to foot impatiently as he wrote, snatching the leaflet from him and reading the sentences before he had time to finish.

"You mean Doctor Ashwood? He's part of the government group overseeing the new wind farm. He's here to make sure the turbines don't cause any disturbance to the local wildlife, and to monitor the—"

"Mr Mason, he's really dangerous!" I gasped. "He's using the wind turbines to do thought control experiments on the islanders!" Even as I said it, I knew how crazy it sounded. Mr Mason gave me one of his puzzled looks and starting writing on the leaflet again. This time I let him finish.

"No, he's not, Max, don't let that imagination of yours run away with you. He's a very nice man, and he's extremely interested in the work of our protest group—he even took some of our leaflets away with him to read."

Took some leaflets...? Great. That scientist had put Mr Mason and the whole protest group on his hit list now for sure.

"Oh. Right. OK. Er…I'm just going out to get some air." I nodded like Mr Mason had been really helpful and hurried out to the school yard. When I got to the main gate I stopped, peering into the night. Clouds were racing across the October moon, the wind whipping across Pykeman Fell, stirring the tree branches and scattering the fallen leaves.

It's a good night for turning the turbines, I thought darkly.

In the brief flashes of moonlight, I could just make out a figure striding away in the distance. His black coat flapped in the wind, reminding me of the dead bats I'd seen littering the Bay. I shuddered, turning back to the warm lights of the school that looked so safe and inviting in the gloom.

It's a lie, I thought, images of David's overturned wheelchair running through my head like a slow-motion horror film. *It isn't safe here anymore. Nowhere's safe now the turbines have come.*

Chapter 20

David wasn't in school the next day.

Neither was Beanie—she was dog tired and spaced out after Doctor Ashwood's signal got inside her head, which was even more worrying. She stayed at home with Mr Brody, and she was still tucked up in bed when I dropped by to check on her on my way to school.

"*What did you tell your mum after Doctor Ashwood's experiment last night?*" Erin scribbled on my notepad as we huddled together by the computers in our classroom pretending to watch our science videos. "*Did she notice that something weird happened?*"

I snorted and wrote back, "*What do you think? Mum's so tired she doesn't know what time of day it is never mind what that scientist's up to. I think living so close to the turbine signal's messing with her head—she spends most of her time sleeping, and even when she's awake she's totally out of it.*"

"*Yeah, my mum too.*" Erin made a face and pointed to the library corner. Mrs Brody was sitting with a reading group of three first-year kids who were taking turns to read a page of their book aloud, but Mrs Brody had fallen asleep, her glasses riding up her forehead as her chin sunk further and further down her chest.

"*My dad's just as bad.*" Erin frowned as she scribbled on the pad, "*The adults are getting so little sleep they can't think straight. Everyone's so wound up that pretty soon—*"

"*World War Three's going to break out,*" I finished for her. "*And it might be the kids who start it...*" I shuddered, remembering the blank look on Calum's face when he overturned David's wheelchair, and the emptiness in Ryan's eyes as he pounded the expensive computer into a pile of scrap.

"*We can't let things get any worse,*" I wrote in big letters so it looked like I was brave instead of a bundle of nerves. "*So how are we going to stop that scientist and his experiment?*"

Erin chewed her lip, thinking hard. Her face was pale with worry, her freckles standing out in a dark band across her nose like the stripes on a snake. They matched her 'don't mess with me, I'm poisonous' hair strands perfectly. I liked the way she looked fierce when she was scared, it made me feel like a superhero with a secret weapon as backup. Erin probably thought she was the superhero with a crap sidekick who kept blowing up every five minutes, but either way we were in this together now.

"*We can't deal with this ourselves, we have to get help,*" Erin decided. "*We're the only ones on the whole island who can't hear the turbines, so it's up to us to do something about it. But we need help. What about telling Mr Mason and the protest group?*"

"*I tried to tell him last night,*" I wrote, "*but he was too spaced out to listen.*"

"*We need to try again. Maybe if there's two of us telling the same story he'll believe us.*"

"What, right now?"

"*Yes, right now!*" Erin nodded eagerly. "*You said yourself that anyone who knows about the turbines and the experiments is in danger. Just look what's already happened to David! We don't have much time.*"

Erin hurried over to her mother, shaking her arm to wake her and signing so rapidly I couldn't follow what she was saying. I wasn't sure Mr Mason and the rest of the placard-waving old folk would be much help, but it would be good to get the secret of the substation experiments off my chest before the ten-ton weight of worry crushed me to death. I had a sneaky suspicion Doctor Ashwood already had his eye on the protest group after picking up their leaflets last night, so Erin was right—we didn't have much time.

"*GOT THEM!*" Erin waved a couple of pink referral forms at me and grinned. "*YOU ME GO SEE MR MASON.*" She used the shorthand sign 'bald' for Mr Mason, but this time I was too worried to feel like laughing.

"*YOU TELL MUM WHAT?*" I blinked in surprise.

"*DOESN'T MATTER. HURRY!*"

Erin headed for the door and I followed, snatching one of the pink forms off her and reading it as we crossed the yard to the main building. "Hey!" I grabbed her arm so she looked at me. "*LIAR! YOU SAY LAST NIGHT I WORRY WET BED!*"

Erin shot me an amused look, and I made up my mind to turn that pink form into an origami version of her. As soon as school was over I'd burn it on the rocks along with about a billion of Doctor Ashwood and half a dozen of Calum and the rest of the gang.

The bell rang when we were halfway down the main corridor. We knew almost as soon as it went off, as doors flew open and kids spilled out into the passage, pushing and shoving to get to their next class. I backed into an alcove by the drinks machine, pulling Erin to safety with me until the tidal wave of kids had washed down the hall.

"*CAREFUL,*" I signed.

After what had happened to David last night, Erin didn't need me to explain any further. There was a strange kind of tension in the air, the hall buzzing like electricity as the kids jostled one another. Their eyes were dark with anger and lack of sleep, and they slouched and growled their way down the hall like a pack of lions on a meat hunt.

When a last dribble of younger kids was all that remained of the flood, I checked the coast was clear then headed for the stairs. Erin gave my hand a squeeze as we climbed to the second floor, and I squeezed back hard, not realizing just how badly I needed reassurance till now. Everything had gone crazy, and this felt like our last hope of saving the island before something terrible happened.

"Oh, crap…" I muttered when we got up to the landing. A line of kids clutching pink forms stretched all the way from Mr Mason's office door to the top of the stairs. Calum and a couple of boys from the gang were at the back of the queue, eying me and Erin moodily and exchanging glances.

I froze, my fists clenching. I hadn't figured out how Doctor Ashwood had targeted his messages at Calum's gang yet, so I had no way of knowing if he was whispering in their ears right now, or how to interrupt the signal. Even if the targeted signal was switched off for now, they might still remember that I'd accused Calum of deliberately breaking David's computer last night.

But Calum didn't challenge us, he just muttered something to Ryan. They snorted with laughter then went back to playing with the game apps on their phones, ignoring us. I let out a long breath and leaned over the stair rail, gazing down at the first floor while we waited.

We weren't there for long before something happened.

The staffroom door at the bottom of the stairs opened, and Mr Mason came out with the head teacher. They were talking to someone standing just inside the doorway so I couldn't see him at first, but when he stepped into the corridor I gripped the stair rail tight in shock.

It was Doctor Ashwood.

I felt Erin's fingers clutch at my wrist, and I didn't need to look round to know she was just as worried as me. As we stared down at the group at the bottom of the stairs, I wished for the billionth time I hadn't gone and got my ears panned in. I could really do with hearing what they were saying right now.

Mr Mason smiled and shook hands with the Doctor like they were agreeing on something, and our head teacher pulled out an appointments diary and started scribbling enthusiastically in it. Doctor Ashwood wasn't listening to her chatter. As Mr Mason headed up the stairs to deal with the queue of students waiting for counselling, the Doctor reached into his long black coat and pulled out his handheld device, plugging his microphone into his ear and turning his head so Mrs MacPherson couldn't see it.

Oh crap oh crap oh crap!

My mind yelling at me was the only thing I could hear as Mr Mason walked up the stairs towards us and Doctor Ashwood began whispering into his microphone and tapping away at his tiny computer. Everything seemed to happen in slow motion after that.

I felt the movement behind me before I turned and saw Calum and Ryan peel away from the wall and head for the stairs. Their eyes had gone blank like last night, but there was a darkness lurking just behind those dead stares. I knew what that darkness meant; I'd felt it myself at the bring-and-buy sale when my hearing aid had picked up the voice whispering in my ear.

As Mr Mason reached the top step, I launched myself across the landing, trying to pull Calum and Ryan back before they could carry out Doctor Ashwood's instructions.

I was too late.

I managed to pin one of Calum's arms behind his back as he was reaching out, but Ryan stepped forward, planting both hands on Mr Mason's chest and shoving with all his strength. Mr Mason's eyes opened in shock as he went sailing backwards, his body twisting and rolling as he crashed down the stairs and landed at the head teacher's feet. Mrs MacPherson just stood there for a long moment staring at the blood running from his nose and pooling on the floor. Then she started screaming.

I couldn't hear the sound, but I could almost feel the echo as my own mind started thrashing around inside my skull, trying to escape from the awful reality. Erin stuck both hands over her mouth to stifle her sobs, and the other kids all gathered round, gazing down in shock at the horrible scene at the foot of the stairs. The weird thing was, no one seemed to be blaming the boys who had done it. It was like everyone had been looking the other way and thought it was just an accident.

"He fell," Ryan was shaking his head in confusion and saying over and over again so clearly I could read his lips. "He fell."

Down below in the corridor, amid the mayhem of teachers running, students crying and office staff calling for an ambulance, Doctor Ashwood stood watching calmly as though everything was going exactly to plan.

CHAPTER 21

The next day at school things were even scarier.

"*YOU HERE!*" Erin heaved a big sigh of relief and pulled me into a chair at the back of the assembly hall, signing at top speed, "*ME THOUGHT TODAY YOU NOT COME. YOU LATE WHY?*"

"*DIDN'T WANT COME,*" I signed back, "*BUT MUM WANT ME POST PRESENT.*" I opened my schoolbag to let Erin see the badly-wrapped parcel full of baby clothes shoved inside. After what happened to Mr Mason yesterday, school was the last place I wanted to be. But the post office was right around the corner from school, so Mum had insisted I go to both. I think she was just trying to keep things normal, but I wasn't sure any of us knew what that word meant anymore.

"Hey, Beanie," I called when I caught sight of her woolly hat over Erin's shoulder. "You feeling better?"

Beanie leaned forward in her chair to say hello, and I had to bite my lip to keep from laughing when I saw she was wearing a pair of bright purple ear warmers. With her bobble hat and her granny's warm winter jumper on, she looked like some kind of knitted Princess Leia doll.

"Bet-ter." Beanie nodded, pointing to the earmuffs. "Sig-nal. Not. Loud."

My grin vanished and I glanced round the assembly hall to make sure no one was looking our way. I didn't want any of Doctor Ashwood's minions listening in when we discussed his experiment. All of the students were sitting in their year groups, waiting for some kind of special assembly. Most of the kids were zoned out as they stared at the games on their screens, ignoring the head teacher's ban on phones during class time. The teachers were too sleepy to enforce it, and Mrs Brody was dozing in her chair at the end of our row.

"WE HERE WHY? DINOSAUR WANT TALK ABOUT BALDY ACCIDENT?" I signed, using the shorthand names for our head teacher and Mr Mason.

"PROBABLY." Erin shrugged.

"WHEELS WHERE?" I asked, frowning when I realised David still hadn't come back to school. We could really use his help to figure out what to do next.

"TODAY OFF. TOMORROW AFTER SCHOOL HE COME MY HOUSE. TOMORROW WE TALK," Erin said, pointing to herself, me and Beanie like we were some sort of secret war council.

"GOOD IDEA," I nodded. "WE MAKE PLAN."

I was just fishing a pad of paper out of my bag so I could write notes to Erin and Beanie during the assembly, when Mrs MacPherson walked on stage. She held up her hands for silence like she usually did, but this time it was pointless, as instead of the usual chatter of voices I was pretty sure the hall was almost dead. Mrs Brody didn't even wake up when the head teacher started talking, so Beanie had to do the translating into sign language for us. Erin scribbled down some of the things I didn't understand on my notepad, so between the three of us we got most of what Mrs MacPherson was saying.

Mr Mason wasn't as badly injured as the rumours the first-year kids spread had claimed—he wasn't dead or paralysed and he hadn't turned into a zombie after all. He'd broken a leg and a couple of ribs and was going to have to stay at the clinic for a few weeks, but considering how bad the fall was, he'd been pretty lucky. The head teacher said there'd be counselling available for any students who'd like to talk about the upsetting experience, and I snorted at that. If I wasn't so worried about drawing attention to myself I might've asked if she'd actually got a professional in, or just got another rubbish teacher with free periods to take over Mr Mason's counselling sessions.

I zoned out for a bit after that, too busy wondering what Doctor Ashwood had been discussing with Mrs MacPherson in the staffroom yesterday to pay much attention to what Beanie was signing. It was only when Erin nudged me hard and I looked up to see her eyes had gone bug-wide that I realised something was wrong.

"WHAT?" I frowned.

Erin signed back so fast she had to repeat herself three times before I understood.

"NEW LUNCHTIME CLUB START SO WHAT?" I shrugged. That wasn't exactly big news. Mrs MacPherson was always coming up with crap new clubs to persuade kids to stay in school during the lunch hour where she could keep an eye on them. So far this year she'd come up with a 'citizenship club', whatever the hell that was, a 'cooking club', and a 'friendship club'. She really had no clue. No wonder Erin and Beanie used the sign 'dinosaur' for her.

But Erin clearly didn't think this was just another rubbish group that would die a death after three weeks when less than two kids turned up. She was nudging me hard in the ribs, pointing frantically to the stage. When I followed her finger and saw the man appearing from behind the curtains, I got such a shock I felt like I'd been zapped by lightning. Doctor Ashwood stepped up to the microphone, smiling his cold, calculating smile at the assembled students.

Bloody hell! I thought, my heart and mind both racing. *The mad scientist's wormed his way into our school and now he's going to carry out his experiments on us in broad daylight!* I turned to Erin to ask what we should do, but she was staring straight ahead at Doctor Ashwood, watching him intently.

It took me a minute to realize he was signing at the same time as talking. He wanted to make sure Erin and me both understood him. He wanted to make sure we knew there was no escape.

"...NEW LUNCHTIME SCIENCE AND TECHNOLOGY CLUB START TODAY," he was signing as I focused on him. "ME TEACH CODING. YOU MAKE VIDEO GAME. WHO INTERESTED?"

Calum and his gang immediately put their hands up, grinning at each other in excitement. They'd all had detention for playing games on their phones in class, so they were looking for any excuse to get more screen time at school. Other kids leaned over their seats, checking with their friends to see who else was going, before putting their hands in the air too.

Doctor Ashwood's pale eyes swept the hall, assessing the number of hands, then he held up a smart phone and added, "YOU COME, GET SPECIAL FREE GAME APP. ANYONE LIKE?"

A ripple of excitement went round the hall, and lots more hands went up. It looked like half the school was going to turn up to his lunchtime club. I had to grab Beanie's hand before she could stick it up too. She'd got so addicted to playing *Sugar Crush* that Mrs Brody had to take her phone off her before she went to bed or she'd be up all night playing it under the covers.

"Trust me, Beanie, you do *not* want to go to that club," I told her. She pouted at me, but I was too busy watching what Doctor Ashwood signed next to worry about her making a fuss. He wasn't speaking out loud this time. He was signing directly at me, the cold smile never leaving his face.

"OTHER NEW APP AVAILABLE. COME CLUB, GET SPEECH TEXT APP. TALK WITH FRIENDS, FAMILY. YES?"

My breath caught in my throat. He was offering me the one thing I desperately wanted, and all I had to do was go to his lunchtime club to get it. For a moment all reason went out of the window. The combo turbines had been here for two months and we still didn't have Wi-Fi or call access on our new smart phones. I was starting to lose hope that we ever would, and I wanted that app *now*. I wanted to talk with my dad and my old gang so badly the thought of having to wait just one more day for the app made my head throb. The hand that wasn't gripping Beanie's arm twitched, reaching up to volunteer. Erin clutched it just in time, and at her touch, it was like a spell was broken, and those pale blue eyes lost their hold on me.

What are you thinking? I wondered, shaking my head to clear it. *That maniac nearly killed Mr Mason, and smashed up David's computer, and now you want to go volunteering for his 'let's turn all the kids crazy' club just so you can get a free app? What's wrong with you?*

When he saw my hand sink again Doctor Ashwood frowned, turning away to flick though a familiar-looking red folder. He found what he was searching for, then set the papers on the podium and took his handheld device from his pocket, adjusting the earpiece and typing in a set of commands. Erin squeezed my arm harder. We both knew what was about to happen.

"Beanie, run back to our classroom, quick!" I called, but it was too late. A shiver ran through the crowd of assembled students, as though a switch had been flipped and an unseen current was flowing through the hall. Beanie clutched at her ears, trying to shut out the noise she was hearing, but after a moment she stopped rocking and her eyes went blank. Whatever that signal was, it wasn't going to be stopped by a pair of furry earmuffs. When she turned to look at me again, the dead look had been replaced with a scowl of anger. She stood up, her fingers curling into fists. All around the hall, groups of students and teachers were turning to growl at each other, their eyes dark and fierce. The rest sat silent and slack-jawed, as if the power to their brains had been abruptly shut off.

Any second now there was going to be carnage.

"WE DO WHAT?" I signed desperately to Erin. But she wasn't standing beside me anymore, she'd run off as soon as Beanie started reacting to the signal.

"Erin?" I called, forgetting she couldn't hear as I backed away from a group of sixth years who pushed their chairs away and headed towards me. Some of the other zoomers in my class closed in, forming a tight circle round me, their fists clenching.

I wasn't a coward—I'd never run from a fight in my life. But I'd never had to face anything that didn't look entirely human before. The kids crowding round me were snarling like a pack of wild dogs, their lips drawn up to reveal their teeth as they reached out for me.

For the only time in my life since the accident in my dad's boat, I was so scared that I couldn't breathe.

I managed to dodge the first punch that came my way, but the second followed so fast I was knocked to the floor before I even knew which direction it had come from. A sharp kick sent me rolling to the other side of the circle where a row of feet were raised, ready to stomp on me. I curled into a ball, throwing my hands up to protect my head, every nerve tensing as I waited for the blows to fall.

They never did.

After a moment I looked up. Everyone had stopped. The students were gazing around in confusion, some with their hands over their ears as though they were trying to shut out an unpleasant noise. That didn't make sense. The signal from the turbines was a silent one; they didn't know they were hearing it. So what were they listening to, and why had they stopped? I jumped to my feet and pushed my way out of the circle, trying to figure out what was going on.

Just then, one of the slack-jawed teachers seemed to remember who and where he was. His eyes went wide and he started shouting something at the students. Everyone turned to look at him, and it was as though the lights behind their eyes suddenly blinked on again. For a second no one moved, and then there was chaos. The fire doors at the side of the hall were flung open, and all of the students ran for the exit at once. The teachers pushed their way through the crowd, trying to restore order and get everyone to line up, but no one was listening.

In the middle of the crowd I saw Doctor Ashwood fiddling with his handheld device, trying to punch in commands to restore his control. But something was interfering with his secret signal. It was only then I noticed Erin. She hadn't run away when the signal started after all. She was standing at the back of the hall with a chair in her hands and a look of grim determination on her face. On the wall next to her was the broken glass panel of a fire alarm. I couldn't hear the shrill clanging of the bell, but I could see the effect it was having on the people in the hall.

When she saw me looking her way, Erin gave me a thumbs up before running to help Beanie out of the hall. I would've hugged her if I hadn't been standing too far away. I was about to follow them when a different image flashed into my mind.

A red folder.

A red folder I'd seen somewhere before.

A red folder that was now sitting on the podium, unattended.

The secret experiment files! I suddenly remembered. Doctor Ashwood had been reading from the folder just before he set the signal off.

He must've been using one of the codes in the files, I thought. My eyes darted to the stage, then back at Doctor Ashwood standing near the fire exit. He wasn't looking at the podium, he was too busy trying to get his device to work and get the students and teachers back under his control.

Before I could chicken out, I grabbed my bag with Mum's parcel inside for the journalist in Glasgow and pushed my way through the crowd to the stage. I took the steps three at a time, rushing up to the podium and snatching the red folder that was sitting there. I didn't even pause to look back to see if Doctor Ashwood had noticed, I just ran for the door at the side of the stage, shoving the folder inside my bag under the parcel of baby clothes.

The corridor outside flashed past in a blur, my thoughts speeding through my head even faster. I had to get to the post office before Doctor Ashwood could stop me. I had to post the files to the one person who could get the story out and help us stop the experiment before it was too late.

I crashed through the main doors and sprinted for the school gates, my lungs on fire and my heart pounding. In the parking lot, three soldiers with guns were getting out of a jeep and heading for the assembly hall. When they saw me run past one of them shouted something, but I didn't stop to find out what it was, I just kept right on going.

I didn't know if Doctor Ashwood had seen me take his folder.

I didn't know if he was coming after me.

All I knew was that I had one shot to send the secret files to someone who could help us, and I had to take it.

CHAPTER 22

After I'd been to the post office, I didn't stop running till I was almost home.

It was the sight of something unexpected in Mr Henderson's field that made me break stride. I leaned against the fence, my breath catching in my throat. Nearly half of the sheep were lying dead. Blood soaked their wool in dark streaks, their eyes open and glassy. The rest were huddled together at the bottom of the field, shivering in fright.

What the..?

It looked like it wasn't just the kids at school who'd been affected by Doctor Ashwood's signal experiment today. Something had got loose and gone mad in the sheep field, and I had an awful feeling I knew what it was. I broke into a run again, heading as fast as I could up the hill to my house.

I had to catch the culprit and hide the evidence of his crime before it was too late.

Twister was paddling in the burn near our back gate, snapping at the tiny fish and having the time of his life. When he saw me his tail went crazy, wagging so hard I thought it was going to drop off. He came running over to lick me, jumping up and getting his muddy paw prints all over my school shirt. I would've been just as glad to see him, if it wasn't for the blood staining his muzzle and dripping down his chest.

It was clear he'd been a very, very bad dog.

"Oh, Twister, what have you done?" I gasped, wondering how the hell I was going to get us both out of this one. His lead was chewed in half, the broken end trailing across the ground. I muttered all the bad words I could think of as I washed the blood off him, feeling sick with dread. I couldn't wash away those dead sheep, and now I was going to have to lie like a pro if I wanted to keep Twister alive.

"Behave, Twister, OK?" I begged as I pulled him up the hill by the collar. I think he would've followed me willingly enough, but I wanted him tied safely to the fence before anyone came asking questions about him.

But when I opened the back gate, I found it was already too late.

Mr Henderson was standing at our door waving a copy of the local paper, his face red with anger. Mum had her arms crossed defensively, and she looked so worried she was close to tears.

Her eyes widened when she saw the mud on my school shirt and Twister's broken lead. "*YOU FIND DOG WHERE?*" she signed.

"He was in the burn playing," I shrugged, trying to look innocent as I tied the ends of Twister's lead together so he was securely anchored to the fence again. "What's going on?"

Mr Henderson launched into an angry rant which I was pretty sure was all about his sheep. He kept pointing at Twister and back at his fields, glaring at me like it was all my fault. Mum signed at the same time to help me keep up, and I pretended I was really surprised to hear all about the dead sheep, like I hadn't just walked past them

167

ten minutes ago. When they were done, I took a deep breath and blurted out the lie I'd been preparing all the way up the hill.

"I don't know why you're blaming Twister," I said. "He's been tied to the fence all week, except when I took him for walks, and I've kept hold of him the whole time."

And that's the problem, I thought grimly. Twister had been out in our back yard for nearly three weeks out of the last four, as Uncle Stuart couldn't find a replacement dog sitter. That whole time, he'd been in the direct firing line of the turbine signals coming from the Bay. Whatever mental sickness was affecting the islanders, Twister had got himself a way bigger dose.

Mr Henderson pointed accusingly at the knot I'd tied in the lead and said something that must've involved bad words, as Mum's eyebrows shot up. I stuck to my lie though, making sure I sounded slow and calm like I wasn't worried about Twister getting put down at all.

"He's been here all morning," I insisted. "I got home for lunch ten minutes ago and took him for a walk, but his lead was frayed and it broke. He ran down to the burn and had a splash about, that's why he's all wet. I had my eyes on him the whole time, so he's got nothing to do with your sheep, Mr Henderson."

I shut my mouth and waited, hiding my hands in my pockets so he couldn't see they were trembling. Mr Henderson went right on glaring, but with me sticking so tight to my story, he'd run out of things to accuse Twister of. He muttered a bunch of stuff to Mum and threw his newspaper down on the doorstep, shooting Twister one more nasty look before he slammed the gate.

I felt so bad for lying I wanted to throw up. Mr Henderson had always been nice to me and the other kids, letting us wander over his land in the autumn to pick the blackberries growing in the hedgerows and eat the apples that fell outside his orchard fence.

Now his sheep were dead and half his income was gone, and I was lying right to his face. If I felt any worse I was going to explode.

Mum was giving me the searching look she'd always use when I was a wee boy and I'd just raided the biscuit tin behind her back. I picked up the newspaper Mr Henderson had left and scanned the headlines to avoid her gaze. Mr Mason's accident hadn't been reported yet, but the paper was full of stories nearly as bad.

'Three Injured in Pub Brawl,' the headlines screamed.

'Local Woman Attacked by Teenage Thugs.'

'Child Bitten by Frenzied Dogs.'

'Bird Deaths—Possible Avian Flu Link?'

'Milk Shortage Worsens.'

'Cow Deaths Blamed on Contaminated Feed.'

'School Suspensions at Record Levels.'

'Police Chief Blames Antisocial Behaviour on Violent TV Programmes.'

There was more local news in one week than there'd been for a whole year, and all of it was bad. I had an awful feeling that when the final phase of Doctor Ashwood's experiment got going, the news would get even worse.

Mum tapped me on the shoulder to get my attention. "YOU TELL TRUTH?" she signed. "JUST NOW DOG LEAD BREAK?" She looked like she was ready to cry. I told her what she wanted to hear, even though lying to Mum hurt ten times more than lying to Mr Henderson.

"Of course it's the truth, Mum. Anyway, how come Mr Henderson runs over here accusing Twister, when he's got two Jack Russells of his own that could've done it?"

"NOT HIS DOG," Mum signed wearily.

"Why not?" I demanded, looking for any excuse to keep Twister from being blamed. "Those vicious wee beasts are always looking for a fight. I bet it was them that got into the fields today and killed the sheep."

"*NO*," Mum shook her head, grabbing a small post-it pad sitting on the windowsill and scribbling, "*Mr Henderson told me his dogs broke into the henhouse and killed a dozen chickens yesterday. When Annie Henderson tried to stop them, they took a big chunk out of her leg. She spent the afternoon at the doctor's. John had both dogs put down last night.*"

"Oh."

There went Twister's best hope of escaping the vet's needle. I was going to have to do a lot of smooth talking tonight when Dad got home if I wanted to keep him alive now. I gave Mum a quick hug and headed up to my room to get my story straight.

CHAPTER 23

That night I couldn't sleep a wink.

When Dad came home we had the mother of all rows over Twister. Dad wasn't stupid, and he didn't believe a word I said when he found out about Mr Henderson's sheep. He was all for taking Twister to the vet right there and then, but Mum managed to talk him into waiting till Uncle Stuart came back from buying equipment on the mainland on Saturday. I sat out in the yard stroking Twister's ears and telling him it would be alright till my parents had finished arguing and Mum called me in to dinner. Dad spent the rest of the night fuming, pacing up and down the living room with a bottle of wine in one hand and a copy of the local paper in the other.

I was desperate to tell them everything about the turbines and the substation, but if they knew I was lying about Twister, then how was I ever going to get them to believe me about Doctor Ashwood's experiments and the danger we were in? The worst thing was, I didn't know whether it was the turbine signal that was making them so angry or whether they would've argued about Twister anyway. I didn't know what was normal anymore, and that scared the living daylights out of me.

Going to bed was pointless. Thoughts spun round my head as fast as the turbine blades in the Bay, images flickering behind my eyelids every time I closed them.

Doctor Ashwood and his handheld device.

The soldiers with their guns.

Calum's eyes going blank.

Beanie rocking back and forth.

Hundreds of kids in the assembly hall all losing control at once.

Twister with his muzzle covered in blood.

And every time I opened my eyes, there they were—the turbines, turning endlessly in the darkness and sending secret signals across the island.

I sat on my window ledge, staring out at the huge shadows in the Bay. I wasn't exactly sure what I was waiting for, but I had a strange feeling that after the drama in the school hall, Doctor Ashwood's experiments were accelerating. By half past two in the morning, I was sick of watching the spinning towers and chasing the crazy thoughts round my head.

Tired and restless, I got up and tiptoed down the hall to check on my sister. Sally was sitting up in her cot, but she must've been crying quietly since she hadn't woken Mum and Dad. I picked her up and carried her round for a bit. She stopped crying straight away, which was pretty unusual as her nappy was smelling ripe and she badly needed changed.

"So you've finally figured out we get on better when you're not screaming at me, hmm?" I whispered, pulling out her changing mat and setting her down on it gently. "Well done, munchkin, it's only taken you eight months, but you got there in the end."

Sally blew a big bubble and looked up at me all wide blue eyes and stinky bum. It wasn't the cutest combination in the world, but after today's drama, I was feeling a lot kinder towards her.

Instead of putting her straight back in her cot when I'd finished changing her, I carried her to the window, letting her squirm about till she found a comfy position. Soon she was fast asleep, her nose squashed up against my cheek. I had to admit, it was kind of adorable.

If my ears were still working, I would've heard noises outside while I was changing Sally. Since they weren't, the first warning I got that something was happening was when I saw a group of kids walking past our front yard and heading for the clifftop. Then the wind sent dark clouds flying across the face of the moon, and I lost sight of them in the blackout.

"What the..? Sorry, Sally, I have to go."

I set my sister down in her cot as fast as I could without waking her, and ran to find my shoes.

Teenage figures were gathering in the dark, staring out across the Bay. Somehow, Doctor Ashwood's whispered instructions were targeting kids my age. If it wasn't for the accident, I might be standing out there with them.

I glanced at the hearing aid I'd stuffed in the half-open desk drawer. If I was braver, I might've put it in to see if I could hear that weird pulsing coming from the turbines. But there was no way I wanted Doctor Ashwood's whispered instructions taking over my brain ever again. I just wished I knew how he was targeting us. It couldn't just be the turbine signal on its own, I mean, it was me and Calum's gang the scientist had set on David, and Ryan who'd pushed Mr Mason down the stairs, everyone else was just sort of… frozen. How was Doctor Ashwood sending different instructions to different people?

And when is this experiment going to end? I wondered, clambering out of the window and onto the front yard wall. *How much worse are things going to get before it does?*

I shuddered to think what would've happened today at the assembly if Erin hadn't set the fire alarm off and interfered with Doctor Ashwood's commands. After seeing what Twister did to those sheep under the signal's influence, it wasn't hard to imagine what the kids would've done to me and the other students they'd targeted. It scared the hell out of me going anywhere near them again with the turbine signal pulsing in the dark, but I had to see what was going on.

I crept down the hill, keeping well back from the group just in case. There were about twenty kids on the clifftop, with more climbing up to join them from the main road. They were walking like zombies, their eyes fixed on the turbines out in the Bay.

"Calum?"

A boy in a familiar red hoodie drifted right past me like I was invisible. I grabbed his arm and shook it, trying to wake him up.

"Calum! It's me, Max! Can you hear me?"

The moonlight glinted off Calum's glassy eyes, and he tilted his head and stared off into the distance like he was trying to hear a radio channel through a burst of static. He pulled his arm away without looking at me, heading over to join the others at the edge of the cliff. Most of his gang were already there, and I recognised some of the other kids from our school who'd volunteered for the lunchtime coding club in exchange for a new games app. I had a sick feeling that whatever they were being taught in this silent after-hours lesson, it was all going to end in the carnage of the final phase.

"Can any of you hear me?" I shouted at the kids, trying to get them to look at me. They all just stood there frozen, staring at the turbines with laser-like intensity. They might as well have been made out of solid stone.

No, not all of them. The smallest figure at the end was rocking on her heels with her hands over her ears. If she took so much as a half-step forward, she was going to go tumbling over the edge of the cliff. I recognised her at once.

"Beanie!"

I raced over, grabbing her round the waist and pulling her away from the two-hundred-foot drop. She stumbled, all disorientated and distressed, flapping her hands to keep me away.

"Beanie, it's OK," I said, backing off to give her space. "It's me, Max."

Beanie stopped flapping and gazed at me in confusion.

"Make. It. Stop!"

"Make what stop, Beanie? The noise?" I asked. "Can you hear the noise coming from the turbines?"

Beanie just whimpered and pulled her hat down over her ears. "Don't. Want. To. Hurt."

"It is too loud? Is it giving you a sore head?" I patted her hat reassuringly. "Come on, I'll take you back to Erin's house, you'll feel better when you're back in bed."

"No…" Beanie's hands flew to her ears and she started rocking again. "Don't. Want. To. Hurt," she gasped. "Don't. Want. To. Hurt…You."

Oh.

This wasn't good.

I turned slowly, looking back at the line of kids on the clifftop. They were all staring at me now, blinking robotically in the moonlight.

Uh-oh.

A sudden shove sent me sprawling onto the grass. Beanie leaned over me, grinding her teeth and clenching her fists inches from my face. "Hurt. You," she mouthed.

Time to go!

I scrambled to my feet just as the group of kids burst back to life, surging towards me like a pack of rabid dogs. I turned tail and ran, my lungs burning as I raced for the safety of my house. I'd almost made it to the front yard when I was rugby-tackled from behind.

Damn. I'd forgotten how fast Calum could run.

Two strong arms pinned me to the grass, holding me down to give the others time to catch up. I struggled furiously, trying to break Calum's grip, but it was like he'd gained superpowers overnight, his hands tightening on my shoulders like a vice. If I didn't get out of this now, I was dead for sure.

"Sorry, mate." I leaned back and headbutted Calum as hard as I could in the face. I was glad I couldn't hear the contact noise when Calum went flying backwards—I didn't want to know if I'd broken anything. He landed in a tangled heap of arms and legs, and something slipped out of his pocket onto the grass. Before the other kids came running up, I caught a quick glimpse of Calum's smart phone lying there in the moonlight, one of the games app icons in the menu screen flashing red like a warning light.

I rolled to my feet and dashed for the wall again, but I was dizzy with pain and didn't see until it was too late that some of the kids had cut off my escape route to the front of the house. I was going to have to find somewhere to hide at the back.

The back door's locked and I don't have a key! I thought frantically. *Where can I go that's safe?*

There was only one place I could get to in time, and that was the garden shed. I could only hope the wooden door was strong enough to keep them out.

I threw myself at the back gate and charged across the yard. I could see the dark shapes of kids pouring through the gate and clambering over the fence as my shaking hands fought with the latch holding the shed door closed.

Come on!

I finally prised the stiff latch open just as the first of the kids lunged at me. I leapt into the shed, slamming the door shut and locking it from the inside. Dust rained down from the roof as a group of kids clambered on top of the shed, fingers poking and prodding at the cracks between the boards in the wall. The moonlight dimmed suddenly, and I turned to see faces pressed against the glass right beside my head.

Oh, crap, I forgot about the window!

The faces disappeared for a second, then the kids reappeared moments later waving rocks, ready to break the glass. The heavy wooden door shivered on its hinges, cracks opening up around the rusty bolt keeping it shut. It wasn't going to hold much longer.

This is it. I'm going to get beaten to death.

My heart almost stopped in fear as the arms drew back to hurl the rocks at the window.

And then, just as suddenly as they had begun, the kids all stopped. It was as though someone had hit the 'off' switch inside their heads. The faces disappeared from the window, the vibrations of feet on the shed roof dying away. The door stopped shivering, the tugging hands vanishing into the night.

I waited for a long time, my pounding heart refusing to believe that it was safe to leave.

Maybe they're just hiding? Maybe they'll jump me as soon as I step outside?

I took a deep breath and opened the shed door a crack to peek out. The yard was silent, empty. I crept out, taking a garden spade with me as a weapon just in case. But there was no one there. I checked beyond the back gate, gazing down the hill to the main road in the moonlight, but everything was still. It was weird. Even though I was shaking with relief, there was something nagging at the back of my mind, telling me something was out of place.

I looked round the garden, trying to work out what was wrong. The plant pots had been knocked over, but none of them were broken. There were footprints all over the vegetable patch, but Mum's carrots didn't look too badly trampled. Everything was in its right place, but a sharp prickling sensation at the back of my neck was insisting I look harder.

I turned slowly, my gaze sweeping the whole of the back yard. And then I saw what was wrong. On the fence by the gate, the end of a thick rope was swinging gently in the wind, the strands chewed through by sharp teeth.

Twister was gone.

CHAPTER 24

"Max!" Erin mouthed in relief when she opened her front door. "YESTERDAY SCHOOL YOU WENT WHERE? ME WORRIED."

"LONG STORY," I signed back, stepping inside. It had been a long night too, and an even longer day.

I'd put my uniform on this morning so Dad would think I was going to school, slipping downstairs before Mum was up. Dad was in the kitchen making a right mess of the scrambled eggs and toast he was trying to cook, and he must've set the fire alarm off, as he pulled it from the ceiling and took the batteries out when the burnt bread started smoking.

"I'm away to school," I'd lied, grabbing the last piece of bread Dad hadn't turned into charcoal and spreading some peanut butter on it. "I'll take Twister to Erin's house on the way there. Her dad has the whole back garden walled off, so he can't get out. I'll pick him up again at home time." I'd held my breath, waiting to see if Dad would see right through my lies. But he'd just shrugged and nodded. He hadn't been out to feed Twister. That was my job. So he didn't know yet that Twister was gone. I still had time to find him before his fate was sealed.

I'd been halfway to the door when Dad grabbed my arm.

"You OK, Max?" he'd mouthed, worry lines digging deep holes in his forehead.

"Yeah, I'm fine, why?" I said it too quickly, and Dad saw the lie from a mile off.

He tried to say something slowly, hoping I'd be able to lip-read, but as usual it was all just a long string of silent mouth-flapping and nonsense syllables. Very deliberately, not taking my eyes off Dad, I'd opened a cupboard drawer and pulled out a notepad and pen. I slid it across the table to him, then stood there waiting. I waited a long time. Dad had stopped talking, looking down at the notepad then back at me. The silent stand-off must've gone on for at least twenty seconds before I finally gave up.

I rolled my eyes at him and grabbed a can of coke from the fridge, stuffing it in my schoolbag along with a couple of breakfast bars. Dad kept pointing to my ear and mouthing at me as I headed for the door. I knew what he wanted, but even if my hearing aid wasn't dangerous, I wasn't giving in to him anymore.

"No, Dad," I'd snapped, "I'm not putting in my hearing aid. I've told you a million times already it doesn't help me hear anything. Anyway, I don't see any point in listening to you when you don't listen to a word I say. If you can't be bothered writing things down for me then you're just wasting my time."

The hurt look on Dad's face had made me feel ten-feet tall for the thirty seconds it took me to walk down the hill to the road. Then the glow of victory faded, and I'd just felt like crap. *Forget it,* I'd told myself. *I've got way more important things to worry about right now than Dad's bruised feelings.*

I'd spent the rest of the day skipping off school and searching for Twister. I must have re-crossed Mr Henderson's fields twenty times, ducking whenever I saw one of the farm hands in the yard. I even went as far as the old quarry on the other side of Pykeman Fell, getting halfway up the slopes of Scarpa Brae before the rain and the thickening mud made me turn back.

I'd been so worried about Twister and what had happened with the kids out on the clifftop, I'd almost forgot about meeting up at Erin's house after school. It wasn't until I'd reached the road again and saw the cottages perched at the edge of the Fell that I remembered Erin said David was coming over to discuss what to do about Doctor Ashwood.

When I'd looked at my watch, it was already quarter past four. I was late. Trying to ignore my sore feet, I'd started jogging towards Erin's house.

Erin sighed in relief when she saw me at the door, pulling me into the living room, muddy shoes and all, before I had time to catch my breath. "*NO PHONE! LAND LINE BROKEN NO CONTACT VERY BAD,*" she signed at me at top speed.

"*DOCTOR ASHWOOD?*" I asked, using the shorthand sign we'd agreed on. With the way he used sound frequencies that folk couldn't hear, and that big black coat of his, the name 'bat' suited him perfectly.

Erin nodded gravely.

I felt a chill of foreboding run down my spine. I was almost certain Doctor Ashwood was cutting off the island's communications before his experiment's final phase began.

David pulled his music player headphones off when I came in, holding them up to show me how he was blocking out the worst of the turbine signal. He looked tired, but he gave me a shaky thumbs up. Beanie was hunched over her smart phone on the sofa playing a game I hadn't seen before. It looked suspiciously like the one the kids who went to the coding club had been playing. When she saw me she put her phone down reluctantly, hesitating before giving me a big hug. I was pretty sure she kept saying, "Sorry, Max," but with her head buried in my chest it was hard to tell.

"It's alright, Beanie, last night wasn't your fault," I told her, trying to disentangle my arms and sign to Erin, "SHE TELL YOU LAST NIGHT WHAT HAPPEN?"

Erin nodded. "BUT SHE NOT REMEMBER ALL. YOU TELL US. AND YESTERDAY ASSEMBLY WHAT HAPPEN?"

"OK BUT ME NOT USE SIGN LANGUAGE," I signed, then said out loud, "Beanie, your signing's better than mine, and I can't stay here too long—translate what I'm saying for Erin, OK? David, you're not going to believe what happened since the bring-and-buy sale."

I told them the whole story, about stealing the secret files at the assembly and running to the post office, about seeing the kids on the clifftop and being chased into the garden shed. The only thing I didn't mention was Twister. I didn't want anyone else telling me the best thing I could do was to have him put down. If I couldn't save one dog then I didn't see how I could help save a whole island. I needed that hope to hold on to or I'd go completely mad.

Beanie scribbled some of the more difficult words down on a notepad for Erin while she signed, and I could see by Erin's frown that she understood everything I was saying.

"SO, JOURNALIST HELP US?" she signed when I'd finished. "SHE TELL POLICE?"

"ME DON'T KNOW," I shrugged. "SHE MAYBE NOT BELIEVE ME, DO NOTHING."

Erin's frowned deepened. "YOU THINK DOCTOR ASHWOOD KNOW YOU STEAL FOLDER?"

I could only shrug again. I couldn't think of any other reason why he'd got the kids to attack me on the clifftop last night. I just wished I knew *how* he'd controlled them like that. I was just starting to ask if the others had any idea why Doctor Ashwood was setting up a lunchtime club at school, and why he was giving kids free games apps to get them to join, when I stopped dead, staring at Beanie's phone with wide eyes.

"I'm such an idiot!" I slapped my forehead. "Of, course, it's the *phones!*"

David's eyes widened in understanding at once. I couldn't believe that I'd never noticed the fierce intelligence burning in them before. Erin and Beanie needed a bit more explanation, though.

"*PHONE?*" Erin signed. "*YOU MEAN WHAT?*"

"We know that phases one and two of the experiment were about using the turbine's infrasound signals to send subliminal messages to the islanders, right?" I said in a rush, drumming my fingers impatiently as I waited for Beanie to relay this to Erin through signs and scribbles on her notepad. "It messed with their sleep, made them aggressive, remember?"

The others nodded, and I knew they were thinking about the way the mainstream kids had turned on the zoomers, and the way the adults were always arguing. My mind went straight to Twister though, and the way he'd changed from a teddy bear into a dangerous monster. I gulped, pushing the thought of what might happen to him if I didn't find him in time away. I had to finish my work here first before I could continue the search.

"The next phase was different though, it was about…" I screwed my face up, trying to remember the exact phrase. "…'Targeted combo mast command response'," that was it. That's what Doctor Ashwood's been doing with his handheld device and microphone. He's been targeting signals and commands to specific people, like when he ordered everyone to zone out while he told Calum's gang to smash up David's computer, and when he got Ryan to shove Mr Mason down the stairs while everyone else looked the other way."

David was swaying harder in his chair in impatience by the time Beanie relayed the information to Erin and she'd asked, "*HOW?*"

"The smart phones! Everyone's been carrying them around with them all day because of the apps. But isn't it a bit weird how the apps work even when we haven't got Wi-Fi? Or at least, the phones are telling us they don't have Wi-Fi access, but that's not what David's computer said. David, did you get sent a phone?"

David made a face that I couldn't interpret until Erin signed, "*BROTHER T.O.M.M.Y. PLAY WITH PHONE. NOW NO PHONE*". David's wee brother was only three. I could picture David's phone lying in bits after that wee troll got hold of it.

"Those turbines are sending out mobile phone signals too, even though Doctor Ashwood's pretending they're still not working. The phones are what he's using to channel his commands from his microphone and that handheld device. And he's got all the islanders carrying them around everywhere because of all the great apps on them."

Everyone turned to stare at Beanie's phone on the sofa like it was a bomb that might go off at any second. I felt sick when I remembered how close I'd come to taking up Doctor Ashwood's offer to join the lunchtime club in exchange for his speech-to-text app.

"I bet those apps all do different things," I said darkly, "and I bet the ones he's loaded onto the kids' phones at his lunchtime club are getting them ready for the final phase. We need to come up with a plan to stop people from carrying their phones so he can't target them, then we—"

"*NO TIME,*" Erin interrupted. "*TOMORROW EXPERIMENT FINISH.*"

"What?" I gasped. "*YOU KNOW HOW?*"

"YOU ASK DAVID," Erin said pointing to the boy who was waiting with growing impatience for us to include him in the conversation. "HE TELL YOU."

David's brown eyes lit up under his mop of sandy hair when he realised he was going to get a chance to speak at last.

"Erin just said you think Doctor Ashwood's going to start the final phase tomorrow," I told him. "How come?"

David grabbed a pencil awkwardly and started pointing at the alphabet sheet on his tray table. I'd seen him with it in class before, but I'd thought he was just trying to learn the alphabet like a four year old, not actually using it to communicate. Erin followed what he was doing, writing down each letter he pointed to. Eventually she had a whole paragraph copied down. She slid it across the desk so I could read it.

"*I bet he knocked out our landlines today. Everyone's blaming it on the coming storm, but he's making sure we can't contact anyone for help. I think he's going to hijack the Halloween party in the Town Hall.*"

"The Halloween party?" I blinked. "Why would he do his final test there?"

David gripped his pencil tighter and went on pointing at the letters while Erin wrote them down one at a time. "*Nearly everyone on the island will be there. He'll use the party music speakers to boost the signal to see what the effects of direct signal transmission are. That's what I'd do if I was running the experiment.*"

"Oh, wow, that's completely…" I ran out of words. I almost wished David wasn't so brilliant at working things out. The thought of all those people being in one place when Doctor Ashwood started whispering into his microphone again horrified me. "So how do we stop him?"

I'd forgotten by now to sign for Erin, but Beanie did it for me. When she finished, we all just sat there looking at each other blankly.

"*FIRE ALARM?*" Erin signed.

"*ME DON'T KNOW.*" I signed back. "Do you think the fire alarm would work this time?" I asked David out loud.

"*I'm not sure,*" he spelled out slowly. "*If he uses the speakers to boost the signal then a fire alarm might not be loud enough to disrupt it this time.*"

"Then we need to make sure he can't use the speakers," I decided, trying to sound braver than I felt. "The party starts at half seven. Erin, Beanie, you come to my house at six and we'll go over our plan, then walk up together. You got all that, Erin?" I asked, waiting for Beanie to finish signing.

Erin nodded and scribbled on the notepad, "*David, your parents are on the council entertainment committee, aren't they? Does that mean they'll be going to the party early to put up decorations and things?*"

David nodded.

"You OK to get there early with them and scout the place out for us?" I asked him, tapping his wheelchair. It must be a total pain to be so dependent on his parents, but David never seemed to complain about it. Or maybe I just hadn't been listening before.

David nodded again, and pointed out another sentence. "*I'll find out what sound system they're using for the music and the best way to knock out the speakers without being caught. You'll need to bring a toolkit or something with you so we can cut the wires.*"

"Dad's got one in the shed," I told him. "Keep your headphones on from now on just in case. Beanie, you're going to need something better than a pair of earmuffs to protect yourself from Doctor Ashwood's turbine signal."

Beanie rummaged in her pockets and brought out a pair of heavy-duty ear plugs. Erin obviously wasn't taking any chances after Beanie had gone wandering about the island in the dark last night.

"These. Work. Bet-ter," she told me, pointing to her ears.

I gave her a thumbs up. "And the last thing, the *most* important thing," I told her, "is to get rid of *that*." I pointed at her smart phone. "I don't care how high a score you've got on *Sugar Crush*, you need to bury it at the bottom of the garden or something, or you'll be the only one of us Doctor Ashwood can target with the phone signal. He can probably turn it on remotely, so it's not enough to just switch it off, you need to either destroy it, or throw it away, understood?"

Beanie gulped hard at the thought of losing her favourite game, but she nodded bravely, her face determined.

"*NOW ME GO HELP MUM*," I signed to Erin. "Sorry, David, gotta get home and help with the baby," I said out loud, feeling bad for lying to them all after we'd just worked so well together. I didn't want anyone knowing I was going looking for Twister, though. Not until he was safely tied up in the back yard and I had a whole pocket full of excuses to get him out of trouble.

Erin followed me to the door and signed, "*TOMORROW 6 O'CLOCK SEE YOU*."

I waved back and jogged down the road, wondering what the hell we were thinking. We were just four kids, for God's sake! How were we supposed to stop a mad scientist from turning our island into a war zone all on our own?

I turned my collar up as the cold wind swept through the fields and shook the trees. The storm was coming alright, and tomorrow it would break whether we were prepared for it or not.

CHAPTER 25

I couldn't find Twister anywhere. By the time I gave up and headed home it was nearly dark, and the wind was blowing so hard I was struggling to stay upright.

My hope was fading with the last of the daylight, and the plan that had seemed so airtight just an hour ago in Erin's living room was looking more and more like a crazy idea cooked up by a bunch of clueless kids.

Whatever happens, we can't do this alone, I decided. *We need help.*

There were only two people I knew who'd spent enough time away from Scragness to have escaped the worst effects of the secret turbine signal—my dad and Uncle Stuart. I was going to have to tell them everything. I could only hope they'd believe me.

Uncle Stuart will when he sees how serious I am about it, I thought, wishing he was coming back tonight instead of tomorrow. *He'll take my side no matter what.* The small spark of hope was just enough to keep me going despite the heavy dread weighing me down.

I made it as far as the fields opposite the burn when something made me stop dead in the middle of the road. A large dog stood by a broken fence, something white and dead clutched in his jaws. My heart sank at the sight of him.

"Twister?" I called softly. "Twister, what have you got there?"

The dog turned to look at me. I flinched back, expecting to see bits of dead sheep on his muzzle and fury in his eyes. But instead his face lit up with delight and he came bounding over, his tail wagging in crazy circles. He dropped the white bundle he'd been carrying so he could lick me, and I nearly choked with relief when I saw it was just a seagull that looked like it had been dead for days.

"Where have you been, Twister, hmm?" I smiled at him now, flipping him over to rub his belly. I'd put a much thicker rope on him after he escaped last time, but he'd managed to chew that one as well. The mud that coated his fur was a pretty clear giveaway that he'd squelched all the way across Pykeman Fell to Uncle Stuart's house and back again.

"You big daftie," I grumbled, "Uncle Stuart will be back tomorrow, so there's no need to go looking for him. Look at the state of you! Mum'll have a fit. Come on, let's get you back to the yard."

I grabbed Twister's collar, glancing back at the seagull on the road with a shudder as we climbed the hill. I could only hope he hadn't done anything worse than play with dead birds while he'd been gone.

I tied the end of Twister's rope to the fence, and he seemed perfectly happy to be back again, settling down to lick the mud off his paws. Dumping my schoolbag in the kitchen to make it look like I'd been to school, I grabbed another can of coke from the fridge, rummaging in the cupboard for a packet of crisps. If I left it up to my parents then dinner wouldn't be till late, and my stomach had been running on empty since the two breakfast bars I'd wolfed down this morning

"Mum, Dad, you home?" I called, heading into the living room. "I picked Twister up from Erin's house on the way back from school. He's been really good and quiet, so there's no need to worry about—"

I got such a shock at what I saw in the living room I swallowed my coke down the wrong way and started choking. Dad was in his favourite chair by the fire, and Mum was sitting on the couch drinking a cup of tea. It was the sight of the man sitting next to her that nearly made me drown on a mouthful of coke.

"*HELLO*," Doctor Ashwood signed. "*TODAY SCHOOL YOU NOT THERE. LUNCHTIME CLUB DIDN'T SEE YOU. HOME LATE. WE WORRY.*" The smug little smile he gave me told me no matter how clever I thought I was, he was onto me.

"What are you doing here?" I demanded, ignoring Dad's frown and Mum's frantic signs for me to be polite.

"*YOU SCHOOL BEHAVIOUR NOT GOOD,*" the Doctor signed smoothly. "*TODAY SCHOOL PHONE NOT WORK, ME COME SEE YOU MUM DAD. SIT DOWN.*" He patted the seat next to him, making it look like an order rather than an invitation. "*YOU EXPLAIN BAD BEHAVIOUR .*" He opened the folder he held, showing me the piles of pink referral forms that Mr Mason had been gathering for the last year and a half.

"I don't have behaviour problems! I get annoyed sometimes because I can't hear, but that's it! And anyway, what's it got to do with you? You're not the school counsellor, you're just taking some random lunchtime club for a few weeks. Mum, Dad—whatever this psycho's been telling you, it's all lies!"

I couldn't believe I'd just said that out loud. It was bad enough Doctor Ashwood had got into my head once before, but now he was in my house turning my parents against me. I could see it in the way

Dad scowled and said "Max!" and the way Mum look mortified by my rudeness.

"YOU FRUSTRATED, ME UNDERSTAND," Doctor Ashwood nodded and pointed to his own hearing aids as though having something in common with me somehow gave him the right to invade my house. "ME TELL MUM DAD HEARING AID SOLVE ALL PROBLEM. WEAR HEARING AID, FRUSTRATED GONE. BAD BEHAVIOUR GONE."

"So I can hear you and your turbine signals, more like!" I snorted. "No way!" I'd gone too far now to back down, so I took a deep breath and plunged right in the deep end. "He's been experimenting on us! The turbines are giving off low frequency sounds, and he's using them to whisper nasty stuff into our heads, making us aggressive and angry all the time."

"Oh, *Max*!" Mum rolled her eyes, signing awkwardly. "BEFORE TURBINE YOU HAVE PROBLEM. TURBINE NOT PROBLEM. NOT USE HEARING AID PROBLEM."

"Mum, I'm telling the truth!" I insisted. "You must've felt those signals too, they've been keeping you awake at night and making you tired and forgetful all the time."

Mum shook her head with what I was sure was a loud sigh. "ME KNOW YOU NOT HAPPY ABOUT BABY. BABY NOT SLEEP, ME TIRED, YOU ANGRY YOU NOT GET..." She trailed off, struggling to come up with the right word. I was pretty sure the sign she was looking for was 'attention', and it made me mad that Mum thought I was making all of this up because I was jealous of my baby sister.

"It's not just people being tired," I snapped, feeling the frustration building and threatening to blow my head to pieces.

"Dad, you've been in a bad mood ever since those turbines came—you've felt it, haven't you? Everyone's on edge and ready for a fight all the time, and then the bats all died and the birds disappeared, and the sheep got attacked and the cows stopped producing milk, and the kids got violent and started fighting and Mr Mason got pushed down the stairs, and it's all Doctor Ashwood's fault because his experiments are using some sort of subliminal messages to whisper into our heads and…"

I trailed off, realizing just how lame that all sounded. I wasn't as good as David at explaining it, especially not under pressure, and my parents were looking at me like I was crazy. Doctor Ashwood just sat there giving me a patronising smile like I was a puppy who'd just peed on the carpet.

I knew right there and then that me and my zoomer gang were on our own. There was no way my parents were going to believe me now. There was worse to come, though. Doctor Ashwood was reaching into his long black coat, pulling out two smart phones. He handed one to Dad, and slid the other across the table to me with a nasty little smirk.

"ME GIVE YOU, FATHER NEW SPEECH TEXT PHONE APP. HELP BOTH COMMUNICATE."

Dad's face lit up when Doctor Ashwood showed him how to use the new app, and my blood ran cold. My dad was one of the very few people on the island who hadn't been interested in the phones—he didn't see the point until the combo turbines were finally fixed and he was able to use his phone to call Mum while he was out on fishing trips. But this new app? It was exactly what he wanted—a way to talk to me without the hassle of having to write anything down. Up until today it was exactly what I'd wanted too. I knew the truth about the phones now, though. Doctor Ashwood was going to weaponise my own father, and he was going to use the very tool I'd been desperate to get hold of to do it.

Dad looked like a little kid who'd been given the world's best Christmas present by Santa Claus himself. He said something into the phone, then held it up so I could see the words that appeared on the screen.

"Hi, Max," his message said, "isn't this great? We can talk to each other properly now."

"We could talk to each other properly if you'd just write things down!" I growled.

"But you can talk to your friends now too! They can just speak into your phone and you'll know everything they're saying. Things can go back to the way they were before."

Dad pushed the other phone towards me with a pleading look.

'Don't be broken anymore, Max', I heard my own angry voice mimicking him inside my head. *'Don't be a zoomer who embarrasses me, just be a normal kid who acts like everyone else. It doesn't matter if this app turns you into a monster, it's better than having a disabled kid as a son.'*

I gave the phone such a hard shove it slid off the table and landed at Doctor Ashwood's feet. "I don't want to be part of your crazy experiments!" I snarled. "Leave my family alone!"

Instead of getting angry, Doctor Ashwood just shook his head in disappointment and said something that made my dad nod hard in agreement. I could guess what it was even before Dad spoke into his phone again and the new message flashed up on the screen.

"Max, go and get your hearing aid. Doctor Ashwood says it'll help you manage your frustration if you practise with it."

"No," I said firmly. "I'm not wearing that thing. It's just part of his experiment to see if his signal can work on deaf kids too."

"Max, stop being so—"

I turned away and raced upstairs before I could read the rest of his message. I had to escape. I slammed my bedroom door and gulped the rest of my coke to push down the lump of anger and fear sticking in my throat. I was shaking so hard I could barely stand up, so I sat on the window ledge, pressing my forehead against the cool glass. At the front of the house I could see Doctor Ashwood leaving. Mum and Dad shook his hand and exchanged a few parting words, and the Doctor pointed to his own hearing aids and nodded. It was pretty clear what he was telling them.

Then they closed the door and Doctor Ashwood walked down the hill towards the substation. The wind had really picked up now, whipping the trees and rushing through the grass like the currents of a rip tide. The Doctor's long black coat flapped around him like the wings of a great bird, and it seemed as though any second he might get swept up into the air and go soaring off over the Bay.

What's he going to do now? I wondered. *Is he going to send more kids to come and get me in broad daylight? Is he going to make my parents turn on me?* The thought sent prickles of fear up my spine. Just then my bedroom door opened and my parents walked in, giving me such a fright I nearly peed myself.

"WE TALK, PLEASE?" Mum signed. "ME KNOW SCHOOL HARD. NOT HEAR HARD. YOU USE HEARING AID, PRACTISE?" She gave me a pleading smile.

"No way." I folded my arms. "I'm not using my hearing aid ever again. That thing's dangerous."

"Stop being so stubborn, Max!" Dad said into his phone, holding it up inches from my face so I couldn't avoid reading his words. His frown was six feet deep, and any moment now he was going to lose his temper. He saw the end of my hearing aid sticking out of my drawer and pulled it out, holding it up for me. "Put it in."

"No."

I tensed, wondering if the scowl on his face was there because I was disobeying him, or whether Doctor Ashwood was whispering into his head at this very moment.

Is this the final phase of the experiment? I thought, backing away until I bumped into my wardrobe. *To see if their soundwave weapons are so powerful they can make parents turn on their own kids?*

Dad took a step forward, holding out the hearing aid again and starting to speak into his phone. But it was another movement outside my bedroom door that got my attention. A streak of brown and black flashed past, there one moment and gone the next. I blinked, wondering if I had imagined it.

"Did you see that?" I asked, pointing at the door. My parents turned round, exchanging glances like I'd gone full-on crazy.

"SEE WHAT?" Mum signed.

"It looked like…"

What?

An animal.

Yes.

A dog.

But Twister's outside.

Is he?

My stomach gave a sick lurch. "Mum, where's Sally?"

"BEDROOM. SLEEP. WHY?"

I bolted for the door before she even finished signing. Running down the hall, I caught sight of a black tail disappearing into Sally's nursery. I threw the door open, skidding to a stop at the sight of the teeth that were bared at me on the other side. Every hair on Twister's back was bristling, and he glared hungrily at the baby that was sleeping in her carry chair just a couple of feet away from his drooling jaws.

"Twister, don't do this," I pleaded. But it was too late. The pulsing turbine signal had finally driven him over the edge. He lunged at Sally, his jaws wide. I threw myself at him, knocking him sideways, and his jaws snapped shut on empty air before they could catch the edge of her carry chair. He rolled across the floor then scrambled up, his furious face just inches from mine. Then he lunged again.

But Dad was there to rescue me this time.

He grabbed Twister by the collar, wrestling him out of the nursery and down the hall. Mum came running in and scooped Sally up, her face so white I thought she was going to faint. "Are you OK?" she asked me over and over, patting my face to check for cuts with one hand and holding Sally close with the other. Sally didn't like being woken up one little bit, and by the look of her screwed-up face she was screaming the house down. For once I couldn't blame her. I felt like screaming myself.

I sat on the floor for a long time with my head on Mum's shoulder and one hand wrapped around Sally's tiny fingers protectively. But then I remembered Twister. I looked up. The hall was empty. Dad must've taken him back outside. Big red warning lights flashed in my head.

"Mum, what's Dad going to do with Twister?"

"DON'T WORRY, DAD FIX THIS," Mum signed with a sad face that told me everything her words didn't.

I leapt up and ran down the stairs two at a time, flinging the back door open and charging out into the yard. Twister was gone. The garden shed was gaping open and a couple of Dad's shovels were propped up on the step. It looked like he had tested them all to find one heavy enough for the job.

My heart was pounding as I raced round the side of the house to the cliff walk. I didn't need to run any further than that. Dad was standing by the wall, digging a deep hole in the ground. His shoulders were hunched so tight with tension it looked like he was going to snap. He looked up when he saw me, holding out his hand to warn me to keep back.

Something was lying scrunched up on the ground. Something that an hour ago had been wagging his tail and licking my face like I was the most important kid in the world.

No.

I leaned against the wall and puked until all the coke was gone and all I had left was a hole in my stomach deeper than the one Dad had dug with his shovel.

I tried to tell them! a voice inside my head was screaming. *Why wouldn't they listen?*

It was too late now. Twister was dead.

EXPERIMENT X01 –
FINAL PHASE

CHAPTER 26

By morning the storm had whipped the Bay waters into a frenzy of white foam. The electricity had been cut off late last night, and now the whole island lay under a thick blanket of silence. No landlines, no TV, no lights. But by the way the waves were crashing across the shoreline, I knew the wind was howling like a banshee round our house.

I sat on my window ledge all day, watching the grey clouds race across the sky and the tree branches lash the air. Down in the Bay the turbines were spinning furiously, their great blades almost a blur. It was clear Doctor Ashwood had timed his experiment's final phase for the day the wind would be at maximum strength.

He was ready for his soundwave test, but I wasn't sure if I was. My head felt like it had been shattered into a thousand pieces. My face was flushed from crying, and my throat was raw from yelling at Dad. Deep down I knew what happened to Twister wasn't his fault, he did what he had to do to protect us. It wasn't Dad I hated, it was Doctor Ashwood. I'd been blaming Dad for a lot of things that weren't his fault since the accident though, and I wasn't about to stop now.

Dad had gone out after dinner to fetch a generator from one of the bigger boats for the Halloween party. I was pretty sure he was just looking for an excuse to avoid Uncle Stuart, but now there was no hope the electricity blackout would stop the experiment from going ahead. Doctor Ashwood clearly had this all worked out in advance. The only places he wanted power on the whole island tonight were the substation and the town hall.

Uncle Stuart would be back from the mainland any minute now. When he found out what Dad did to Twister, he'd be furious. And if Doctor Ashwood's signal tapped into all that rage, then Dad would be in big, big trouble. They were both carrying the new smart phones now, and Doctor Ashwood could whisper straight into their heads. I couldn't bear to think about what might happen if they turned on each other.

Erin and Beanie arrived before I could work out the best way to break the news to Uncle Stuart. Beanie was wearing a long white sheet for a ghost costume, a white woolly hat pulled down over her ears. I lifted one flap and grinned when I saw the earplugs screwed tightly in place. She gave me a thumbs up, but her face was serious. Erin had hastily thrown together a witch's outfit from black tights, boots and a long black cardigan. Her cardboard hat had been blown to pieces in the wind, and she dumped the remains on the coffee table.

"LAME COSTUME, ME KNOW," she grimaced. "MORE IMPORTANT THING WORRY ABOUT."

"ME TOO," I nodded, looking down at my own football top that wasn't really even a costume. "YOU READY?" I asked, pulling on my jacket.

Erin nodded. "YOU GET TOOL?"

I opened my schoolbag so she could see the toolkit I'd swiped from the garden shed. Inside there were wire-cutters, screwdrivers, a couple of spanners and a hammer. It wouldn't be much fun carrying all that lot into town, but if it helped us stop the turbine signal from the speakers then it would be worth it.

"*YOU GET RID OF PHONE?*" Erin asked. "*SOMEWHERE SAFE?*"

"*THREW DOWN CLIFF.*" I signed. I'd chucked mine over the edge this morning, but Dad had his in his pocket all day, so there'd been no chance to pinch it before he left. Mum had been asleep with Sally on the sofa until dinner time, one hand curled round her phone with the nursery rhyme app going full blast. I could only hope Mum was too exhausted for Doctor Ashwood's final experiment to have any effect on her.

Beanie couldn't hear me with her earplugs in, so I signed to her, "*YOU PHONE GONE?*" She pouted at me and signed back, "*ERIN BURY BACK GARDEN.*" She clearly wasn't happy about losing her favourite games. I gave her arm an encouraging squeeze and called up the stairs, "OK, Mum, that's me going now. See you later."

Mum had been wandering around in a daze since Dad left after dinner, folding laundry all wrong and tripping over baby toys in the living room. I wasn't sure where she was now, though.

If my ears had been working and if Erin hadn't been deaf, then one of us would've heard the water running upstairs and gone to investigate. But neither of us heard the sound of the baby bath being run for Sally.

"Mum?" I called again, "I'm going to the Halloween party, remember?"

Still no sign of Mum. That was when I noticed Beanie peering out of the back window. "*YOU SEE WHAT?*" I asked when she turned round.

"*YOU MUM UNCLE SHOUT, NOT HAPPY,*" she signed, looking worried.

Crap!

I dashed through the kitchen with Erin close on my heels. We skidded to a stop in the back yard just in time to see Uncle Stuart slamming the door of his pickup and driving off in a cloud of dust. Mum was standing at the gate, tears streaming down her face. I could guess what had just happened.

I gave Mum a hug, wishing I'd heard Uncle Stuart arrive and got the chance to explain things myself. "Did you tell him about Twister?"

Another tear slid down Mum's face, and I took that as a 'yes'. My heart sunk right to the bottom of my football boots.

"WHAT HAPPENED?" Erin asked, gazing at the disappearing truck and trying to work out what the fuss was about. All I could do was point to the end of Twister's lead still tied to the back fence and shake my head. Erin understood instantly, and her eyes widened. She squeezed my mum's hand and said, "I'm so sorry," out loud in her mumbled voice, but it was me she was looking at.

I had to take a big gulp of air to stop my throat from tightening up. "Come back into the house, Mum, it's too windy out here."

It was already getting dark, and the storm was sweeping its way across the island. There was no rain, but the raging gale snatched the leaves from the trees and sent them whirling round the yard like giant red confetti. It wasn't a good night for a party, but it was perfect for the turbines. I led Mum back inside and sat her on the sofa to calm her down while Erin fixed a pot of tea for her.

"What did Uncle Stuart say?" I asked.

"HE VERY ANGRY!" Mum signed. "HE NOT LISTEN. HE GO TOWN SEE DAD."

"Wait, Uncle Stuart's going to the town hall?"

Mum nodded, running a hand through her tangled hair and trying to pull herself together. "ME GO," she signed. "STOP FIGHT."

"No, you need to stay here with Sally and have a rest. I'll deal with it. Uncle Stuart will listen to me. I'll make sure they...wait. Mum, where's Sally?

The playpen in the living room was empty, my little sister nowhere to be seen.

"Is she upstairs sleeping? I thought she already had a nap and you were playing with her?"

Mum frowned, all sleepy and confused like she couldn't remember what she'd been doing before Uncle Stuart came round. "ME TIRED," she signed at last. "WE GO BED EARLY. FIRST SHE BATH."

"A bath?"

Mum realised what she'd done about half a second after I did, but I was already flying upstairs before she could get off the sofa.

Oh, God! How long has she been in there on her own?

By the time I charged down the hall and into the bathroom I could hardly breathe from fear. The first thing I saw in the dim light was Mum's smart phone propped up on the windowsill, the nursery rhyme app flashing. I snatched it up, smashing the phone against the wall and shattering the casing. Then I saw Sally's baby bath sitting in the tub, water overflowing from the taps Mum had left on. Something baby-shaped lay submerged at the bottom, the plastic ducks above it spilling out with the excess water.

I lunged for it, blinking in confusion when instead of my wee sister I pulled out one of her dolls. It took me a minute to realize Beanie was standing by the sink with Sally in her arms, drying the baby off with the edge of her ghost costume.

"Not. Safe." Beanie mouthed, nodding at the overflowing baby bath. "Too. Much. Wat-er."

Mum came running in, her face turning chalk white when she saw the plastic bath that was full to the brim. "It's OK, Beanie's got her," I said quickly before she could have a fit. "She's fine."

Mum looked like she was ready to faint with relief. I knew exactly how she felt.

OK, that does it, Sally's coming with me, I decided. *She's not safe here with Mum in this state.* Getting rid of Mum's phone might put an end to the targeted commands, but that wasn't enough to stop the turbine signals that were blasting through the house from across the Bay. Keeping Sally out of harm's way was yet another thing I had to worry about now. I didn't know how many more balls I could keep in the air tonight, but if I stopped juggling then my family was going to be in real danger.

I turned the taps off, making a mental note of all the jobs I had to get done in the next hour. *I need to bring Sally to the town hall with me, get Dad's and Uncle Stuart's phones off them and make sure they don't get into a fight, then stop Doctor Ashwood's final experiment. Oh, yeah, and stop Mum collapsing with exhaustion.*

I grabbed her arm and propped her up, leading her back to her room.

"You need to get some rest, Mum," I said, tucking her up in bed. "Don't worry, I won't stay out too late."

"NOT SLEEP, NEED TO...BABY WHERE?" Mum signed clumsily, trying to get back out of bed again.

"She's fine, I'll look after her. You go to sleep."

"YOU GOOD BOY, GOOD BROTHER," Mum signed before her eyes closed, her face relaxing and the tension draining away.

I knew that wasn't true. I wasn't good, and I was a really crap big brother. But I also knew if I didn't get moving and stop those turbine signals, then everyone was going to turn evil. The only people standing between the islanders and the coming apocalypse were me, Erin, Beanie and David. Oh, and now Sally was coming with us too.

Great, four zoomers and a baby, that's our army, I thought bleakly. *We're going to lose this war for sure.*

Chapter 27

The main street in town was completely dark. The street lamps were dead and the moon was covered with a thick blanket of cloud. Apart from a few cars, the only lights in the night shone from the carved jack-o'-lanterns the kids in costume were carrying to the party. The wind was too strong for candles and the kids had replaced them with torches, their light flickering out of the pumpkin eyes and casting shadows of witches and goblins on the walls.

We were late.

By the time we got to the town hall, a lot of the party-goers had already arrived. So much for stopping the experiment before the islanders gathered. The hall was half full already, kids crowding round the buffet table to admire the giant haunted castle cake and checking out the list of party games posted on the wall.

I looked around warily, trying to find David in the crowd and frowning when I saw that every single person in the room had their phone out. The parents sitting at the back of the hall waiting for the party to start looked tired and grumpy, playing games and checking the weather forecasts while the kids took pictures of each other's costumes and posed for selfies.

"Oh, crap!" I muttered, biting my lip nervously. If we didn't get the signal stopped in time and those adults got violent with the kids, there was going to be a blood bath.

Before I could go looking for my dad and Uncle Stuart, we spotted David waving to us from an alcove by the emergency exit. He pulled off his sound-cancelling headphones and switched off his music player as we hurried over.

"Sorry we're late, David. Things got kind of complicated at home. Nice costume, by the way."

David grinned out from under his Dalek helmet. His whole wheelchair was covered in painted armour plates made of cardboard and papier-mâché. It must've taken him and his parents weeks to make. Sally reached out to grab the ping-pong ball off his hat's eyestalk, sticking it in her mouth to taste it before dropping it on the ground. At least she wasn't crying for once. She was having the time of her life, gurgling in surprise at all the exciting things to see and dribbling down my shirt.

David frowned at her, but it wasn't because she was messing with his costume. "It isn't safe for her here," he spelled out on his alphabet sheet as quickly as he could.

"It's safer than her being at home right now, trust me," I told him. "It's the rest of my family I need to worry about. Have you seen my dad or my uncle Stuart? I need to find them."

David shook his head. "Sorry. But no time now," he spelled out. "We have to break the sound system."

"Right, I've got my dad's tools. We'll get to work." I handed Sally over to Beanie and asked David, "Where are the speakers?"

He tapped my arm and pointed. I was getting better at reading his expressions, and right now he had an 'uh-oh, this is all going sideways' look on his face. I followed his shaking finger to the stage where the sound system was set up. Calum and his gang were sitting there taking pictures with their phones and comparing high scores on their games apps. There was no way we could get to the speakers with them in the way.

"Crap crap crap," I muttered. "NOW WE DO WHAT?" I asked it out loud as well as signing it for Erin, as I was pretty sure David was the only one who could come up with a plan to fix things now. He frowned for a bit, then started pointing at the alphabet sheet on his tray table again.

"Generator. Back room," he spelled out. "Go."

"We can't take out the speakers, so we knock out the generator instead," I nodded. "David, you're a genius."

David threw me a 'yeah, I know' grin.

"STAY HERE LOOK AFTER BABY," I signed to Beanie, remembering she couldn't hear a word I was saying with the earplugs she wore. "YOU ME BREAK GENERATOR," I told Erin. "David, keep an eye out for Doctor Ashwood while we're gone."

I grabbed a hammer and a pair of pliers from Dad's toolbox and Erin picked up a heavy spanner, and we made our way to the storage rooms at the back of the building.

As soon as we left the main hall we plunged into darkness. The corridor lights were off to save on generator power, and we couldn't risk turning them on in case we drew attention to ourselves. When our eyes grew used to the dark, we could make out a light coming from a room at the far end of the passage. We tiptoed towards it, drawn like moths to a flame. I could feel a strange vibration under my feet as I got closer, and a quick glance at Erin told me she felt it too.

"STOP!" Erin warned me before I walked straight into the back room. I peered round the door, holding my breath when I saw it wasn't empty. A huge dockyard generator was sitting inside, a bundle of cables snaking across the floor. Two soldiers were guarding it, checking the connections and making last-minute adjustments.

"WE DO WHAT?" I signed awkwardly to Erin with my tools tucked under my arms. She shook her head and mouthed, "Don't know," back.

We couldn't just stand there watching the soldiers all night, so we tiptoed back up the passage to the main hall. As soon as we got there, I knew things had gone from bad to worse.

The music system must've been switched on, as there was a group of kids bopping about on the dance floor. Calum and his gang had moved from the stage so they wouldn't get deafened, but they'd been replaced by something a whole lot worse.

Up by the speakers, half hidden by the stage curtain, Doctor Ashwood was looking out over the crowd. The third soldier stood beside him, his gun slung over his shoulder. The Doctor was wearing a white lab coat, and they looked just like a couple of ordinary islanders dressed up as a scientist and a soldier in combat gear. Halloween was the perfect night for them to hide in plain sight.

"Bad. Men." Beanie shook her head and hugged Sally protectively.

"Yeah, they are." I threw my hammer back in the box in frustration. "How the hell are we meant to stop them now?" Erin and me both looked to David for help. It was agonizing waiting for him to spell out his last idea one letter at a time, but in the end it was worth the wait.

"Break the main signal box," he spelled. "Destroy the source."

I grabbed a small notepad and scribbled my answer back. With Doctor Ashwood in the hall it wasn't safe for us to use sign language anymore. "*You mean the device Doctor Ashwood's holding?*" I wrote. I didn't see how we were going to get him to just hand it over, not when he had an armed bodyguard watching over him.

David shook his head in frustration, and Erin grabbed the pen and wrote, "*No, that wouldn't work, that thing's just a computer to channel the remote signals into commands, isn't it, David?*"

He nodded, relieved to see at least one of us was keeping up.

"*So we have to break the thing sending the signals?*" I guessed.

When David read the question I'd scribbled he nodded even harder.

"*Wait, you mean we have to break the turbines? Are you crazy? How the hell are we meant to do that? Even if we could get out into the Bay, there's no way we could...*" I trailed off, letting the pen slip from my fingers.

David was looking at me the way I looked at Sally when she dribbled her lunch all down her clothes that I'd just washed. He went back to his alphabet board, his forehead scrunched up in concentration as he moved his trembling fingers between the letters as fast as he could. The seconds were ticking away as we leaned over to see what he was spelling. Any moment now Doctor Ashwood would turn on that signal and start the final experiment.

"The combo turbines just provide the infrasound carrier wave and mobile phone radio waves," David spelled out. "The signals for transmission on those waves are being generated in the substation."

"Of course!" I slapped my head, then grabbed the pen again. "*I'm a moron. Those big aerials I saw coming out of the second hut were sending the signal to the turbines to get carried out on the waves! We have to get to the substation and destroy the signal generator there.*"

David nodded, rolling his eyes and giving me his best 'God, it's hard work being surrounded by idiots' look. Erin glanced up at Doctor Ashwood to check he hadn't spotted us, then wrote, "*We need to get moving.*"

I snatched the pen off her again and scribbled, "*We'll never make it to the substation in time.*"

Erin wrestled the pen from me and wrote back, "*Then we'll have to take the short cut from the harbour.*"

I raised an eyebrow. I had a nasty suspicion I knew exactly what she meant, but I made her write it out just to be sure.

"*Take your dad's boat. We could get from the harbour to the substation in ten minutes.*"

"*No way! Dad would kill me if he found out! And anyway, I haven't been on the boat since...*"

I didn't need to finish that sentence. They all knew what I was struggling to say.

"*Please, Max?*" Erin pleaded. "*We're out of options here.*"

She was right. It would take us way too long to get to the substation on foot. Even if Erin and me ran all the way, I couldn't leave Beanie behind with my wee sister, not when I wasn't sure if her earplugs would protect her against the signals.

"*Fine, let's go,*" I decided. "*Beanie, bring Sally and come with us, I need you to look after her for me, OK?*"

Beanie looked at what I'd written then nodded seriously, making sure Sally was wrapped up securely in her ghost sheet.

"David, you'll have to stay here I'm afraid, mate," I said out loud now, pointing apologetically at his wheelchair. "But if Doctor Ashwood even looks like he's getting his signal device out, then you take this hammer and you break the fire alarm by the door there.

It worked in the assembly hall, and it's the only other option we've got. Think you can manage it?"

David tested the weight of the heavy hammer with both hands. It wasn't an easy job for him, but I knew he'd give it his best shot. The fire alarm wouldn't mask the turbine signal, not with the speakers going full blast, but it might cause a bit of a disruption and buy us some time. He pulled his headphones back on and turned up his music player volume for protection, then nodded.

"Right. Let's go," I mouthed to Erin and Beanie.

I grabbed the toolbox just in case we needed it, and we made our way out of the side door into the dark street. The Halloween party was in full swing now, and the main road was deserted. The only other building that had any lights on was the pub on the corner. Candles flickered in the windows, silhouettes moving behind the glass.

I was just about to cross the square and head for the harbour when someone came charging round the corner, nearly knocking me flying. I could see from the way Uncle Stuart was swaying that he'd had a bit too much to drink already.

"Where's your dad, Big Mac?" he demanded. For once he didn't bother writing it down, but I managed to make out what he said.

"He's gone back home," I lied. I knew Dad must've gone to the pub after dropping the generator off, as I could see his car parked at the top of the street. "Look, what happened with Twister, it wasn't Dad's fault, he—"

But Uncle Stuart wasn't listening. He'd spotted Dad's car too, and his face went rigid with anger.

"Uncle Stuart, wait!" I called as he made a beeline for the pub. I was just about to run after him when Erin grabbed my hand.

"WE GO BOAT MAX," she signed. "NO TIME."

"But..."

She was right. As soon as the turbine signal was switched on there'd be nothing I could do to stop Dad, Uncle Stuart, and all the people in the hall turning on each other. We had to destroy the source.

I glanced back just once as Uncle Stuart disappeared into the pub, then I set my shoulders to the wind and raced for the harbour.

Chapter 28

The water in the Bay churned with froth as I drowned, the pressure in my head so strong I was sure my skull was going to cave in. The darkness was coming for me, closing in on all sides as the broken winch line dragged me deeper. My arms were turning to lead, my frantic flailing slowing. There was no escape.

The first mouthful of water hit the back of my throat like acid, burning its way down to my lungs and sending shockwaves through my body. My mind was screaming silently, begging me to keep fighting, but I had nothing left to give. Fireworks were going off behind my eyes, the final celebration of a life cut short. My dad's last cry echoed in my head as the world collapsed, the sound that had started as a scream now fading to a whispered prayer.

"MAX!"

"*Max…*"

*

"MAX!" Erin waved a hand in front of my face to get my attention. "LOOK! WE GO TOO FAR!"

I didn't need to check the dashboard coordinates to know she was right. We were heading too far out to sea. I swung the wheel, turning the nose of the boat back towards the island, the nightlight sweeping the headland for signs of the small substation jetty. My hands were clammy despite the biting wind whipping round the main mast, and my legs were shaking so badly with cold and anxiety I had to lean on the instrument panel to stay upright.

I wasn't sure what scared me more—memories of the accident, Doctor Ashwood's experiment, or imagining Dad's fury when he found out I'd taken the trawler from the harbour myself. Either way, I was half dead with fear by the time Erin spotted the small wooden jetty in the dark.

"THERE!" She pointed. "ALMOST! KEEP GOING."

It wasn't like I had any other choice.

I steered for the substation, feeling the wind lashing the side of the boat and the powerful current tugging at the propellers.

Keep it together, Max, you've done this a hundred times before! I told myself. *Just another minute!* I begged the grumbling engine. *Just get us to the substation to end this experiment and I swear I'll never mess with you and the sea again.*

Erin gave my hand a squeeze as I reached out to reverse the propellers and edge the boat alongside the jetty. She was trying to be reassuring, but in the glare of the nightlight I could see the glint of fear in her eyes too.

"OK, Beanie, we're here!" I called down the hatch where she'd hidden away to keep Sally out of the wind. I didn't want to leave her in there with my baby sister while Erin and me broke into the substation in case we couldn't get the signal stopped in time. Beanie didn't hear me with her earplugs in, but she looked up when the hatch was opened.

"Cold," she grumbled, hugging Sally tight as she clambered up the steps. She'd taken her sheet off and wrapped Sally in it as an extra blanket. Unbelievably, my wee sister was fast asleep. I wished I could be that oblivious to what was going on around me.

I anchored the boat and jumped down onto the jetty, tying the mooring rope up and making sure Dad's trawler wasn't going anywhere till we got back.

"READY?" Erin asked, handing over the toolbox and grabbing a torch from the cockpit cupboard.

"YES," I lied. "COME ON."

We helped Beanie down and then hurried to the padlocked gate barring our way into the substation. I tried to cut the chain with the bolt cutters from the toolbox, but the steel links were too thick. The army clearly didn't want anyone getting in. Erin attacked the wire fence with a pair of pliers, and between us we managed to prise up enough of the netting to squeeze under.

"KEEP CLOSE," I signed when we'd wriggled through and pulled the toolbox in behind us. "KEEP EYE OPEN."

The three soldiers were with Doctor Ashwood in the town hall, but there might be reinforcements for the final test tonight. I had no idea what we'd do if we ran into more soldiers out here in the dark, but I filed that thought away under my ever-growing list of 'things I'll worry about later'.

We crept through the maze of transformers, the feeble torchlight flickering off the metal pylons and straining cables. Everything was shivering in the wind, the high-tension wires pulled so taut it looked like they were going to snap. Moonlight flashed through the racing clouds, throwing great shadows of the turbines across the compound before plunging us in darkness once more.

"HERE." I tore my eyes off the spinning blades and hurried to one of the huts. "THIS GENERATOR SHED."

Even without me pointing it out, it was obvious which building housed the source of the signal. The door and the window were bolted shut with steel plates, a giant padlock turning the hut into a fortress. My heart sank when I looked up and saw that the aerials on the roof had been fenced in with a roll of razor wire two feet high. It was going to take us hours to cut our way through that if we wanted to knock out the signal.

"YOU CUT?" Erin asked, signing and pointing to the enormous padlock on the door.

"MUST TRY, NO OTHER WAY. HOLD LOCK," I told Erin. "ME BREAK CHAIN."

I threw all of my weight into trying to snap the steel links with the bolt cutters, but this padlock and chain was even thicker than the one on the gate. Soon my hands were aching and my arms were groaning in protest but the heavy metal refused to give. Erin tried forcing the lock with a screwdriver, but nothing we did made a blind bit of difference to the steel barring our way inside.

Beanie paced up and down restlessly as we worked, rocking Sally back to sleep whenever she woke up and trying to shield her from the worst of the wind. She was miles better at this whole baby thing than I was, even though I'd had eight months' practice.

"Wait! I think I've done it!" I yelled out loud. I felt something give under the last squeeze of my bolt cutters, and I pushed harder, ignoring the pain in my bruised hands. Without warning the bolt cutters burst apart, the strain just too much. I was left holding the two broken ends and cursing in the dark.

"NOW WE DO WHAT?" Erin asked. We were out of useful tools, and now we were both out of ideas too. I kicked the door in frustration while Erin rummaged about in the toolbox, frantically searching for something that might help us get inside. I was halfway to giving up when Beanie tapped my shoulder.

"Bon-fire," she mouthed.

At least, that was what I thought she said, but it was so random I thought I'd got it wrong, so I ignored her. Her hands were full of baby, so she couldn't sign what she wanted to say.

Beanie tugged my sleeve this time. "Bon-fire," she said, so clearly I couldn't mistake her.

I really wasn't in the mood to play games. "*NO, TODAY HALLOWEEN, NOT NOVEMBER 5TH,*" I signed quickly, turning my attention back to the locked hut.

"But—"

"*NOT NOW, SHH! ME ERIN THINK PLAN. YOU QUIET HOLD BABY, OK?*"

Beanie wasn't about to give up. She shuffled up till her face was right next to mine and I couldn't look away.

"OK, OK, you've got my attention. What?" I snapped out loud even though she couldn't hear me through the earplugs.

"Burn. It. Max," Beanie mouthed slowly and clearly right in my face.

"Burn what? You mean the…" My mouth fell open. The hut was made of wood. We couldn't get the door open or get near the aerials on the roof, but if we sent the walls up in flames it would take the signal generator inside with it.

"*YOU GENIUS!*" I grinned.

But Beanie didn't smile back. "No!" she wailed, thrusting Sally at me so fast I nearly dropped her. Beanie's hands flew to her ears, and a shiver of dread flashed down my spine.

The experiment had begun.

"*YOU OK?*" Erin tried to hug her, but Beanie couldn't focus on anything except the signal that was loud enough to carry through her earplugs. This close to the source there was nothing she could do to resist it. She gave one last gasp, then her face went blank. She stood up slowly, pulling the earplugs out and throwing them on the ground. Now she caught every pulse of Doctor Ashwood's silent signal, and she closed her eyes and swayed on her feet as though listening to music only she could hear.

"*ME BURN HUT DOWN!*" I signed awkwardly to Erin with the baby in my arms. Sally had woken up and was squirming about, crying at the top of her lungs. She clearly didn't like the silent noise any more than Beanie did. I passed her over to Erin and signed, "*ME GO BOAT GET PETROL.*"

I didn't wait for an answer, I just bombed across the compound like my legs were on fire. I should've taken the torch, as I nearly ran head-first into the fence in the dark and had to scrabble around looking for the loose section we'd prised up. By the time I found it and squirmed back through I was almost sobbing in fear.

All those people in the town hall, what's the signal going to make them do? my mind was yelling at me as I ran down the jetty and leapt back into the boat. *Are they going to kill each other? What about Dad and Uncle Stuart? What if..?*

I'd nearly gone crazy by the time I found a can of petrol in the hold and lugged it back to the fence. I dashed back across the compound, taking a couple of wrong turns round the transformer boxes before I finally found my way back to the middle hut. The torch was lying on the ground by the door, and by its light I could see Erin backed up against one of the pylons, holding a spanner in one hand to ward Beanie off and shielding Sally as best she could with the other. Beanie was crouching on the ground before her like a guard dog ready to pounce. I was pretty sure she was growling.

Erin's eyes fixed on mine, then darted to Beanie's trouser pocket. Through the grey fabric, I could make out a rectangular bulge and the familiar warning flash of an app being activated. If I'd just checked Beanie's hands earlier, I would've seen the tell-tale signs of dirt under her nails. Erin may have buried her phone, but

Beanie had dug it up again, the temptation of her favourite games too strong to resist.

Doctor Ashwood had a direct line straight into her head, and any second now he was going to give the command to attack.

I hesitated, not sure whether I should rescue Erin and Sally, or set the hut alight first. Erin decided for me by pointing at the hut with her spanner, her eyes wide with panic. I pulled the cap off the petrol can and splashed it against the walls, making sure some of the sharp-smelling liquid went over the roof and the aerials up there. Then I reached into my pockets, and froze.

I didn't have a lighter or a box of matches.

Of course I didn't. I was only fourteen, and I didn't smoke.

Beanie edged forward, getting ready to throw herself at Erin and my baby sister. I was sure the people in the hall were all doing pretty much the same thing right now. Any moment now there was going to be carnage.

"HEY!" I waved to get Erin's attention and signed, "DOESN'T WORK! ME NOT HAVE—"

Before I could sign 'fire', Erin dropped her spanner and pulled a lighter out of her pocket along with a bundle of paper figures. She edged away from Beanie and threw them over to me, and I gathered them up so fast I nearly fell over. I'd forgotten all about Erin's origami bonfire fetish, and I'd never been so glad that my only friends were a bunch of crazy zoomers with weird hobbies.

In the dark I could see the origami people were all tiny models of Doctor Ashwood and the soldiers. I'd never taken so much pleasure in setting anything on fire before. I used the burning paper to light the petrol-soaked walls, the flames licking their way up towards the roof and the aerials on top. I didn't get to enjoy the bonfire for long. Just as the wind stirred the flames and the whole hut went up in a blaze of orange and yellow, Beanie lunged for Erin.

I got to her just in time.

"Beanie, calm down!" I yelled, trying to keep a firm grip on her. She kicked and struggled in my arms, her eyes flashing in the firelight. It was like the signal was giving her ten times her usual strength, every one of her muscles firing on full power. She pulled away, lunging for Erin and Sally again, this time going in for the kill.

Before she could reach them, Beanie suddenly went limp, sinking to the ground like a puppet whose strings had just been cut. She sat in a heap for a whole minute, her body trembling. Erin and me just stood there staring at her, not knowing what to expect.

"YOU OK?" I asked Erin at last.

"YES," she nodded. "YOU?"

"YES," I signed, even though my shaking hands made me look like a liar.

I checked Sally over, making sure she hadn't been hurt. She was howling at the top of her lungs, but luckily Erin and me were immune to her screams.

"Beanie?"

I crept closer, not quite trusting her yet. She looked up at me at last, her lip quivering. I knew right then and there we'd got our Beanie back to normal and stopped the experiment in its tracks.

"Don't. Like. It," Beanie sniffed, tears streaming down her face. "It. Hurt."

"It's alright, Beanie," I said, kneeling down to give her a hug. "It's over now, but just in case, we need to get rid of this for good, OK?" I pulled the smart phone out of her pocket and shoved it in mine. She was too drained to protest, burying her head in my shoulder instead.

Erin brought Sally over to join our group hug, and we sat looking up at the flames rolling through the hut as the electrics inside caught fire.

"YOU THINK SIGNAL STOP BEFORE..?" Erin signed. She didn't need to finish. I knew what she was afraid of. It scared the hell out of me too.

"ME NOT KNOW. WE GO BACK SEE."

And get out of here before Doctor Ashwood and the soldiers come back to find out who's been messing with their signal generator, I added to myself.

Just as the flames were spreading in the high wind, licking at the other huts and transformer towers, bright lights suddenly lit up the sky above the Bay. There were heavy-duty helicopters ploughing through the storm clouds, and they were coming our way.

"LET'S GO!" I signed, running for the boat. I didn't know whether there were more soldiers in those helicopters, but I knew we mustn't get caught in the blazing substation with wire cutters and a near-empty petrol can in our hands.

By the time we'd got back on board the boat and fired up the engines, the helicopters were landing on the scrubland behind the substation. I kept the main lights turned off, using the dashboard systems to guide me in the dark as I drove full speed for the main harbour. Halfway there I threw Beanie's phone into the sea as hard as I could. I couldn't risk that thing hurting any of my friends again.

Did we stop the signal in time? I wondered as I gripped the wheel and peered out at the seething water.

In a few short minutes we were about to find out.

CHAPTER 29

By the time I got the boat back to the harbour, the flames from the substation could be seen for miles around.

The quayside was so full of boats I had trouble finding an empty docking berth. Police motorboats vied for space with harbour patrol launches, and there was one big ship that looked like it belonged to the navy. The jetty was crowded with police officers, and as I slipped Dad's boat into a corner space as far from them as I could get, I saw a squad of soldiers disembarking from the naval vessel.

I exchanged glances with Erin. I was pretty sure my face was as pale as hers in the moonlight. I killed the engine, docking silently at the far end of the quayside.

"WE GO ROUND THAT SIDE," I signed, pointing to the shipping sheds facing the harbour. As long as we kept to the alleyways between the sheds and stayed off the main road, we should be able to get back to the town hall unseen. Erin and Beanie nodded, but they didn't look any more confident than I did.

We clambered off the boat and hurried back into town through the shipping yards and back streets, trying not to think too hard about what might've happened while we were gone. When I saw the flashing lights of the police cars and the soldiers surrounding the town hall, my heart sank.

I scanned the crowds of people filling the square. They were looking dazed and confused, but I didn't see anyone who was injured and there weren't any paramedics running about. Then I caught sight of someone who made my heart leap in hope.

Alison Parker.

The journalist from Glasgow.

She was standing in front of the town hall, facing a man with a TV camera and talking into a microphone. As soon as she'd finished filming, I passed Sally over to Erin and ran up to her.

"Alison!" I panted, "it's me, Max! Did you get the files I sent you? Did you call the police here to stop the military experiment? Are you telling the world our story? Did—"

"Shh!" Alison put her finger to her lips and drew me away from the swarm of people who were crowding round to watch her filming. When we found a quiet spot, she pulled a notepad out of her bag and started writing me a message. My heart sank when I read it.

"*I got a tip from a colleague last week about Doctor Ashwood's secret experiment, but I didn't believe it until I got your files this morning. I contacted the police and told them there was a bomb attack scheduled to take place in Scragness tonight—it was the only way to get them to act fast enough to evacuate everyone. They had no way of contacting the island as all the phones are down, so they sent out police and bomb squads as soon as they were able to. I got a TV crew together to make sure we recorded everything so they couldn't pretend it never happened,*" Alison had written.

"What? A bomb threat! That's a load of rubbish!" I snorted. "You have proof it's a secret military experiment—you're a journalist, you need to get the truth out there!"

Alison made a face and wrote something else on her notepad. "*My colleague who gave me the tip vanished last night. I think the military took him away for questioning. When we got to the harbour we found the army had already taken over the police operation. We're being watched, Max, so be careful what you say.*"

"But now you've got the police and the TV crew here you're going to tell the world what's really going on, right?" I asked.

Alison shook her head. "*It's not as easy as that, Max. I've only got one set of files as proof, and the military can easily claim it's a forgery. They're already covering their tracks—by tomorrow it'll be as if Doctor Ashwood never existed. According to the information my colleague gathered, that's not even his real name. No one knows what it is. Apparently, this has all happened before—he'll disappear for a while and then he'll pop up somewhere else with a brand-new identity and a new set of experiments.*"

"But—"

"*I can't do anything more right now with the military crawling all over the place. I've got a five-month-old baby, and I've already been threatened.*"

"Threatened? By who?" I asked.

Alison shook her head. She wasn't willing to say any more. "*I've done my best,*" she wrote, clearly as frustrated as I was about not being able to tell the world the truth. She gave my hand a sympathetic squeeze, but there was a warning in her eyes I could read clearly. "*Don't go making trouble, Max,*" she was saying. "*You won't win.*"

Huh. We'd stopped Doctor Ashwood's experiments on Scragness, and by the looks of it we'd managed to do it before anyone got badly hurt. For now, that was as close to a win as I could've hoped for.

I let Alison get back to her TV crew and ran to show Erin and Beanie the notes she'd written for me on her pad. Erin screwed her face up when she read them, but Beanie just nodded and gave me a hug. She always knew when I needed cheering up.

"LOOK!" Erin grabbed my arm and pointed to the other side of the street. David's parents were standing by their van with his little brother Tommy, ready to load David's wheelchair in after talking to the police. We crossed the road and crowded round, eager to know what had happened. When David grinned and pointed out, "It's all OK," on his spelling board, I was so relieved my legs nearly gave out on me.

"Did you break the fire alarm?" I whispered so his parents wouldn't hear.

David nodded and pointed to the fire truck parked up on the kerb. "Made a big noise when the signal started," he spelled out on his alphabet board. "Bought you some time."

"Good work, mate, if it wasn't for that brain of yours, we'd never have stopped Doctor Ashwood. Where is he, by the way?"

We all looked round. At the end of the dark alley by the town hall, Doctor Ashwood stood tapping at his handheld device, shaking his head and frowning like he couldn't figure out what went wrong. A military jeep drove up, and a short man who looked like some kind of high-ranking general got out and spoke to him, pointing off in the direction of the substation. Doctor Ashwood's face turned pale like he was about to have a fit.

Then he glanced round, and our eyes met. He knew right there and then that I'd beaten him, I could see it in the fierce glare he threw at me before he climbed into his Land Rover with the soldiers and drove off.

Sorry, Doctor, but I'm not letting you hurt anyone on my island ever again, I thought with a scowl. I was pretty sure once the Doctor got back to his secret base and found out what we'd done to it, that would be the last we ever saw of him.

"WE GOOD TEAM," Erin signed, grinning at David and giving Beanie a hug. "WE LEAVE SCHOOL INVESTIGATE CRIME GET MONEY."

"YOU JOKE, YES? ME LAST TIME WANT INVESTIGATE ANYTHING," I signed right back. "BUT THIS TIME MAKE THREE FRIEND NOT SO BAD," I added. And I meant it. It was the first time in ages I'd felt like I wasn't alone. Maybe being a zoomer wasn't so bad after all.

Just as David's car drove off, we saw Mr and Mrs Brody searching through the crowds for Erin and Beanie. It seemed like everyone on the island who hadn't gone to the Halloween party had now turned up to find out what the hell was going on.

"ME GO FIND DAD UNCLE," I told them. "YOU GO HOME SLEEP."

Sally had woken up and was chewing my finger hungrily in the hopes of finding a secret milk stash. I shifted her onto my shoulder and headed across the town square that was rapidly emptying of people now that they'd given the police their statements and the drama was over for the night.

"Come on, munchkin, time to see if we can find Dad and Uncle Stuart."

CHAPTER 30

"Dad! Uncle Stuart! There you are! I was really worried."

I found them sitting on the low wall outside the chip shop. They weren't talking, and they both had their arms folded defensively like they were really mad at each other, but at least they weren't fighting. I hurried over.

Dad turned round, his look of relief hardening into a frown when he saw I was holding Sally. He reached out and took her from me, checking to make sure she was alright.

"Yeah, I'm fine too, Dad, thanks for asking," I muttered.

Dad and Uncle Stuart weren't looking so good. Dad had a bruise under his eye and a fat lip, and Uncle Stuart had a cut on his chin and a couple of burst knuckles. It seemed like I'd shut the signal off just in time before they killed each other.

"What happened here tonight?" I asked.

Uncle Stuart reached into his pocket and pulled out his notepad and pen and started writing. "*It was weird. Everything in the pub was normal, then all of a sudden the mood changed and we all got really angry. Some of the guys started knocking lumps out of each other, and...*" Uncle Stuart rubbed his eyes like he was really tired. "*Then the police* and army arrived from the mainland and sent a bomb squad into the town hall. Everyone's saying it was a fake bomb scare, I think that's why folk started fighting—they were just frightened."

"That's not what I was asking. I meant what happened with you two? You look like you've gone ten rounds in a boxing ring."

Dad and Uncle Stuart exchanged glances, and Uncle Stuart started writing again. "It's fine, Max, it's all been sorted. I was really angry about Twister—" he stopped and bit his lip for a minute then went on, "But I get why your dad did it. If Twister went for Sally then there's nothing else he could've done. I knew Twister wasn't right these last few weeks, and some of my friends' dogs were even worse, attacking people and killing sheep. I don't know what got into them. I was just hoping he'd snap out of it, you know? Before..."

I nodded and looked away with a lump in my throat. He didn't need to finish. I'd been hoping the exact same thing.

"Where have you been, Big Mac?" Uncle Stuart wrote. "We went looking for you when the police came, but we couldn't find you anywhere. And how come you brought Sally with you? It's way too late for her to be out."

"Mum fell asleep and I wanted to give her a break. I didn't mean to stay out so late with Sally, but like you say, it's been a weird night. I wasn't in the hall when it all kicked off though, I was...helping my friends take care of something."

Dad frowned. He always knew when I was lying. He pulled out his phone and tried to use it to speak to me, but all of the apps were dead and unresponsive now. He started firing questions straight at me instead, talking way too fast for me to have a hope of keeping up by lip reading. I wasn't going to let him get away with it this time, though.

"Don't start that again, Dad, you know I can't understand you. And no," I scowled, "I'm not wearing that stupid hearing aid ever again. It doesn't help, it just makes everyone think they can speak normally and ignore the fact that I'm deaf. You can't keep pretending I'm not, and that things will go back to the way they used to be, because they won't, not ever!"

Dad opened his mouth to say something else, then shut it again, blinking at me like I'd just slapped him. I wasn't about to let him retreat back into silence again. Not this time. I grabbed Uncle Stuart's notepad and held it out to him defiantly.

"You get one last chance, Dad. Either write down what you want to say, or from now on I'm going to act like you don't exist either. I'm sick of trying to talk to you when you don't bother making any effort for me."

Dad shifted Sally and took the notepad awkwardly, starting to write then stopping and looking at Uncle Stuart like he needed help. Uncle Stuart leaned over and whispered something that looked like, "Tell him, Sean," and Dad nodded, passing him the pad. I was just about to explode with anger, when Uncle Stuart shook his head, writing something down quickly and showing it to me.

"Your dad's dyslexic, Max, he finds it really hard to read or write anything."

"Oh." I stood there for a long moment just blinking, trying to take it in. *What? Dad's never been able to read or write properly? How come I'm just finding out now?*

I thought back to all the times Mum and me went to the library together when I was small, and how she used to read me bedtime stories and Dad never did. Then I remembered how he always looked so uncomfortable when he put the TV subtitles on for me, or when I asked him to write things down. No wonder he was finding me being deaf a lot harder than Mum did.

"But you never came with us to Mrs Brody's to learn sign language, Dad, not once," I said, the lump in my throat making my words all thick. "Why not?"

Dad was avoiding my gaze, staring at the ground and saying what he wanted to say to Uncle Stuart who wrote it down for him. It was a start, I guess.

"*I'm not good with languages, son, I didn't want to embarrass you in front of your teacher,*" was what he said.

"But Mrs Brody teaches all the kids with special needs!" I frowned. "She's got loads of dyslexic kids in her class."

"*Yes, but...*" Uncle Stuart paused, waiting for Dad to go on. When he didn't, he filled in the rest of the sentence himself. "*Your dad was in a special class all through school. The other kids used to wind him up something terrible for it. He was always getting into fights and being suspended when it wasn't his fault. I think you being in a special class now has brought all of those bad memories back. You get what I mean?*"

I got exactly what he meant. And I'd never been so relieved in all my life. All this time I'd been thinking Dad stopped loving me because I was a kid with special needs, when he'd been one himself and was scared of me finding out and thinking less of him.

We'd both been total idiots.

"Dad, I don't care if you spell worse than Sally, I just want to talk to you! Will you try?" I begged. "Will you learn sign language with me and Mum and write things down for me, even if it's hard?"

Dad took a deep breath like he was trying not to cry, then looked up at me and nodded. It was the first time he'd looked at me, and I mean really *looked* at me since the accident. And it was only then that I realised that all this time Dad had been feeling every bit as alone as I had. He pulled me into a big hug, squashing Sally between us as we held on to each other as though our lives depended on it.

Sally woke up and looked around with wide eyes. For a minute I thought she was going to start bawling, but instead she did something she'd never done before. She squirmed around on Dad's shoulder, holding her arms out and trying to get back to me. I lifted her up, letting her rest her head against my neck and suck my thumb. In a couple of seconds she was fast asleep again, holding tightly to my hand.

"Look at that, she doesn't hate me after all," I laughed. "Though that'll be easier to believe when she finally stops dribbling all over me."

Dad smiled back and nodded to the car, raising his eyebrows a bit so I'd know it was a question. "*Time to go home?*" he was asking.

Uncle Stuart ruffled my hair and left us to it. I could see he was still upset about Twister, but some things just took time to fix. We'd done a pretty good job of patching things up tonight, there was no sense in pushing it.

Just as Dad and me were heading to his car, I caught sight of Calum and some of his gang standing around on the corner. When they saw me they nudged each other and exchanged glances. They'd clearly been talking about me behind my back.

I tensed, my fists clenching and my heart speeding up. They weren't going to start a fight with my dad watching, but that wouldn't stop them making stupid comments or laughing at me. Calum didn't look like he was about to pick on me, though. He was writing something down on the back of a party ticket, and he handed it to me as I walked past.

"*The guys are coming back to my place to hang out,*" he'd written. "*You want to come and stay over?*"

It was what he used to ask every Halloween.

Back in primary school, me and the gang used to go round the town trick or treating, then head back to Calum's house to watch horror films and tell spooky stories. Halloween used to be a lot of fun back when we were best friends.

"Nah, not tonight, I got to—" I started, then I stopped. Calum used to ask me all the time to go to his place or play football with the rest of the boys. I felt awkward about not hearing what they were saying and having to ask for everything to be written down, so I always said no. After a while he just stopped asking. Then the gang started whispering about me behind my back. They were probably just wondering why I didn't want to hang around with them anymore.

I'm such a moron! I thought. It was like a lightbulb had blinked on in my head and I could see things clearly for the first time since the accident.

Calum hadn't dumped me after all. I was the one who'd got so wrapped up in my own frustration and embarrassment about being deaf that I'd dumped him and the gang without meaning to. Maybe I was the one who needed to make more effort.

"OK if I go over to Calum's tonight, Dad?" I asked as casually as I could. I didn't want to sound desperate or anything. "It's still Halloween, and the party wasn't much fun."

Dad hesitated for a second, glancing around at all the police officers still milling about the square as though trying to work out if it was safe to let me out of his sight. But then he nodded. "OK, Max, I'll—"

I missed the last bit that Dad said, but Calum scribbled it on the back of the ticket for me to read. "*He'll pick you from my place tomorrow. You coming? My dad's got a generator, so we can watch films. I got the new Night Freaks one. It's got subtitles.*"

"Yeah, sure," I said, trying not to sound too eager. "Let's go."

As we walked down to the harbour together, people were gathering round the police boats at the dock, watching the flames from the substation lick the sky. The helicopters had taken off again, their lights disappearing across the dark sea. I was willing to bet they'd been sent to collect all the secret experiment equipment before anyone found out what was kept in those huts. Too bad for them it was all burnt to a crisp. I was pretty sure that Doctor Ashwood was in one of those choppers, making his getaway.

"*What do you think happened?*" Calum wrote for me on the ticket,

"The party was crap, so I went and set the place on fire for something to do," I shrugged. "Can't trust us zoomers not to do mental things when we get bored."

Calum threw me a sideways look, then burst out laughing. "Whatever you say, Big Mac," he grinned.

I know that's what he said, as he always used to say it when I told a bad joke. I laughed too, but when I stopped I found there was a bitter aftertaste in my mouth. No one was ever going to believe what Erin, David, Beanie and me had managed to do tonight to save them.

No one except Doctor Ashwood, that is.

I gazed out across the harbour, watching the flames devour the last traces of the military experiment. Out in Wicklin Bay, the turbines turned in the wind, silent and harmless now the secret signal was turned off for good. I smiled to myself in the darkness, then turned from the water and walked off into the night with Calum and my old gang.

CHAPTER 31

"MAX!"

Erin nudged me and pointed at the computer screen. We were almost out of time.

I quit daydreaming and typed in my last answer. Beanie hit the enter key before the last second ticked down, and the score blinked up. Thirty-three to thirty-two. We'd just kicked the backsides of Calum and his gang. Again. That was the third time this week. David cheered and spun round on his wheelchair in what I think was meant to be a victory dance. He nearly ran Beanie over, and Erin had to pull her out the way before she got flattened.

Calum and the boys groaned, complaining yet again that it wasn't fair as it was David's computer and he probably got loads of practice in at home. It didn't stop them coming back for more at break, though. It was too cold now for football, and since they'd discovered how addictive the games on David's new computer were, they'd been hanging out on our side of the school yard a lot more at break. Calum made a face and chucked his empty coke can at me.

"Don't mess with us zoomers, mate," I grinned, "you'll just embarrass yourself."

"Jeez, Big Mac," Calum grumbled, writing, "*whose side are you on anyway?*" on the cover of my maths book before I could pull it out of reach. I hit him over the back of the head with it and dodged out of the way before he could throw a play-punch in my direction. The bell rang and the guys grabbed their bags off our unit's wheelchair ramp and headed back to their mainstream classes, yelling something about a rematch tomorrow. Calum hung back as the zoomers came hurrying back to our unit to escape the cold, scribbling something quickly on the notepad he'd started carrying around so he could talk to me.

"*I'm going down to the youth club at the community centre on Friday night. They've got a live band playing and pool tables set up. You want to come and check it out?*"

"Sure," I nodded. "Can I bring the gang along?"

But I didn't mean Calum's gang. I mean my gang. Erin and David and Beanie.

Calum made a face, but he didn't say no. He knew whose side I was on. I was on his side, but I was a zoomer too, and I wasn't ashamed of it anymore.

I waved to Calum as he ran off, watching the winter wind stirring the wild grass across Pykeman Fell and wondering how fast the turbines in the Bay would be spinning. A new energy company would be coming soon to rebuild the substation, but the turbines weren't causing any more problems. The government had told everyone that the fire was an accident, but instead of continuing the combo-tower experiment they were paying a telecom company to put up proper mobile phone masts across the island as compensation. After Christmas we'd have replacement smart phones that worked for real, and me and my zoomer gang could investigate Doctor Ashwood ourselves. I wasn't sure if he'd ever come back to Scragness to experiment on us in the future, but one thing was sure: if he ever did, we'd be ready and waiting for him.

I pretended to tie my shoelaces as the other kids filed into our unit and the main building, putting off going back to class for as long as I could. School had been a bit less awful this past month since the experiment ended, but that didn't mean I wanted to spend a double period filling in Mr Mason's worksheets. He had a limp and used a cane to walk for now, but that didn't stop him coming back to bore us to death. I wasn't exactly over the moon at wasting more of my break times trying to dodge his counselling questions, but lately I'd been giving in and just telling the truth. Sometimes after I got angry and frustrated and blew up, it actually helped to have someone to talk to.

I just hoped he never found out I said that.

At least me and the zoomers would be in some of the mainstream classes this afternoon. Erin wasn't keen on sitting at the same table with Calum in Biology and Geography at first, but she warmed to the idea when everyone figured out how smart she was and how she always got us extra marks for our group projects. The two girls she hung out with must've just been messed up by the turbine signals, as they're the best of friends again. The one called Heather had a really nice smile. I noticed it in our Religious Studies class the other day when she passed me a note asking if she could copy my homework. Mr Mason was too busy droning on about Hindu festivals or something to notice. I might ask her to go to the school dance with me at Christmas.

Maybe.

I might even tell Dad about her next time we go out on the boat.

It was much better at home now that Dad made more of an effort to write things down and we were laughing together again. He was learning sign language too, which was going really slowly and driving Mum up the wall at the dinner table as we kept knocking things over, but I was pretty sure if he stuck at it, we'd get there. Sally was sleeping through the night now, so Mum was a lot less tired. We went to the park together the other day and had a picnic in the freezing cold. It was kind of embarrassing being out with my parents and everything, but kind of nice and normal at the same time. It was so funny how excited Sally got when I sat with her on the baby swings. Just as well she had her nappy on or I would've gone home with a big wet patch all down my jeans.

It wasn't all happy ever after or anything, I mean, I was still struggling with being deaf, but lately I'd been having a lot more good days than bad ones.

And that just left Beanie.

It hadn't exactly been a fairytale ending for her either. Her granny stayed in hospital for three whole weeks, and it took an island petition to shame the council into putting money aside to get her a part-time home help so she could move back home and look after Beanie herself. Beanie still stayed at the Brodys' several days a week to give Granny Lewis a break, and I went over quite a bit now to do my homework with them and help Erin look after her fish tank. Erin might have the patience of a saint with us, but I was pretty sure she still made wee paper dolls of me and Beanie sometimes and burnt them out on the rocks when no one was looking.

Maybe I'd go over later tonight, but right now, I had to go to class.

I waited till the yard was empty to trudge back up the ramp, watching the seagulls swoop down to fight over the fallen crisps and snack crumbs the kids had dropped. I knew they were making those high-pitched cackling sounds I used to hear out in the Bay, but now I didn't mind too much that everything was silent and I had to use my imagination to fill in the soundtrack. It was kind of peaceful.

I didn't mean the birds were peaceful. They were dive-bombing the litter bins and fighting over the scraps like frenzied sharks in a tank full of tuna. I just meant I was sort of…at peace with the silence. Watching the flutter of wings against the pale sky and the flash of winter sun off the school windows, I felt like I was finally brave enough to face the fear that had been eating me up from the inside ever since the accident. I knew I had it in me. I hadn't just fought a war against the wind turbines and the military's secret experiments.

It was even better than that.

I'd won the war I'd been fighting against myself.

GLOSSARY OF SCOTTISH WORDS/PHRASES

Boak—a feeling of nausea. "It's giving me the boak" = "It's making me feel sick".

Bogging—dirty, but also 'disgusting' when referring to food.

Burn—a small stream.

Cack up—mess up.

Clatbag—some who is dirty.

Gurning—whingeing, crying.

Manky—dirty.

Panned in—broken, smashed up.

Scaldhead—someone who is bald or has a shaved head.

Skelly-eyed—cross-eyed, squinting.

Space cadet—someone who is not 'with it', or is lost in their own world like they're on another planet.

Wazzer—a stupid or annoying person.

Wee—small

Zoomer—some who's a bit crazy, eccentric, or just 'different' – similar to 'space cadet'.

ACKNOWLEDGEMENTS

Writing can be a long, hard, and sometimes lonely slog at times, and there have been many people who have given me support and encouragement along the way. As always, my mother and brother Martin have gone above and beyond the call of duty to help me reach my goals and achieve my dreams, and I can't thank them enough. The list of family and friends who deserve a personal mention is too long to detail here, but hopefully they all know how much their encouragement has been appreciated. I'd like to say a special thank-you to Carolyn and Shona who have been with me on my writing journey for the last twenty-five years, and whose friendship has been a great source of support, joy and comfort during all the ups and downs of life.

Huge thanks go to Archna Sharma and Jade McGrath at Neem Tree Press for all of their hard work throughout the publishing process—their enthusiasm and great ideas have made for a wonderfully positive publishing experience, and the effort they have put into this book has been very much appreciated.

Finally, I'd like to thank the British Deaf Association for reviewing the novel before publication to ensure the Deaf characters' stories were portrayed sensitively. In order to support their work campaigning for equal rights for Deaf people and empowering Deaf people to achieve access to their local public services,

20% of the author royalties for this novel will be donated to the British Deaf Association.